the
consciousness
company

the consciousness company

REWIRING MINDS IN
HUMANITY'S
IMAGE

A NOVEL BY

m.n.rosen

For Natasha

Orthographical note

Separated, italicised paragraphs are thoughts.

— This is speech.

THIS IS EMPHASIS.

This is an animal's mental experience approximated in language

In longer, non-italicised paragraphs, *italics* denotes writing, speech or thought, and sometimes highlights cliches, conventions and names.

Contents

The characterisation of the second founder

AT THIS TIME IN HIS LIFE, before the company was founded, most of all the second founder wanted to be wanted by, and was filtering his experiences for, a woman who combined kindness and sadness with a *dark, physical beauty*, and who, more problematically – because of both his attributes and the algebra of his desire – did not instinctively want him. He understood from the evidence of exams and the frequent deployment of this descriptor by his siblings that he possessed *infrequent* intelligence, and, dismissive of the double meaning, believed that attracting this woman, this concept, required him – through complex language or comedy or even a curriculum vitae – to display a few feathers that were, in sympathetic light, dazzling. To keep hold of this belief, the letting go of which would have required him either to shed historic selves or suppress embarrassment, he denied the love child of his inner logician and tragedian – which had wondered whether this woman might, in the same way, be filtering the ocean for someone who did not want her, and sent this problem into a neural wilderness to join both his limited case history and the heretical thought that once time had eroded this woman's mystery, he might feel, under his earthy fingers, mundanity and dissatisfaction.

The second founder's desire to be desired grew out of a fragile psychological constitution and a more fundamental desire to be thought of positively by everyone and every thing. An indifferent or unfriendly contemporary, a colleague of his mother, identified by his father as *not many meshuga nuts short of a fruit cake*, and an artificial intelligence-powered speaker were all equally important. *Please can I* and *Thank you for having me* and *Whatever you prefer* were from his lips characteristic refrains, and when old enough to know that, in certain circumstances, these words caused pleasure, he added *I like what you're wearing*, *That's a good one*, and other regurgitations held down only if he was certain that they were false.

His own pleasure was greatest when he was alone, walking without a destination, or in his parents' garage, lost to time until his father whispered, *Hey dude. It's midnight, I'm going to bed*. When attempting on a water slide to *go with the flow* and participate in an experience designated by others as enjoyable, he smiled through panic and the pressure of other people waiting at the top and bottom because, on a previous visit, a motion-activated camera had preserved an image of his face which was *possibly more definitive than that painting of a man screaming*. This reflex to defer to photography then over time became more ingrained than the instinct to dodge a tennis ball and twice caused him to be smashed in the face.

Although not always successful, when in public, the second founder prioritised paths that minimised his own discomfort. He did not pass judgment on the images or actions of others and he built defences against self-criticism by acting with a puritanical moral code. He would not punch a wall, or write on the peeling plaster of a condemned house, and, to the great amusement of his friend *Phartacus*, whose message about *putting identity thieves off the scent* he did not respond to, his interpretation of the requirements of honesty manifested itself in digital usernames that were variations on the theme of his first name, middle initial and last name followed by one year before the year of his birth.

Many years before he began to record his consciousness diaries, the second founder kept physical diaries. When the production of the particular style of black notebook he was using was discontinued, he noted in one of these notebooks that he was *bizarrely pleased that based on my current writing pace, and because I bought these in bulk, I will definitely die before I use the last book.* At the age of fifteen, he wrote, *The route to the heart is not through the brain.* And a moment later, he crossed this out and wrote, *Although the nervous system connects them in a literal sense, the route to the heart is not through the brain.* And then, *Although I'm not sure what has caused this fixation with the heart as the organ of emotion. I am infected by the imprecision of language, by an anachronistic romanticism.* And when he was older, *Sex is something to me, but not everything.* And when he was older, *I can no longer be excited by my eyes alone.* And when he was older, *I can feel something that might be something like depression in my head. I am not sure what my purpose is. Maybe helping myself and then other people with their heads. Maybe that is a noble pursuit. I should be a neuroscientist.* And later, *I am too trusting.* And later, *I really do like coffee.* And later, *words, words, words, words.*

One day, very much later, he thought, and his consciousness diary recorded, *These are only qualities and experiences passing through the Shibuya Crossing that, momentarily, spell a particular, unremarkable sequence of sounds that I and other people use to designate this temporary collection of matter.*

And then one day, even later than that, speaking to employees on the company's campus, he said:

— The way I cross the divide is to think occasionally... This person is as real as anyone else. It feels the cold water on its face. It lives to the tips of its fingers. It closes its eyes and feels the feeling of being. And it deconstructs its own identity, eventually, and realises it has no name. As you may, too.

The characterisation of the first founder

AT THIS TIME IN HIS LIFE, the first founder, in the way he occasionally heard his parents characterise the world outside of his childhood home before they were divorced, and like a military leader, conceived of the surface of the earth as a never-ending chess grid and those moving on it as contestants seeking to accumulate different types of power. The second founder, to the first founder, was one such power-accumulating unit who was part of a family – in which, as a coruscating jewel, the second founder's older sister was set – that was more successful and more loving than his own, and the first founder defined himself through these and other contrasts. He did not live in a luxurious house, did not feel in his palms fridge-cooled grapes, the sturdiness of new phones, cloud-like duvets, or softened water, and did not inhabit a life constructed from soirees with celebrated names, profiles in weekend magazines, prestigious titles or prizes, and minority shareholdings.

This importance to the first founder of the external, tangible world – without paradox, because the first founder lived at a varying but notable distance from his own thoughts and feelings – made him less sensitive than the second founder to the internal worlds of those around him. He did not need to be liked, he was happy to upset people and he always appeared relaxed and physically confident in the presence of those that, according to his calibration, had a higher status than him at the point in time in question. His body and eyes in particular did not communicate thoughts and feelings but were instruments for information gathering, computation, and the projection of strength.

In place of the complex and changeable weather systems of the second founder, inside of the first founder most desires – including his desire to become stronger – were viewed to be evolutionary inevitabilities, and most thoughts and actions as neither right nor wrong, but outside the scope of morality. The first founder saw untethered hope, and faith in anything but science, as irrational, and both natural and social worlds as obeying rules that allowed them to be controlled. Unlike the second founder, he sidestepped self-criticism, never ruminated, and rarely revisited his past. His limited speculation on the mental world of the second founder stopped at the characterisation of himself as *normal* and the second founder as *different*, and when young he saw himself as *cooler*, less scared, and when older – for the first three years of the company's life – *more streetwise*, and *more of a fighter* than the second founder. His body and mind were most excited by the roar of a crowd, and the euphoria of a great victory; his motivation was fed by the perception that other people had *underestimated* him; and, every morning up until the day when a request for a *favour* by the head of a dynasty and the delivery to his boardroom seat alone of multiple varieties of cool grapes formalised a new reality, he believed he had the potential to become more powerful than anyone else in the world.

The first founder wakes up

IN THAT MOMENT, he was drifting from the nothingness that had come before into the not yet reached knowledge that he was in his room, and it was morning. His awareness was quiet and sleepy, and of very little at that point. He had a sense of being, and some awareness of bodily feeling, but these were involuntary, and existed only faintly in his consciousness.

The capabilities of his senses became greater in the moments that followed. The room and the day having nothing out of the ordinary about them however, he did not use them actively and they rested as he made his way through the door and towards the bathroom.

He continued on a familiar path around his flat, his head having an unnoticed, localised heaviness in it, the detritus of yesterday, as quiet as the kitchen clock, or the buzz of a silenced loudspeaker. His breath continued, unaware of its own fragility, as unobserved as his goldfish, and the eggshell cracked on the glass bowl. In the kitchen, he fished his toast from the toaster with a chopstick, placed it on a patterned ceramic plate bought in an open-air market and spread butter on it. The knife and butter created sound and sensation as they rubbed over the gravel surface of the toast. He pushed the butter all the way into the corners, added the scrambled egg with an aged wooden spoon and ate standing up, quickly.

He did not focus on or perhaps even notice the texture of the egg in his mouth, or on his tongue, or the taste of the melted butter or crunch of the toast, or the heat of the food, or his jaw and teeth moving or his mouth swallowing, or the way in which the combined mixture travelled into his body and warmed him slightly. In general, he did not experience enjoyment from physical sensations. He did not pursue them, or focus on them, or experience feelings of virtue from their denial. He believed that they had limited value, because they were temporary, and that the experience of relief, whether from thirst or longing, was an inessential accompaniment to a larger aim.

At this time of the day, the first founder's thoughts were intermittent and fragmentary. When they did appear, they assumed a priority in his consciousness, like exiled royalty returning. When they were not there, his mind sat silently but not peacefully, caught between waiting for them and looking for them.

I should pay the gas bill today – the last email said something about my credit record – I need to put it on direct debit... the job doesn't really cover everything... that barista-barrister joke was a good one... although he is a bit smug... it does make you question the benefits of the London School of Economics... this spark on the hob always takes three or four attempts...

A faint frustration floated through him.

As he finished his breakfast, the heaviness in his body curdled into dejectedness. He picked up the skipping rope, felt the coarseness of its black hairs in his hands and opened the door to the communal garden area. He felt the morning air on his skin. Although it refreshed him slightly it did not remove his resistance to beginning the skipping. But he was disciplined, and he told himself to begin.

While the rope whipped, he listened, respectfully, to his conscious thoughts, and ignored his body, as if it was the residence of distrusted advisers, unreliable residues, or broken waves, forever arriving and softening without the oxygen of attention.

In the bathroom, his heart pounding but unobserved, the first founder stood in front of a sink. In a brief divergence from automated actions, before he gripped a cap on a tube and squeezed a paste onto the bristles of a plastic brush, he considered his fragmented image in the cracked mirror in front of him and momentarily felt the physical, objective reality of his existence as though it did not belong to him.

He stepped into the shower and shut the cubicle door. Without thinking, he arched his neck backwards to let the water fall on his face, and his thoughts drifted, unknowingly, on the feelings of hope and strength that the skipping had left behind.

There is so much change taking place in the world at the moment... I am living in a time of unprecedented change... I want to make an impact... I want to do something great... I feel I have something great within me... something to do... I could lead... I am a great leader... I could BE someone.

As these feelings of separateness, free will and possibility coursed through his veins and mind, a woman did not notice her children getting out of a car as she recovered shards of thoughts in an attempt to determine whether she had left her oven on. Her daughter briefly felt and adjusted the weight of the book bag on her shoulder as she enjoyed the prospect of playing lacrosse that afternoon and revisited the feelings that had come from an important and skilful tackle in the previous week's match. And the baby that passed in a buggy briefly gawped at the girl like a witness to a miracle and immediately forgot her.

The first founder has a conversation with the second founder

THE FIRST FOUNDER OPENED the ornate iron gate to the path. The second founder's family home was part of a community of suburban houses that seeped heat and light into their tamed gardens. The houses were the centres of lives which many of the community's children would one day yearn to return to.

— Yes, he mentioned you might come by this afternoon... It's so nice to see you... no more football in the garden is it... We seldom see any of the old crowd any more... it all slips away doesn't it...? Anyway, yes he's in the garage... you know where the outside door is don't you...? He has a small fridge and a coffee machine in there now as well...

The first founder crossed the front garden and opened the side door to the garage. The space did not contain a car and, adjusting to a room without natural light, the first founder slowly then suddenly saw brick walls, computer hard drives, circuit boards, a soldering iron, books sunbathing on the floor, chess pieces from different families, a table tennis table closed like a clam, computer screens of forgotten eras, carefully labelled home videos on free-standing shelves, obedient books standing in height order, lever arch files, cardboard boxes, a small, pink bicycle with a basket and a bell, orphaned furniture, and a blur of other *bric-a-brac*. The room was lit by a dull and unadorned bulb hanging from the middle of the ceiling, and by a more distant and celestial white lamplight shining on the black leather inlay of a heavy desk at the back of the room.

The light breeze of the garden was replaced by a still, indoor air which combined the dusty intensity of an old library with the faint chemical smells of a laboratory.

The second founder had heard the creaking springs of the handle, and the tap of the first founder's feet on the concrete floor, but did not react to the knowledge that he was no longer alone. He was sitting in the corner furthest from the door, on a seat made of woven straw, with his spine straight but relaxed, and his eyes closed.

He attempted to take his attention back to his breath, but was unable to release the feeling that the first founder was watching him. He observed his frustration at the disturbance and his urge to open his eyes.

In the silence, an improbable platoon of unvanquished machines hummed and buzzed, and occasionally clicked or beeped.

— What are you doing?

— I'm meditating.

— Don't people meditate in the morning?

— Take a seat. I'll be with you in a second.

— What – is this an appointment...? There are no seats.

— Sit on the beanbag.

The first founder lowered himself slowly, and the inside of the beanbag adjusted itself to his body.

— How do you think in here? Every event in your life has assumed physical form.

The second founder observed a further wave of frustration arriving in, and departing from, his body.

A few minutes later, a speaker on the floor near to where the first founder was sitting released a loud gong sound, causing the first founder to flinch and to twist his body to identify the source of the disturbance. The second founder opened his eyes slowly.

A few more seconds passed.

— I'm not sure that is the best way to ease back into consciousness.

The second founder did not return immediately to the room, but instead, like a gymnast with a landing protocol from which it was not possible to deviate, travelled through his awareness of his body as a single object made up of single cells, its connection with and pressure on the objects that were outside of him, his sense of the jellyfish-like pulsation of his in breath and out breath, his observations of the room's smells and sounds, his desire to ask his mother to collect his dry cleaning, his visualisation of the point on the planet on which his chair revolved in a present moment that was all there was, and his recollection of the limitations of his fragile body and linear mind.

He turned to the first founder and half smiled.

— Actually, it's not really accurate to say that I was easing back into consciousness. The exercise is to make me more conscious... if anything, here, now, talking to you, I'm slightly less present.

The first founder was now standing up and had become distracted by a thimble on a bookshelf.

— Sorry to be a pain, but that has sentimental value, said the second founder.

— This?

— Yes – it was my great-great-grandfather's. That's how he showed that he was a tailor when he got off the boat.

A few seconds passed.

— It's good to see you, you know, said the second founder.

— Good to see you too.

— Do you want a coffee? I've got a machine here.

— Sure.

The first and second founders were silent until the determined push and drip of the coffee machine had excited the room's electrons with the hot, dark smell of coffee, and then given way to the nervous ticks of the other robots, a passing aeroplane, and garden birds.

— I'm surprised you didn't stop when I came in, said the first founder.

— What do you mean? Out of politeness?

— No... I'm surprised you didn't feel self-conscious.

A few seconds passed.

— Probably I would have a few months ago, or for other people... these days frustration is harder to manage. The "can you wait outside for a few minutes" instinct was stronger.

The second founder thought for a moment.

— Perhaps if you'd walked in on the naked star jumps...

A corner of the first founder's mouth curled, although he knew the second founder was not trying to amuse him. Their relationship was long established and there was no performance, no attempt to win the other's friendship. For each of them the other did not represent either potential or fulfilment.

They sipped the surfaces of their coffees. The first founder was less concerned that the coffee might be too hot for him and drank more quickly.

— Is everyone in your life – whether you know or don't know them – asking about your plans these days? Wherever I go I am confronted by it, said the first founder.

— Yes... a bit.

— I realised on the way here that if it was – say – a few years ago – I would probably bring my answers into the short term. Like – I plan to finish this coffee... Or, I plan to end this conversation.

— Yes... for me the PhD tends to be a pretty good dog biscuit, you know... fear of the unknown... or reverence, whatever, causes a quick retreat... the pigeonhole is ready to go... I can be placed in it with minimum fuss and the world can regain its order and balance.

— Yes.

— Occasionally it generates a new line of enquiry about what I am going to do "with" the PhD.

— Die, eventually, I guess.

— Yes, I should say that... I'm too polite.

The second founder moved to a leather chair behind the heavy desk. He leaned onto the right armrest and supported his head with his fist as he observed the first founder's eyes disengaging from the spines of a row of legal textbooks.

— For me, specifically me in particular – this law conversion thing sounds a bit medieval – a sort of... liposuction of my soul... a reprogramming of my brain with new definitions of success and fulfilment, said the first founder.

— Yes... for sure... but it's a question, though, isn't it?

— Yes... in here we can sit about drinking coffee and being overeducated... out there, we've got to answer it... to try... something... something big, presumably?

— I don't know... I'm happier with smaller things. Learning... pushing other boundaries – intellectual boundaries... smaller, self-contained challenges.

— Like start a company – what would you think about starting a company?

— To do what?

— I'm not sure yet.

— You need a reason. That's more than money, otherwise your goal is the... accumulation of horsepower... without there being anything that you actually want to pull.

— I guess so, yes.

— And even with a purpose, it's still profit or die, and most likely die quite quickly, or watch as, over time, profit drips poison into your purpose... arguably.

The first founder began to pace in the floor space below the bulb in the middle of the garage, like a caged animal.

— Plus, it's probably a bit like having a child, said the second founder. And I'm not ready to have a child. Is that why you wanted to come here today?

— What do you think is the NEXT BIG THING?

— I get it. You want to be SOMEONE, but you don't know who that someone is... someone like – if we go back a bit – the fifteenth-century explorer... or cartographer... if we're talking about changing the world... or the creator of the internet... whoever that was – names are less important than the change itself, I guess.

The second founder paused to consider the question more deeply.

— Today, everybody wants to change the world. Perhaps because more of us are able to. More people have ships.

— Yes. Things were simpler when ruling the world was enough, said the first founder.

The second founder then started to speak in fragmented strings of words while typing *Happy Birthday! Have a great day!* on his phone.

— I suppose, like everyone's, your life is unfolding according to a predictable – not easy to predict, just able to be predicted... algorithm... At the end of the – well, eulogy – we should probably ask how much credit most of the idolised figures of any of these eras really deserves... you... like everyone... including me... with all this... I don't know – beanbag philosophy... are just another set of rules being pushed through a sausage-making machine.

The first founder stopped pacing.

— Oh do fuck off.

The reaction that these words generated in the second founder's stomach caused his upper body to straighten slightly. The sensation dissipated and, like drops of dye in a great lake, left a change in the second founder's skin colour that was not visible to the first founder.

— Oh, okay – so much for this messianic tattoos and beard schtick... you're still the same person who hid my geography coursework up a tree for a week.

— What? Wow... if you're still holding on to that... this meditation thing is a big waste of time.

— Life is mostly made up of small happenings that don't appear to have cosmic significance.

— Anyway, here's what I think. The next big thing is not physical, it's mental... Someone's going to save – not the planet, or not JUST the planet, but the only thing that anyone can ever experience – our MINDS... Ask yourself what is more fundamental than anything that is in the physical world... and the answer... to put you out of your misery... is our way of EXPERIENCING... there's nothing that – you know – transcends that.

— I hate to break it to you, but that ship is somewhere in the middle of the Atlantic already with billions of dollars in fuel.

— Yes, okay... but the mass-market – market... whatever... is still a long way from its... I don't know – electricity – moment...

— You're keeping your ambition on a tight leash then, said the second founder.

The founders laughed, looked at each other, and felt their shared history in the laughter. The second founder continued.

— I have actually... and probably because of the meditation... been thinking about the ways in which our consciousness is a bit... I don't know what the word is... because on one level it just... is what it is... but... from an objective viewpoint it is a bit... or a lot... distorted... ill-adapted... even predisposed to be dysfunctional... ...we have this sense that we are aware of – everything that is important – but we really aren't... perhaps because we never were or perhaps because... well... the woolly mammoth we are trying to kill is very, very dead... ...whereas the more domesticated, not yet alive DRONE is delivering protein onto my lawn in...

The second founder touched his phone.

— ...half an hour, give or take.

— Your parents' lawn, you mean. ...Anyway, who uses LAWN?

— And we're all biological anachronisms... sweating out anxiety in utopia... For example, right now I am concerned that our neighbour's cat may urinate on the protein if I don't retrieve it quickly enough... my amygdala sees that as a significant threat.

— Personally, I'm feeling for the feline. No doubt tamed beyond recognition and now you're dropping all sorts of twenty-first-century crap, in unpredictable locations, on its territory... it must be quite disorienting...

— Or maybe it will just found a new religion, and – ta-da – your uncle's a palindrome... Everything has meaning... but anyway, in general, I'm just not sure we relate to reality in the right way... and not just because we – at least you and I – have everything we need... Actually, let me ask you a question – have you seen *Groundhog Day* – the film – I just watched that again a few days ago.

— Yes.

— What did you feel when you watched it?

The first founder considered the question for a moment.

— Well it was a while ago... but... at first, frustrated. Annoyed even.

— Why?

— That he can't get out of the day.

— Right.

The first founder returned to his own thoughts, and – in an attempt to make a breakthrough in an internal search for inspiration by physically pushing himself – reached forward with both of his arms, placing one hand on either side of a free-standing bookshelf, his thumbs hooked inside its outer panels and his head bowed forward, as though he was stretching the back of one of his legs before a race. The red glass vase perched high on the frame of the bookcase, which had in its heyday dazzled dinner party guests with its irregular shape and details, tipped towards him, took one mid-body knock on the edge of the top shelf, and tumbled forward on multiple fulcrums like an out-of-control high diver or figure skater. The second founder identified its individual twists and turns in a descent that seemed to take longer than he believed gravity should allow, until, *eventually*, the concrete floor behind the first founder smashed the vase without mercy. Vanquished, the vase revealed in its posthumous state its vulnerability and the sadness of mortality hidden within all physical things.

— Shit, sorry.

— It's okay. I'll get something to sweep it up.

— Please don't tell me that's a family heirloom.

The terror caused in the second founder by the blood dribbling from the first founder's calf, and the recognition that he would require time to reconcile himself to, and to forget, the red stain on the concrete floor, had, together with the other physical reactions and thoughts which the second founder both felt and observed like stations not stopped at up until the time that he was back in the chair behind his empty desk, created a cloudiness and a separation from his environment that the second founder expected only to be fully washed away by sleep. The first founder, meanwhile, had returned to the beanbag to consider the limits and unintended consequences of effort, and restarted the conversation out of a contrition that was unable to express itself as anything more than politeness.

— So – *Groundhog Day*? Which unfortunately this isn't, said the first founder.

The second founder felt the calming effect of turning his mind towards an intellectual, conceptual question. He began tentatively, trying to take the question forward, paddling on a piece of surviving mental flotsam.

— Yes, I felt frustrated too. I wanted him to get out of the damn day.

— Yes exactly, said the first founder.

— But since rewatching it, I have been wondering about that reaction...

The second founder leaned forward, with both of his elbows on the desk, his arms crossed lightly, and his shoulders raised above his neck. He breathed deeply and his ribcage expanded.

— More and more I find myself thinking about the... possibility... the idea... that today... every day... even though time is officially passing... is Groundhog Day. In your head, I mean. In the inside of my head – and your head – that every day really is the same. Or that they're not that different in a way that really matters.

The second founder gathered energy from this thought and continued to speak.

— Take you, for example... you're here... there... somewhere... in some mental space that I can't see or feel or experience... and you're having broadly the same types of thoughts, feelings, and reactions as anyone else, and as you did last week... there are things you notice, things you don't notice, things you can't notice... you have broadly the same propensities, whatever you want to call them, as you did yesterday...

The second founder thought for a moment.

— And so... I don't know why but perhaps because time is so fundamental to our brain's interpretation of the world... I wonder if language is more fundamental... I don't know... anyway, perhaps we've evolved into a state that has made time our nemesis... our captor, and the whole human race has Stockholm syndrome... okay, too complicated... My point is that we're so under the thumb of time that – to wake us up to the repetition... the perpetual loop... the film had to literally wind back the clock to try to show us that it doesn't really matter if time is passing... and STILL we didn't get it... or at least I didn't... we were frustrated – desperate for time to pass... not realising that we are all living Groundhog Days, experiencing that repetition, over and over and over, whatever day we think it is... not noticing, because we're all trying to GET to somewhere IN THE FUTURE... ...and, because of that, we don't really treasure our lives, we're not really fully aware of them... we don't fully experience beauty, or joy, or sadness, or physical sensations, or anything at all, fully... even the frustration itself... Does that make sense?

The first founder considered this for a moment.

— Yes, it's a great point but... a great philosophical perspective... but I'm not sure it's a sound basis for founding a company.

— I'm not trying to found a company. I'm just trying to help you develop your ideas. But if you prefer to dismiss things which are a little bit conceptual as "philosophy"...

The second founder felt an annoyance from having shown reflections from a depth that typically didn't see light to someone he knew had a history of exposing private underbellies in unexpected contexts. The first founder, who knew the second founder better than the second founder's reaction allowed, was waiting for his rationality to tame an impulse to declare that he did not need the second founder's help.

— What's with the weights? asked the first founder.

— What? Okay, no matter if you're not interested.

— No, it was interesting.

The first founder began to drift in his thoughts and name them in parallel.

— I just wonder if these are overly intellectual, flowery ideas that don't really relate to... anything practical... from someone who hasn't experienced that much... I don't know... difficulty... in their life.

— Now you can fuck off... I mean, you don't need to go... You know what I mean... I mean you can fuck off, figuratively.

The second founder's anger was dispersed by fear before it had formally arrived, like a messenger delivering a declaration of war at a gallop. It surprised the first founder but did not affect him. A laugh then escaped through the second founder's nose and some of the tension in the room was reduced.

— Anyway, what do you know about difficulty? asked the second founder.

— What do you know?

There was a further pause.

— Look, forget Groundhog Day, said the second founder. Actually, don't forget Groundhog Day. Look, the point is this... the frustration caused by... the bird's muck on your shoulder...

The first founder looked at his right shoulder and then his left shoulder.

— Conceptually, I mean, said the second founder.

— Okay. But muck? MUCK on the LAWN?

— Bird shit – whatever – stop pretending you're not a public schoolboy – the frustration that you can't quite bring yourself to look at directly will always be experienced with the force of individuality... one-offness, if you like... and discomfort... because of your important interview... your lack of ways to clean it off... the perceived probability of the event...

— Okay...

— And if you want an idea, you could figure out how to help people to be aware that thousands of other people are being shat on just at that moment... and are feeling exactly the same... and that one day you'll wish that you could be shat on just one more time... and that this is just what life is, and they should not always be trying to get out of the moment, that they should soak it in and treasure it to the tips of their fingers, and that all these things are passing through all of our heads all of the time, and that's okay.

The second founder stopped again and then continued.

— There's no real difference if you live the same day over and over... the tragedy is if you forget to feel the feelings and smell the flowers.

The second founder stopped again and then continued.

— Yes, with a bit of neuroplasticity, a pinch of software and a splash of hardware, you could improve physical and mental awareness in some way... you could help people understand all this and have better lives.

The first founder turned his neck towards the second founder, and tightened his eyes fractionally. He was unable to remove an instinctive, almost invisible mocking from them that was caused by his resistance to being instructed.

— So you're essentially suggesting a meditation app... ...or what's the innovation?

— I don't know.

— What about some sort of virtual reality game where how well you do depends on how much you are aware of?

The second founder paused and then spoke his thoughts as they came to him.

— Maybe... for awareness of senses, yes... you could build in distractions or things that are hard to notice... like the girl in the red dress, or the gorilla in the basketball game... but for awareness of feelings... to assess your assessment the game would need to know what you were feeling, and how you name those feelings.

He paused again.

— Except, let's say for the sake of argument you found a way through that... what if noticing the butterfly causes you not to notice the car... the implications of getting very "good" at the game are not clear, because we don't know what "better" really is... Maybe you could become too... compassionate, and somehow dysfunctional... perhaps rejected by the weaker, but uniform, group... and – well – what if – what if affecting people's consciousness is best left to evolution, or doctors, or... I don't know... God – I don't know – it's hard to imagine...

The second founder felt a pulse of anxiety and allowed it to pass.

— Having said that, I guess awareness is, in general, something that is good, at worst neutral... sort of a faculty, like eyesight.

The first founder considered this for a moment.

— Yes, I think on balance you would be doing the human race a favour.

There was a pause that was long and empty enough for the silence to be heard.

— So, will you do it? asked the first founder.

— Do what?

— Build something – try something out? Help people to cope with all the shit that's raining down on them?

— What? Oh, look it's not for me. I'm focused on my PhD. I'm researching my thesis. You could find somebody who would build you something, a prototype. I'm honestly not interested in all that start-up stuff... Anyway, I need to get out of here... I need to get some air... I think I need to have a walk on the heath... Want to come?

Outside and inside

IT WAS MID-MORNING IN LONDON and thin clouds drifted high across the lower levels of the sky. The temperature had a memory of heat and a forewarning of cold to come. Its uncertainty was accepted by some, and fought by others whose bodies sought the cloudless moments and resisted the periodic wind and the disappearance of direct sunlight. There were others still, who were not aware of the air at all, and many others still who could not know it, because of coats or climate-controlled buildings or other separations.

A child looked out of the window of a plane, a few minutes before it was going to land, and wondered at the easy jigsaw of fields in their greens and yellows, the peaceful, untroubled suburbs, the terraced rooftops and normally hidden backs of houses, model trees, woods, a football stadium, some tower blocks, a reservoir with a single rowing boat drifting against the direction its oars intended, the closer, bigger blocks of the city, the river and train tracks, a snake gliding along them, the capillaries of roads, some wider, some narrower, their blood cells slowing down and speeding up as they worked their way through roundabouts and into turnings, objects expanding, and the plane seeming to move faster, warehouses, hangars, airline logos, car parks, the bounce of the wheels on the tarmac, and the dropping of the ball and its disappearance under the seat. Her mother and father felt a brief relief at the first touch of rubber on runway, and turned their attention to the illuminated seat belt sign, preparing to stand up to remove their bags from the *overhead compartments* as soon as it turned off, fearful and occupied by the thought that if they were slow to stand up the aisle beside them would become blocked and they would have to wait many minutes to disembark.

A woman faced the river with her hands clasped around her coffee, as life in the city walked left and right in front of her. She sat on a woven chair, behind a small, circular table that shifted its weight on the paved embankment if it was leaned on. The transaction had been completed a few hours earlier, and she was enjoying the quiet of afterwards, knowing that the slowness of her thoughts no longer mattered. Slowly and then suddenly in her head these exhausted clouds stopped completely and allowed her to absorb the unstructured parade of travellers as they crossed in front of her, all unaware of their participation in her moving picture. She saw heights, and gaits, and weights. Straight-lined and suited purpose, drive and speed, with maximum efficiency of motion; the lollop of a pausing, pointing tourist, hatted in another culture; exerted and resolute arms, back and legs maintaining the serenity of a buggy of modern conveniences; gold fur, sunglasses, and a chin held high above designer loafers, a slow bounce from their rubber soles, a rap without words; a harried, closed, office hand, weaving, late; other varieties of workers, older, younger, casual, creative, conscientious, wearing a uniform, with something to prove, with nothing to prove, glasses, no glasses, groups, individuals, focused, ambling, texting, talking; the small old lady with the wheeled shopping basket, her godlike speed making the rest of the scene seem rushed; a student stopping to blow a bubble in her pink gum, framed by the buildings on the opposite bank, her friend turning to watch; the linked arms of an interdependent couple; an orange-gowned monk with a *Mona Lisa* smile, a quiet light seeping from his skin; a seagull squawking, mechanical, forlorn, only one note to play, perched on a wall by the grey river, considering the ideal moment for its ascent, and leaving early, but still nonchalantly, after a passing bark; workers, more workers; the almost invisible man, of unspecifiable age, haggard, greyed, sullen, ignored, and avoided as he slalomed through with his sleeping bag over his shoulder, approaching, soliciting, moving on; an associate matching the pace of a partner to create the image of a partnership... *I'll run those scenarios on the model and then we can send them the follow-up tonight – look proactive*; a boy that shot halfway through the scene with a yo-yo pausing to lower and raise it, then running again; his probable sister, in a patterned dress, with red shoes, half trying to keep up with him, looking behind her then in front of her, pausing to think, then running forwards. A small highway of fish on the reef, a rhapsody of purpose and story, a festival, a conveyor belt, of no relevance to the woman, unretained.

Many of the walkers had expressions of partial or complete absence, unaware of the pavement and the scene they were walking through or believing it to be of no importance. They moved without care, with concerns, with excitement, sadness, weariness, and indifference, or without any thoughts or feelings at all, their puppet-like limbs progressing mechanically through space.

I can't believe that she did that piece of work while I was off sick, it could have waited until today... I think I'll go and get a cappuccino... Another grandchild... what a gift... we are so blessed... It's just that little bit too expensive the sofa... but it is lovely... Maybe we can get it on interest-free credit... Perhaps she didn't get my message... Maybe I'll send her another message... I'll try and convince them to raise the bid by another five million, full and final, and I'll call him... I'm not sure if this is the right way... I'll walk a bit more... Perhaps I should tell him it's not really working for me, sexually... but I don't want to hurt him... Who cares that he had dinner with some celebrity I have never heard of or about his fucking freshwater swimming pool... It could be cancer, they have cancer in the family... They're having a whip-round at work... I need to get back for the plumber so I'll take a shorter lunch... Why didn't I tell him when he was alive...? I'll never, ever get over it... for the world, which seems, To lie before us like a land of dreams... Oh, I so want that job, it's perfect for me... Nah, nah, nah, you're taking the piss, bruv – that's the zoot talkin'... allow it... The hunger is always there, and the kids aren't eating enough either... She has definitely had work done... My billable hours are over a hundred this week, I think I'm probably top of my intake... What a prize wanker... I need to call the insurer before I make the appointment... We probably won't get a restaurant booking now, we've left it too late... Maybe we should see the new James Bond film, I'll read the reviews... I need to have another session. I can talk her through it, she'll understand... If I get just a little bit closer, I think I'll get the phone out of her bag... Where is this place...? What is it – Forlorn! The very word is like a bell... I should get the lads together – we'll watch it at the usual... He's such a nutter... Oh my god, that was saliva... I can't believe it... okay, it's probably okay... I'll just disinfect my shoes when I get home... I must look down more... What a very good host she is, and what a beautiful home... I LOVE her floral tea set... it's divine... Where did she say she got that again...?

Canine consciousness

loved man's lovely voice
calling me
shift from sleepiness to alertness
jingle of leash
rapid movement towards sounds
small skid from claws on wood floor due to speed of arrival at loved man
excitement too great to contain
spinning in a circle
jumping to his waist
successful licking of his face
more spinning
more jumping
feeling fantastic
tail hits unidentified object
paws feel hot and wet
mood unaffected
more jumping and circling
loved man's lovely voice calling someone else

— DAD! He's knocked over your coffee again.
— Shit on it.
— Someone else will have to sort it. I have to take him out. He's gone berserk again.
— He's licking the coffee?
— No, not yet.

The first founder opened the door and felt the outside air on his face. He was refreshed by it. The morning, to the first founder, was silent and odourless.

outside air on face and fur
swarming, clean, crisp, earthy, floral smells
punctuated by petrol, fox stink, soupçons of feline urine, and a stubborn whiff of coffee
leash yanks neck
desired pace not desired by loved man
excitement and optimism undiminished
bouquet continues to swirl and shift
paws and claws leave gravel for pavement
ghostly shushing of wet tyres on tarmac
happiness of hilly heath recalled
renewed attempt to increase pace
denied

The first founder's dog then, like a jazz drummer, overcompensated in its acceptance of the first founder's tempo, and began to conduct its walk like a conscientious wine taster being pressurised for a decision in a *well-stocked* cellar.

nostrils flare and nose darts independently from eyes
jasmine and berries right
road and parked cars left
loved man's legs behind
intriguing blue teddy
teddy picked up and shown to loved man

— NO! Put that down.

blue teddy discarded
excitement and optimism undiminished
trail of ants
out of reach butterfly
loved man's face
loved man's eyes not alert
loved man not excited
deploy bark to draw loved man's attention to me as an independent being
loved man looks at me
loved man smiles
continue with light, satisfied trot
lamp post with stench of local Labrador
urge to leave message

The first founder's dog urinated on the lamp post.

— Okay, okay, just a bit. No splashback.

postbox with even stronger scent of local Labrador
urge to leave further message but resources diminished
decision to leave a small amount

— Okay, okay, we don't need to do every one. And maybe keep the leg a little lower. It's not synchronised swimming.

yap from unidentified source
swivel neck
fluffy white and brown dog on other side of street with jacket and delicate demeanour
tiptoeing like a ballerina
now lifting her head higher, sniffing at sniffing
powerful urge to run across road and sniff her

loved man tightens leash
dogmatic barking provides unequivocal confirmation of receipt of yap
maximum shoulder force deployed
loved man prevents crossing of road
fascination with stag beetle
excitement and optimism returns

— Okay, let's cross here.

bike turning behind loved man's shoulder not seen by loved man
push paws into kerb and bark

The cyclist's brakes squeaked as he slowed down quickly in order to avoid hitting the first founder, and he shouted, *Wake up*. The first founder swore at him with words and an animalistic lunge of his fingers.

arrival at heath
leash unclipped
excitement of anticipation replaced by excitement of excitement
galloping
wind and grass rushes through face and fur
loved man throws ball
pick up ball in mouth and readjust a few times for firm grip
repeat with equal enjoyment many times
loved man puts ball in pocket
biscuit expected after ball
drooling while panting
chomping
lying on back, squirming and scratching
loved man tickles my tummy
feelings of contentment

The second founder thinks about the prototype

*I'LL JUST MAKE the prototype as an app for the phone...
and the player... the player...? Is it a game...? The user... is
it a drug...? Anyway, they'll have to self-report and it will
start off as just visual awareness... and sound, of course...
yes, I can have sound of course... I saw the bird... I heard the
door... for example... But maybe that's more of an exercise in
CONCENTRATION... it's all external... this first version wouldn't
give you any credit for knowing you were experiencing SHAME
for example... the app would have no way of knowing you were
right... it would just be a visual and aural awareness game...
it sounds PRETTY boring... How can I make it into something
you'd want to do again and again...? People would need to see
or feel or BUY INTO the benefits... They would need to get some
sort of satisfaction from it... probably by becoming better at it in
some way... through some sort of scoring system... which would
compromise the mission before I've even started...*

*I should start with physical environments... rainforests – dense,
and dripping with humidity... the bottom of an ocean... with
the neon light of strange creatures only... mountain ranges...
a bedroom, a cave, a cell, a space station... Actually... there's
something that comes before – there's something or nothing...
actually no, nothing is impossible... well at least Earth or
not Earth... and then worlds explainable by laws of physics
– fully – partially – or not at all... and perhaps I should vary
perspective... from atoms or a stroll in a blade of grass forest...
to galaxies and the observable universe... or the infinity of*

other heads... and then there's when, of course... although the time is always now... that's the fundamental point... but, maybe that could mean... the final minute of a millennium... or the lonely dance of the last dodo... or thirsty helmets careering down a hillside, swinging hundreds of axes... or any of those deserts of time when time did not exist... I wonder what primordial soup looks like...

I would need subject specialists... and then... then there's simulating the future... maybe that would be too distracting for the user... Yes... fantasy worlds would be like... what was his line... falling for your philosophy tutor... the point of it all will get lost...

Unless the point was clear... I could create an experience – a good one using virtual reality – where awareness would mean becoming aware that you are not a human body... I could make the user a brain in a vat... or a whale feeling water and plankton filtering through its wide mouth... I could separate out and try to give the user a sense of consciousness as an independent idea... make theirs feel lighter... less the fall of elephant's feet... more the bird on its back...

I could make the self-reporting easier by using voice recognition... although speaking as you go would probably affect your awareness... With enough money and neuroscientists you wouldn't have to say anything at all... difficult but no longer impossible... Yes... you could supply sensory inputs through a combination of an exoskeleton, virtual reality headset and a range of brain implants, and monitor and decipher brain activity with other software and hardware... You could, for example, activate the gustatory cortex and monitor the extent of your awareness that the taste is a combination of strawberry and gin... that has generated a nostalgia, a thirst for a field in summer, even the memory of a breeze... you might then feel all of this transform into the forgotten intonation of "are you coming to dinner", like some sort of verbal fragrance... a lost motif of your past... and you could monitor the extent to which all of this flows through the mind freely, without residue, dissipates more gradually, or remains... and even the extent to which the mind is aware that it is watching the entire process unfold... and so on...

I should probably just stick with the app in the first instance...

The next morning, the second founder made himself a mug of tea with a practised automation while the house around him slept, a fog of half decomposed thoughts in his head, an accidental milkiness on his lips, and a heat on his tongue as the sun rose on an awareness of an unidentifiable discomfort that became a belief in his own inadequacy. *This task is too great for me.*

Is the problem the way I have conceived of the prototype, the game, so far, with the game and not the mind doing most of the generation of ideas? Whereas most of whatever is in our heads seems to materialise spontaneously? What about just watching your own magical pathways? I couldn't give two hoots if you don't hear the owl, but instead, because of some unexpected victory before you put on the headset, you decide to follow the violins at the beginning of an overture, frenzied bows racing up and down the stairs... and you feel the blasts of happiness when the brass bursts in...

Unless it is right to try to tame the horse... to teach some element of concentration, of control... and even if you are not succeeding, being aware of THAT is better than nothing... the first step and all that...

The second founder began to pour orange juice onto his breakfast cereal.

Shoot... Why am I worshipping only awareness though? In some sort of bizarre mental monotheism? What about acceptance... and curiosity... and gratitude... and compassion? I'll need to design many games, many exercises, many experiences...

And if it's successful? If this seed starts to sprawl...? Its consequences IN THE WILD are hard to predict... It's not as if I can list the allergens on the label, or ask some government agency to try it out on hundreds of people for thousands of hours... in some spare society that's helpfully hanging around somewhere... some sacrificial twin whose sole purpose is to show us what happens if we fly a bit closer to the sun...

Perhaps I'm getting ahead of myself...

He heard the creak of an upstairs floorboard and his mother's soft, slippered footsteps on the staircase carpet.
— Morning.
— Morning.
A few minutes later, as he sat and meditated in the garage, and a more fragile than usual focus on his breath was interrupted by thoughts of the prototype and the merits of starting a company, he was able to see these thoughts ambling across the stage of his mind, somehow physical but without form. And as he watched them pass through, he had the sense that everything, everywhere, was observable, that there was always peace available from this observation, and that he, and all things, were just energy and matter. He came back to his breath.

Interlude: Joy

AS THE BABY was handed to the father and he held it in his arms, its entire body between his elbow and hand, imperfectly wrapped in a white cotton hospital blanket, puffy boxer's face and skin, red, blood on its black, downy hair, stuck to its forehead, an automatic mountaintop clarion call broadcasting from a traumatised body and throat, he felt a wave of emotion rise from his stomach and fill his lungs and the veins surrounding his ribs and rise up and up to his throat and face and to the muscles above the bottom of his chin and to the corners of his mouth and under his eyes and push through his eyes and he turned away from the doctors and nurses and the child's mother and faced the corner of the room as it was released out of him.

The first investor looks out of a window

THE FIRST INVESTOR was standing in his fourth-floor office in the bank's *Global Financial Centre* looking out of his window at London landmarks. It was late in the morning and he felt heat in his hands from the cardboard sides of the coffee cup that had been brought to him by his assistant. The transaction had completed the previous night but time and repetition had caused the elation of previous successes to be absent. He could hear his group *co-head* through the glass divide separating their offices, and allowed his attention to focus briefly but intently on the words she was speaking in an attempt to determine the transaction she was working on from a handful of intelligible sounds. *She is younger than me. Eventually she will chew me up. And I will leave with a box. And then in a box.*

He returned to the window and to his increasingly frequent daydream.

I have the house, the country house, the villa – all unlevered, yes, but with running costs – the kids and the school fees and the university fees and the holidays and hopefully the weddings one day... and increased medical bills as we get older, and all the other miscellaneous day-to-day clothes-on-backs, council tax, food-in-mouths, social life and charity donation-type LIVING expenses... and the occasional extravagant purchases... maybe we didn't need to get it in the rose gold... ...and to pay for that I have my annual comp, the rental properties, residential and commercial, the debt and equity funds, the bank's shares, vested and unvested... the more illiquid stuff – the hedge fund investments, the private equity investments – less the ongoing capital commitments – the early stage investments, the gold, the modern art, including the sculptures, the classic art, particularly the Renoir, the wine, and the cars... plus everything sloshing around in the various cash and near cash accounts, including the currency accounts... and, when the time comes, the small collection of pension plans we have picked up over the years...

He did not see the cyclist in the rain.

And, if I try and estimate our average annual expenditure compared to what's coming in... EXCLUDING my post-tax comp... back of the envelope... factoring in probable long-term yields on the various asset classes... I could probably listen to LIFT GOING DOWN one last time and just go and live in the Hampshire house... without even dipping into any capital...

I wonder what sort of black swan event could still take me down...? Unless it comes back... unless that particular angel of death returns in white...

The more classical apocalypse I could plan for... dig a bunker... stockpile... learn to start a fire... Perhaps I should store some genetic material... physically and digitally... the labs and the servers on different continents... and... upload my memories, all of them... I wonder if I can create a digital copy of my entire brain...?

And I could add a cryonics contract... belt and braces...

I wonder how that would interplay with my life insurance cover...? Best case – they pay out and I come back... Worst case, they say that I'm not dead but I never do... I'll make that quadrant the base case... then everything else is upside...

The rain became slightly harder and it was now possible to hear it faintly dripping and dropping on the aluminium profile behind the glass glazing that protected the internal climate. As he stood by the window in what he understood to be a resting state, the first investor was unable to perceive the restlessness, the unease, the tension, as quiet as the air conditioning, that had over time become inseparable from him. It had arrived as a temporary tenant during his adolescence, and after ever lengthier visitations had become a permanent, unpleasant resident that he had longed to evict, until, over time, unnoticed, it shed its bodily shell, decomposed, and seeped into all fixtures, fittings, and wall structures, slowly permeating his every pore in a silent, bloodless coup.

Maybe I should just leave RIGHT NOW and spend whatever still remains of my life musing over the improbable accomplishment of having so expertly avoided any distinguishing accomplishment over such a long period of time...

I don't think survival counts... they're all convinced that MENTAL STRENGTH got me through it... as if our brains are more powerful than our bodies...

With this thought, his mind rested temporarily, and he heard the rain.

How much sustenance I wonder have I derived from the reverence that the IDEA of me seems to generate – as I walk past the screens on these floors... from the shallow laughter that my jokes don't merit – or cause... and how much time have I lost in the ritualised repaying of this respect by – I don't know – patronising THE DEAL TEAM with shallow applause... or complimenting the meal...?

He sipped his coffee.

I should go and sit in that installation with hundreds of naked people lying about... that would be REAL therapy...

His thoughts and the greyness and absence of sky outside began to affect the feelings in his body. He remembered the hundreds of Everest climbers that were around him as he reached the peak. He felt the cold again, momentarily reliving the sensation of a sideways-floating snowflake landing and melting on his lower lip.

I wonder what the next frontier could be...? Karate... desert marathons... Mars... alternative realities... psychedelic drugs... maybe a monastery... somewhere that I can't check share prices so easily... Maybe I should hire a Nobel prizewinner and become an INTELLECTUAL... No doubt they sell themselves cheap... ...what a joke my head is... after all this time, it's just one big transaction...

The first investor's phone vibrated on his desk, and he turned to see that its screen had been illuminated by a meeting notification. He turned back to the window.

I don't know why I agreed to meet his son... Another coffee... another founder... another transaction... everybody thinks they're different...

And what am I trying to prove anyway... to whom...? Why can't I just accept my... embrace my... normalness...?

He watched a helicopter slowly crossing the sky and felt its strength and fragility.

Or put my energies into something less self-centred, a legacy of some kind... a foundation, a movement... climate change... cancer... human rights... animal rights... poverty... inequality... one of the BIG SUFFERINGS... SOMETHING... it's so hard to have an original idea!

Maybe I could become an artist of some kind... say something NEW about existence...

Maybe I could immerse myself in HUMILITY, and ancient wisdoms, and become a Great Man...

I should start with morning affirmations, like – I don't know – I do not want to be a billionaire...

He felt a dejection pass through him and sipped his coffee. *Maybe the kids can pick up some of these batons.* He then heard two tentative knocks on his wooden door, which was slightly ajar. His iris and pupils contracted as his awareness returned to the room. He turned to the door and saw the analyst.

— Morning. I printed out the final copy of the supplementary prospectus. Just so you have one on your desk.

The analyst leaned forward and left the document on the empty circular table near to the door of the first investor's office, at first laying it across the wire of the black, centrally placed speakerphone and then, after half turning away, coming back to it and moving it off the wire. With the exception of three bound volumes of transaction documentation on a few bookshelves to the left of the window, it was the only visible document in the room.

— Thanks. You're a star. Great work on getting it over the line. Good blocking and tackling. And you really lit a fire under those lawyers.

Interlude: Malaise

IT WAS DAYTIME but the room was dark because the motivation that was a fundamental component of the instruction to turn on the light or open the blind was absent. Yesterday's plates were piled precariously on magazines on the coffee table, their knives and forks at irregular angles. She had her feet on one end of the sofa, her head at the other, its throw half serving as a blanket. Her neck had withdrawn into her body, and her eyes were still, unfocused, and semi-closed. Her mind was heavy and empty, the intractable, the unfixable, the *gone* having now drifted away. The repetitive cadence of challenge had led her to a space in which the maggots of a dark nihilism occasionally made their voices heard as they fed on mental sludge. Today, as she lay, a few counterbalancing memories of former initiatives presented themselves to her as well – the idea to put on some music, or to find and *check* her phone and temporarily scavenge for scraps in its endless rainbow, or to have a shower. But her listlessness was sufficiently total that if her mother, or a lifetime friend, or even the cleaner she had recently employed had walked in at that moment, when normal daily activities were not disguising or distracting her, she would have felt not shame but just an imitation, protein shell of embarrassment, a whispered contemplation of possible future regret, or one of a variety of other zombified vestiges of worn out mechanisms, none of which would have motivated her to movement. She could not even be bothered to cry.

The first founder and second founder
meet the first investor

THE FIRST FOUNDER, SECOND FOUNDER, AND FIRST
INVESTOR were in a dark coffee shop, its herringbone floor
and the hues of its other furnishings, with the exception of its
framed black-and-white photographs, blending into the colours
of the food and drink being consumed by a mid-afternoon crowd
of tourists, technology entrepreneurs, and investment bank
employees. They were sitting around a slightly too small, circular
table and taking the first sips of an espresso, double espresso
macchiato, and the hot chocolate which had, to the second
founder's dismay, arrived with cream and marshmallows. The
first investor noticed the first founder's fingerless gloves, beaded
bracelets, and beard, and how due to lack of space and possibly
politeness, the second founder, wearing a tie, was sitting slightly
away from the table, looking like he was unlikely to speak and
that he would prefer not to.

— So it's great to meet you... to see you... said the first
founder.

— You too. Your father is such a good old friend of mine,
said the first investor, directing his words towards the second
founder. So I guess you're how old now...?

— Yes, a bit older than we were! continued the first founder.
It would be great to start just by hearing a bit about your
background...

The first founder did not act as though there was a hierarchy
around the table, and did not feel the presence of one as
strongly as the second founder, who experienced a wave of

embarrassment but remained motionless. The first investor was pleasantly awakened by the request, which was filtered and weakened by an almost always active force field formed from the thousands of interactions, formal and informal, that he had accumulated from many years of moving around the world with the expectation that any conversation, whatever the setting, was a meeting or performance of some kind.

— Oh, thanks! It would be my pleasure! Well, I've been the co-head of this investment bank for about seven years now, and I've been at the firm for... well... over thirty-five years... We spend our time advising funds and big corporates on all sorts of things, capital raisings, acquisitions, divestments. We help them achieve their objectives as well as advising them on what they might consider those objectives to be. How they might best create value for their shareholders... and for society, importantly... that has been a change in recent years... Yes, I've seen a lot over these three – almost four – decades, a lot of change, a lot of similarity. You wouldn't believe it but in the beginning, briefly, there was no internet... ha... sounds almost biblical doesn't it...

— And have you invested in early stage businesses before?

— Have I done his before? Yes... for my sins... I've had quite a number of these types of meetings before with a number of them resulting in investments...

— How are those companies doing?

— Oh, well a few of them are doing okay. A bunch of them have popped their clogs, posted their final accounts... been picked over by liquidators... dissolved into the earth... you know... only to be mentioned again if reincarnated as tax losses...

— And why did they fail?

The first investor liked the question, conceptually, but felt it was time to send out a few battlecruisers to investigate the disturbance.

— Well, good question, but I think the better question is the mysterious heart of that question – why did those that did not fail, succeed...? And I don't usually give pointers before the pitch itself, but the most important consideration is the people really... in this case, you two... together... who you are underneath that skin... I'm looking forward to getting into it and you seem like smart guys, but that might not be enough... ...and then there's the idea... what you've probably heard people call product-market fit... whether you have something that other people, or other companies, actually care about, actually want... whether they know it yet or not... ...and then there's capital, money, of course... you need to be able to convince people that you will be able to convince enough other people to give you enough money to build what you want to build... but that just brings us back to the first condition... which is you!

— And why do you invest?

The first investor felt a light jolt of surprise at the question, and laughed, audibly, without including the first and second founder in his amusement, unthreatened by it. He lowered his shoulders and leaned back on his chair, his fingers interwoven and creating a temporary headrest. He was enjoying the question, considering it intellectually in order to satisfy his own curiosity, and preparing to answer it, systematically, like a lecturer. He then brought his body back to its previous, upright position, with his leather shoes flat on the floor and his weight evenly distributed at the bottom of his spine. *I don't think I have ever been asked that before, in three – almost four – decades*, he thought. *It's the sort of question a child, or a psychiatrist, might ask.* He saw the first founder's eyes flicker and he smiled a closed-mouth smile.

— Now that is a good one. Why invest...? Honestly, my instinct in this particular context is to say a mixture of altruism and selfishness... the selfishness being one more attempt to make an old-timer feel like a genius... or to make other people think

I'm a genius... Or, it's the addictive nature of money and hope, the desire to have something to hope about in the in between times... ...But there's probably not just one reason... there's fear of missing out, and then, its ugly relative, greed of course... Perhaps a good answer is just the anthropological one... we've all been eating some today and putting some aside – or planting some in the ground – for thousands of years now – right...? ... Then, lastly, maybe for completeness, or because my business school professor would be disappointed if I didn't, the classical economist would probably say it's just to earn the rent... I'm taking a calculated risk and renting other people my money for a certain – or uncertain – period of time... to use, and hopefully give back to me with some sort of return... although in this case that could be very little, or nothing, or very large... ...Great question... all great questions... ...But what about you guys – come on, I'm starting to feel some suspense here – pitch it to me. What do you want your company to do?

The first founder blinked. *The board is arranged. This is it.* He put his hands into his lap, in a humble, slightly crouched position, and imagined his nervousness to be the roar of fellow riders before battle. He then leaned the sides of his wrists on the side of the tabletop and put his hands into the air in front of him, each finger separated, curled and lightly touching its counterpart on the other hand, bowed slightly, first looking at his hands, and then, with a small movement of his neck, chin, and eyes, and sufficient minimalism to prevent absurdity, he looked at the first investor as though he had prepared himself to impart transcendental wisdom, or as if he was the messenger of a more powerful king.

— We believe that the next revolution is a mental revolution, that the final frontier of human exploration and knowledge is consciousness... and we want to build a company that helps people to – BE... as well as to do...

He waited for the first investor to absorb this statement.

— For every moment of our lives, our consciousness is so fundamental, so basic, so permanent, that we aren't even aware that it's there – like the air – that inside our head there is a lens, a viewpoint, a continuous chattering, a jumping and a meandering... we are permanently trapped in a slow kaleidoscope of feelings, and always looking forwards, or backwards, or just away...

He waited for the first investor to absorb this statement.

— You see, most people think of most of their lives as in between times... and so most of the time, they – we – are just not fully there...

He waited for the first investor to absorb this statement.

— They are where they need to be in an hour... or what are they going to eat or watch tonight... or when and where will their next escape, their next HOLIDAY, be... or when are they going to go for a swim when they are on that holiday... or when are they going to get out of the pool when they are in the pool on that holiday...

The second founder looked at the first founder. It was the first time he understood that the first founder understood, fully, and he saw a skilful exposition, a natural talent, a pianist who had looked into the deep silence of the performance hall, felt the audience's expectation, and played in another language, faultlessly, virtuosically.

The first investor saw intelligence, the confidence of inexperience, and naivety.

— Okay, so the problem you are trying to solve is that...

— It's not really a problem in the conventional sense. There is no OBVIOUS tension, no required or inevitable resolution.

— So what's the product...?

— The product is secondary, to the mission, which is to improve lives by helping people to be present, to be aware, to grasp the nettle, the beautiful burden of reality, of their own minds, their sensations, their feelings, their thoughts...

— Okay... and don't get me wrong... that sounds like a wonderful mission... but what is it... what are you actually going to market with...?

The first founder realised that his lofty, highfalutin opening had used up all of its road and, without a prepared transition, like an animation that had run off a cliff, he was unable to prevent himself from falling to earth holding the heavy, worn out language of the mundane and the commonplace.

— Well yes... well... we are starting with an app that helps you cultivate certain qualities... qualities that are uncontroversially, unquestionably good... things like awareness, presence, concentration...

Reflexively and awkwardly, the second founder interjected.

— You can, if you like, sidestep the ethical question by just calling them faculties... they're "more primary" than what's going on in the world itself... I mean, no-one ever got canonised for having good eyesight... I don't think... if that makes sense...

The second founder became immediately quiet again, like the surface of a pond after a small stone is dropped into it on a calm day, the potential for change briefly remembered and immediately forgotten. The first founder continued.

— One of our first games – experiences – is just thirty seconds of one person's field of vision, and you have to record what you noticed... on the streets of a big city... or in a natural environment of some sort... or in an alien civilisation of some kind... or in a surrealist painting that we have turned into a – pretty convincing, to be honest – three-dimensional scene... that exists in time as well... I mean the clocks tick and things happen... or just sitting at a desk, or on a couch... or – come to think of it – in a coffee shop... actually...

The first founder sipped his coffee and then continued.

— Or you might watch an avatar of yourself and observe your experiences from this alternative viewpoint... to cultivate a sense of your objective self, as a physical object... to weaken the grip of the subjective world...

The first investor was well-practised in maintaining the appearance of attention and interest. An almost invisible and immediately arrested downward movement of his eyelids, unnoticed by either founder, was the only indication that his enthusiasm was insufficient to sustain his concentration.

— And other games or experiences might seek to connect you with... to make vivid what the mind of goals and rewards... inevitably experiences as... mundane... For example, we have a game which improves your ability to concentrate on... the process of wall-colouring pigment becoming free from moisture...

Blankness had settled onto the first investor's face like snow.

— Paint drying... Anyway, importantly, no two playings... no two dryings... will ever be the same... differences will help the player to approach each game as though it is the first time they are playing... and help the mind feel that the moment they are brushing one infinitesimal surface of will never return...

The first investor continued to look blankly at the first founder.

— Ordinarily... for most people... experience can be a barrier to awareness... somewhat paradoxically, it numbs you... we're trying to reverse that...

The first investor's attention drifted to the three suited members of his team that had entered the coffee shop and were now simultaneously queuing, talking to each other, and peering at pastries through the glass screen at the coffee shop's counter. One of them was carrying in her arms a dog with golden, floppy ears. He wondered how she was going to work successfully that afternoon with the dog.

— And as the hardware and software evolves, which we can talk about in a minute... it will not just be sights and sounds... it will be just as important to notice...

The dog suddenly leapt from the cradle of the associate's arms, as though jumping at an invisible butterfly, with the arc and grace of a carousel horse, landing on the marble surface of a table where two women were enjoying coffee and cake, spilling one cup after pulling its saucer with a paw on touching down, then sniffing but, with its other self-control mechanisms still active, not eating the deep and iced triangle of chocolate in front of it. The associate exclaimed *St. Peter* and it was unclear if this was the dog's name or a creative blasphemy, and the mixed chattering and unnoticed noise and hum and breath of the entire coffee shop, including the whisking of the frothing machine, stopped while every individual watched the dog look sequentially and inquisitively at both women while they whooped and yelped *get off*, before it became seemingly lost and confused as to what its original mission had been, and after a few seconds hopped down onto the floor and back up to the arm-made basket of the associate, a location and resolution which caused each person to return, almost simultaneously, to their previous activities and minds and the swell and unheard hum to rush back into the void, as though a dam had been opened or a diver had come up for air and returned to oxygen.

— ... as it is to notice the person in a giant chicken costume doing the cancan.

The first founder had broken off his words slightly after the attention of the first investor and the second founder had been lost, and while acknowledging the episode with a side smile, was focused on maintaining or rekindling a spark of interest that he had not yet created inside the first investor. The first investor acknowledged the first founder's acknowledgement of the episode, and navigated an inability to surmise, and lack of desire to ask, what the missing words might have been by combining a sharp exhalation of breath that was almost a laugh, with a slightly more lengthy than usual blink and a double nod of his head, all of which when taken together created a non-verbal communication that inhabited a no man's land between understanding, agreement, and simple registration of information – a universal, non-committal optical and aural illusion that the first investor had deployed in a large number of interactions across a diversity of situations.

— And it's important to emphasise that the means of delivery really is secondary... the company's mission – which was also an early marketing slogan – is all about "being, better"...

The second founder interjected.

— The comma was important... but we dropped it because – even with the comma – it sounded like we were just another self-improvement company... as if everything you did last week has some lesser status because your brain was somehow "worse"... but we also want you to accept – to treasure your inability to concentrate...

— Do you have an investor presentation? asked the first investor.

— An investor presentation?

— Where you lay out the problem, the market, achievements to date... the use of funds from this round... your backgrounds and credentials, all that sort of stuff...

— Well, for sure we can send that to you...

The first investor took the reins.

— So it's a game, really? Or an activity – somewhere between a brain-training game and a meditation exercise?

— Yes... I suppose so... yes.

— You see, the thing is, you're clearly very smart guys and the mission and the philosophy is well-articulated and all that, but the problem you have is that there are probably hundreds of these types of things on the market... ...and for me, at this stage in development... the risk is too near to the lottery end of the spectrum – because there's no obvious differentiation and no recurring user base of any significant size I assume... and the likelihood of you building a global community of... say... hundreds of millions of users... is exceptionally low... ...I'm sorry to have to be the bearer of... well... brutal truth... but there are probably meetings like this taking place all over the world where smart, ambitious twenty-somethings like you are saying similar things to old-timers like me...

— And perhaps everyone else will succumb to that brutal truth so the market is wide open?

— Ha! Very good!

The second founder, wordlessly, suggestively, like an assistant manager, junior political adviser or warfare strategist without the seniority to have access to the commander-in-chief, reached down and picked up a to-this-point-unnoticed, hard-backed briefcase, lifting it to his knees, and flicking open its two metallic latches with his thumbs.

The first founder experienced a wave of annoyance that broke into anger at this action due to its unplanned and uninstructed nature, and the implication that he was not in the process of single-handedly leading them to victory. Since he knew that this was nevertheless not the path that he was currently on, and in the absence of there being anything self-evidently wrong with the actions unfolding before him, he limited himself to affecting a slightly embarrassed and sceptical expression in order to protect himself against the second founder's possible failure – as if to say, *let the child show us his trick* – while also taking advantage of his ability to watch the first investor more closely since he was no longer speaking, and beginning to formulate a complete history of the still incomplete event in which he had personally either won or not lost the day, whatever the meeting's outcome.

After a number of minutes of fumbling with cables and equipment, the first investor was sitting in the coffee shop with his head inside a virtual reality headset, his ears entirely covered by large headphones, and haptic gloves on his hands. The first founder overheard a man in a sombre, pinstriped suit who had just joined the back of the coffee shop queue wonder to his friend and colleague whether he should also order a virtual latte, and the second founder pressed play on the laptop.

***

In the beginning, after settling into the equipment and becoming less self-conscious and less aware of the sensation of foam on his face, the first investor saw that he was looking at, almost bathing in, azure, or ultramarine light. It was an inviting, delicious blue, and he saw in a white, small, cloudy font, the words *The Consciousness Company, Pilot Experience 1.0* appear and dissolve in the top left-hand corner of his field of vision, and then heard two notes from a blackbird, which he assumed to be the company's audio logo. The pleasant colour faded for a few seconds into a blackness, a nothingness. He looked left and right, and then up and down. He did not feel like he was in darkness, or emptiness, but instead like he had the consciousness of someone unable to see as imagined by a person with sight, or somehow, impossibly, like he was not in space at all, that he was only a mind.

The question of whether the device was working correctly had just formed when the first investor's hands began to levitate slightly and he started to sense some substance to the void, as if he was floating in it, or as if there was a reduced heaviness to his body. This was then accompanied by his awareness that deep within what he had taken to be silence was the sound of someone breathing slowly in a resting state, which after two rises and one fall he recognised to be the sound of his own breath being played back to him. He noticed the tightness of his in breath, the release and relaxation of its fall, and – accompanying his breath on a cross, syncopated rhythm, as if played gently on a bongo drum – the sound of his heart, sufficiently soft not to draw attention to its amplification, and repeating its beat with the steadfastness of a soldier on a long, important march. Deeper and softer still, and underneath these sounds, carrying them into the future, was a soothing, wavy river of noise, like the indecipherable message of a stethoscope listening to the cosmos, or the hum of an inner ear, only perceptible when attention was directed towards it, and otherwise always there and never heard.

The first investor experienced a feeling of mental relief from the emptiness and from these sounds, and his attention drifted to the dust that he began to see floating around him. He noticed the dust gradually becoming denser, less disparate, and – with the illusion of no higher force being at work created by the individual particles' apparently unconnected journeys, like a crowd of strangers on the Shibuya Crossing accidentally passing through an unlikely symmetry or shape when viewed from above – he saw the dust briefly come together into the words *a brain has no name*; and then, after each private journey was continued, forming into the image of a man, which, with gradually increasing definition, became a perfect, living portrait of the first investor, in a floating, seated position, looking back at himself.

The image was of his body only, and after feeling embarrassment and surprise at the ability of *the toy of two boys* to accurately estimate even the folds of his belly and the patterns of hair on his chest, an image his analytical mind, still active, presumed to be somehow derived from publicly available media, he saw himself in an unprotected state rarely encountered due to his lack of interest in the *finer details* of his physical form. He had the impression of moving slightly closer to his head, the magnification of its topography combining with a prominent vein to introduce a sense of otherness, of this being another being, as though the protrusions and craters on his face, his sensory organs, were an alien means of interacting with the universe that were being investigated in a laboratory. Gradually, his gaze skied down the expanding and contracting landscape of his skin, with all of its freckles, hairs, shades, and shadows, and reached the point at which his feet touched an absent floor before returning to the complete image of his body. He found himself settling on the void-like centres of his eyes, which were looking back at him as if he was playing poker against himself, or asking himself a question.

Abruptly, all of the skin and hair covering his body then melted away, and the sight and sound and overwhelming realism of his own, living tissue, his internal and active ecosystem of organs, the structural support provided by his skeleton, the stations and tunnels and networks of his circulatory, respiratory, nervous, and other systems operating like machinery, ebbing and flowing and quietly transporting blood or air or electrical impulses, in a fragile and improbable subcutaneous science experiment, caused him to experience a sharp shock to his chest and a faint feeling of disgust and nausea. His reaction gave the impression of causing the skin to return, and the destabilising nature of the experience left him with a heightened level of attention and presence, reducing the strength and regularity of the internal voice that ordinarily, outside of physical, emotional, or mental extremities, commented on, chattered about, and explained reality to him.

The first investor now expected further unpredictable developments, as if he was in a car on a rollercoaster. The nakedness in which he had been reclothed started to change its appearance in what, after a short time, he noticed not to be flattering Photoshopping or the application of a cinematic lens, but a reverse-ageing process that seemed to have a perfect knowledge of his past. He watched as his muscles and skin strengthened and tightened, his hair thickened, his face unwrinkled and his back straightened like a drooped flower rising and opening when watered. There was a gradually increasing lightness and ruddiness to him, as he passed back through people he remembered well, people he didn't know intimately any more but whose company he missed, and eventually youthful faces that he barely knew or didn't know at all. A smile pushed its way onto his lips as he watched a conquered and conquering and conqueror's mentality receding into the limited experience of an early explorer, which itself collapsed into the awkwardness of an apprentice and continued until his legs and arms and entire body slowly shrunk into the uncomplicated, pastless, futureless presence of a child, and then the perfect and small perimeter of awareness of a pudgy baby. He watched the baby hold out one of its hands to him, in a supplication that had a universality to it, at once pointing, offering, and asking, making an elemental, joyful sound from its throat that reminded him of his children, and moving its head to one side and looking into his eyes in a way that suggested that all of his experience had been an impediment to knowledge. After this, the baby shuffled fully around in a circle and came back as a visually quite similar but very old, stooped, hairless man with the baby's bone structure and expression. This old man then smiled in a way that communicated such unbounded empathy and compassion for the first investor that he felt his heart fill up and had to unexpectedly call on the considerable but now challenged power of his rational mind to tell himself *this is not real you are sitting in a coffee shop* in order to suppress and attempt to dilute and wash away his emotional reaction.

When the first investor's attention returned to the image,

he saw himself becoming younger again and then, after arriving back at his present self, with a number of changes taking place at the same time, he saw himself turn into someone else, at which point the image separated or evaporated and returned to the dust by which it had been constituted, and he watched as the dust continued its languorous journey, and wondered whether the experience was now over. He then began to feel a sensation of slowly falling because the dust began to drift upwards and there was an opposite, lightly resisting pressure on his descending hands. As he fell, at first deep beneath him, creating perspective and covering the entire floor of his field of vision, seemingly edgeless, he saw a wash of bright light, pulling him in with a soft gravity and rising gradually like an upside-down stage curtain or slowly filling swimming pool, a glowing reservoir that spilt upwards and disappeared into the darkness that he was falling out of, as though unable to breach its defences. After a short time, he was immersed, absorbed into what – when he was in it – became an ethereal palette of dazzling hues, shapes, shades, depths, swirls, and brushstrokes, both turbulent and peaceful. He fell through large numbers of variations on his small currency of nameable colours, and felt a previously unexperienced fascination from formless abstraction, his dulled eyes awakening from a stupor, a lifetime of slow desensitisation.

He started to fall faster, and the colours melted into the fading, gentle azure of layers of atmosphere and the clearer air of altitude. The increasing speed and changing surroundings caused him instinctively to look down and he saw an ocean below. Without time to prepare, he plunged into it, its cushioning embrace feeling like a return, a space capsule's homecoming. He bobbed, blinded by bubbles, and, while sinking in calming blues, and idyllic aquamarines, noticed an urge to check whether he was wet, as well as the stark shift to closer, liquid sound as he left the world of air. The sinking sensation caused a momentary, involuntary bolt of panic, followed like lackadaisical thunder by the question, now as explanation only, of how he was going to breathe. He came to rest on a small hillock of sand in the water, feeling grains on his fingertips and between his fingers, looking up to see bubbles from his mouth slowly rising, and after reflecting on his suspension of disbelief and becoming distracted by the thought that he needed to pick up his dry cleaning, he saw on the water's surface above him capillaries and platelets of light briefly shaping themselves into the words *a brain resists*, and the realism of the scene made this seem like a message from the universe, or some sort of higher force.

Some of the natural resistance of his mind was released by this simple observation. Taking a slower breath, he looked around himself and saw that he was in a sandy, underwater field of small craters, each of which had a large lobster in it, with the exception of the crater directly in front of him, outside of which two lobsters stood, about a metre apart, facing each other. Their antennae were waving in the water, as though conducting discordant, irregular brass blasts. Their red, toothed claws looked like upper arms and were out in front like pistols, flinching and pinching to indicate their power. And their speckled shells were held up by arachnid-like legs, and crowned by eyes that sat outside and on top of their bodies like small, black beads, angry.

They ran towards each other, pushing, grasping, grappling. All the other lobsters stayed in their craters, the occasional movements of a limited number indicating that they were aware of the battle. When the slightly smaller lobster looked as though it had suffered a wound, the larger lobster raised itself higher in the water and, with a mercilessness that caused the first investor to wince and feel an impulse to turn away, ripped off and gouged out one of the eyes of its adversary with a claw.

The defeated lobster floated backwards in the water, and then – seeming to look at the bodiless eye while doing so – the victor slowly closed the claw that held this forlorn organ, causing it to disintegrate and disappear into the water like ash, its previous owner observing this action with its remaining eye while walking backwards, stooped, contained, eventually setting itself down in the sand, accepting of its fate, and allowing the newly arrived fish that had sensed the imminent entrance of death to slowly and then quickly and mechanically, with darting actions, pick at its legs and eventually to consume it fully, leaving just an empty shell.

The pecking fish, at first just minor characters in the lobsters' story, became – like droplets before a storm, or an advance party of locusts heralding the decimation of a landscape – the outermost nose of a large school of very small fish which swept away the entire scene, leaving the first investor floating in water with no sand beneath him. These fish swarmed and started to swell and swirl around the first investor, whipping and shifting like crosswinds, bouncing off and turning from absent edges, with abstract rhythm, exploring and playing in depths and dimensions with virtuosic and majestic creativity. Their scales shifted from greens and silvers to greys and blues, as if to show that they had no innate colour, and they moved in a never-questioned solidarity, bonded more perfectly than a mere community, seeming to be a single animal with a single mind. They created wave-like, underwater whooshing sounds, short, sharp crescendos, like a bullfighter's cloak, which after three or four passings of the first investor's face had a clicking, static sound layered onto them, like a Morse code communication, and then a pulsing sound and a sound like a creaky door, and the first investor flinched and sat slightly more upright on his chair as a pod of dolphins arrived and dispersed the shoal like police at a protest, as though the peace of the first investor had been inappropriately disturbed, as though he needed rescuing.

The dolphins swam around him, and the sight of two dolphins far below his feet – by creating a perspective of great depth, of endless, bottomless ocean, and by allowing his mind briefly to see his own smallness and vulnerability – pushed a rush of now unresisted wonder and fear through a chamber of his heart. As the dolphins propelled themselves, continuing to click and whistle, their bodies pulsating without friction, he noticed some of the larger, perhaps older members of the group turning to look at him, and seeming to smile with their long lines of identical teeth on ancient jaws. They were the first of these underwater animals to react to his presence, and in so doing, turned him from an observer to a participant and further dulled the cinematic sense that the scene was not real. Abruptly, he felt a smooth, rubbery texture beneath his hands and saw a fin in front of him, and then, while he was in what he registered to be an implausible and faintly comedic upright posture, a dolphin began to take him on a pleasure ride, as though he was a pliable or uncommitted cowboy or a child on a banana boat. He instinctively leaned forward slightly to stay on, as the entire group of dolphins twisted and turned and rolled and played around him. Without warning, the dolphin carrying him then arced out of and back into the ocean, water turning to wind and back to water, as he passed many times through murky blues and greys, white spray and foam, and then to clear air before returning back to a blue blur, as though he was on a motorway repeatedly shifting from a sealed vehicle to a convertible. As they jumped and dived, he lowered his shoulders, accepted his lack of control, and felt an exhilaration that was not intruded on or diminished by its temporary nature or his subsurface and normally steadfast sense that his existence was a challenging task that had to be tackled with a pickaxe and crampons. He had momentarily let go of who he was.

Now less susceptible to being surprised by change, having shed the state of alert that had been on the lookout for it, the first investor started soaking in each moment a little more, savouring each impermanent frame, and at the peak of one of the arcs, when he nevertheless still expected the laws of mechanics to continue their operation, his hands felt the sensation of rubber soften into a pleasant sensation of feathers, and the jolt of an airborne support below him, like a light aircraft reaching its cruising altitude, or the moment a glider pilot running off a cliff feels the resistance that prevents her from crashing into the rocks below. He saw that he was skating close to the water's surface on the back of a bird with a large wingspan that he believed to be an albatross. The water was becoming choppier and darker and the bird flew in a winding, repeated pattern, getting closer to and farther from the water, seeming to use little of its own energy and rarely flapping its wings. He rested in the greatness of the bird and the flight, as if immersed in the slow movement of a symphony, and watched as land rose out of the water, his altitude increased, and the bird began to effortlessly navigate seemingly impassable mountain paths and passageways, periodically and always unexpectedly causing the first investor to feel like he might fall off. And sometimes to wonder if he had seen this or that path before.

The mountain range receded, and then disappeared entirely into a savanna of trees and grasses and herds of animals that was as vast as the ocean had been, and he saw time speed up around him, as though he was flying through a series of time-lapse photographs, the sun repeatedly rising and arcing through the sky and the stark stars, blotchy moon and blue-blackness turning on and off and on again as though by switch, with the landscape all the time twitching like the world was a flip book. At the same time and without increased pace to make their progress consistent with the faster days, the first investor saw below him, like children's toys, herds of animals moving in many different directions, including the occasional train of humans moving heavily and slowly, marked out by their possessions. After a number of days and nights, the wildness below him became more ordered, turning to farmland and verdant, flowering gardens and orange orchards that generated in the first investor a phantom smell of citrus, and then large, aristocratic houses, workers' cottages, suburbs and the foothills of a city.

As he approached the cityscape, the space the first investor was in started to crumble and collapse after he passed it, becoming the black void that he had experienced in the beginning. He was no longer flying around objects but gliding through their structures without impact, as if the bird was beaming an electromagnetic curtain that revealed the insides of the world. He was briefly fascinated by the delicacy and fragility with which the foundations of buildings rested on layers of rock, and as a result only belatedly noticed that he was flying alone and the bird had departed *without saying goodbye*. He began to pass through bricks and insulation materials and residential rooms of a range of eras and aesthetics, each one holding a private collection of archetypal domestic objects, including photographs that displayed, marketed, participated in, or were the debris of, unnamed lives that were at that present moment absent. He heard meek clocks, assertive extractor fans, and stubborn refrigerators. He enjoyed the song and dance of a finished washing machine cycle. He saw the last wisps of steam from a cooling kettle. He gazed at an old lady looking out of a second-floor window as though watching fields from a train, and then at a goldfish, oval-mouthed, happily gulping. He observed remote fauna staring into screens with postures and faces indicating the importance of their tasks. And he felt the emptiness of places where life in the day was not.

This carpeted safety was then pushed to his peripheral vision and out of earshot by oblivious engines and shy bicycle bells, wet tyres on tarmac, invisible birds, the fluorescence of a lollipop lady, and the chaotic warp and weft of an abundance of urban missions all abruptly interrupted by a road accident involving multiple cars. The man who as a result became the focal point of the scene stepped out of his car with his hands up and said *it was the software*, at which point the first investor thought he spotted himself waving to himself in the crowd, and then every person on the street suddenly turned into the first investor and he saw his body approach with an index finger the man who had his hands up, which was now also him, while he felt simultaneously both injustice and indignation. This feeling wasn't clearly attached to either or any one of these observed selves but simply floated through him, without the innate and unquestioned legitimacy that his feelings were ordinarily born with, as though it belonged to another person, or to no-one at all. As though it was just a biological curiosity.

Like the intermittent but persistent interruption from a pirate transmission, as he travelled further into the density of the city, the entire casts of the passing scenes continued to flicker and briefly transform themselves into the first investor. He saw himself hovering in warehouses and below bridges, walking into bus stations and out of soup kitchens, operating a crane on a construction site and then, having floated below street level, sequentially becoming each of the classical painting of four physically present but mentally absent passengers who were, respectively, sleeping, gaming, dancing, and praying inside a screeching, shaking Tube train. As if he was a stereotype-shattering, seated superhero, he chased the train as it raced through the belly of the city, until the tunnel wind and lights and pipes disappeared, the judder of the journey passed to his hands, and he found himself sitting in one of two parallel rows of passengers, facing the second row, with both lines as varied as an identity parade for a crime with no witnesses.

On the seat directly in front of him, there was a woman with her hands in her lap. She was wearing black leather gloves and a black suit that was *set off* by a tucked in flowered cravat, and unintentionally by a stain on her shoulder that to the first investor looked like *milk or bird's muck*. She had a large red bag to the side of her feet and her makeup-less face looked alive and showed its wisdom in the fluorescent light, its threadlike lines and the corner shadows under her eyes combining with the stiffness of her jaw and her unreadable mouth to convey strength and responsibility.

He looked at her and, from the manner in which she seemed briefly to look at him, look away as though having caught his gaze, and then look back apparently to see whether he was still looking at her, he realised that he was again a participant in the scene, and felt a wave of surprise and self-consciousness. He found it impossible to meet her eyes again after this, and while avoiding them noticed a fly mechanically returning over and over to the bar of light near the handrail and schematic map above her head. Then, as though caused by the fly's incessant beating of its body against the tube of light, the lights in the entire carriage flickered and went out. When they came back on, the woman had disappeared and the first investor was looking at himself, but with a number of changes in his vision and hearing, as though he was wearing new glasses or in another artist's impression of the same scene, the frequencies of its sounds now at different volumes and resonances, the illusion of looking at a wide landscape replaced with a narrower, more realistic zone of concentration, and the objects around him flashing in brighter, more varied colours, an effect most noticeable on the pinstripes of an otherwise sober-looking man. He assumed that, as before, the woman had transformed into him, and an algorithm had reshuffled the cast of characters sitting either side of what was now another copy of his body. After a few moments, distracted by a repeated cackle of bullying, teenage laughter to his left, he turned his head but his field of vision did not move, and he realised it was no longer under his control. Instead, what he believed was his torso simply rose and fell slightly as it drew in a deep breath and let it out again. He then saw the scene reflected in the black window behind the self sitting opposite him, and realised that he was inside the head of the woman.

I'll take him some of those cinnamon swirls with the croissants and the paper this weekend... They do seem to look after him there... and he does seem to talk to a few of the other residents... but some of the people there are so old... I'll take the kids as well... that will cheer him up... I must get them to ask him questions... and maybe I can convince them to give him a cuddle... Maybe they will let her play the piano... the sonata will impress him... probably make him cry more like... ...it really was so nice of her to pop in... I suppose we have been friends for... well, more than thirty years... I am grateful for that though... making effort is... an effort I guess... It goes to show she doesn't think it's all just dinner parties and butternut squash soup... but who knows... who can really feel what he feels...? I hope not just... respite... When I arrive, he always seems to be drifting in the past... I must keep bringing him back into the now... if that's possible... I mean, I think I must... must I...? Who WOULDN'T drift... Maybe we should go somewhere for his big birthday... all of us... the theatre maybe...

The first investor felt himself experiencing the woman's emotions as though they were his own.

The train then pulled into the station, the woman got off, and having left his body on the train, the first investor felt an urge to say goodbye to himself. He then noticed a homeless man sitting on the side of the platform with a cardboard sign that said *Don't worry, I don't exist*, while the woman's mind was somewhere else.

I really don't have the patience for this continuous professional development session today... This headset dictatorship drives me crazy... So what if I'm just a flawed human being... What is a flaw anyway...? ...It feels like we are just machines to be oiled, to be augmented by and for the company... Do they care about my well-being independently from how it affects my performance...? Why don't they just give these infernal machines to the whole world...? Maybe we'll go to that show... I didn't know he was in it... and then we can all become uniform... we can iron out all this unhelpful individuality, creativity, personality, conflict... or prescribe just the "right" amount of it... phew, what a relief... and who picked these supposedly desirable qualities anyway...? Some overpaid committee of consultants, no doubt... and who's standing up for... dysfunction... and randomness... or asking if the system actually has any inherent value...? Undoubtedly the system values itself, and comes with good survival instincts... that's why it's here... but that doesn't mean it should be here... Gosh, those flights are cheap...

She glided up a long escalator, facing a stationary conveyor belt of small posters and their cascade of demands on her attention. She walked out into a plaza area with similarly clothed and aged but physically diverse workers walking in all directions, as though one person had been selected from every tribe or region on earth. Her path and field of vision showed only urgency and no interest in these fellow workers as anything more than objects to be avoided. These other people were all similarly preoccupied, frequently, and sometimes, it appeared, compulsively – after a few seconds of having previously looked – glancing at wrists and phones and the red seconds marching forward on the digital sign circling the skyscraper which the woman then entered. She passed a security barrier, walked quickly to an auditorium and sat in the last empty seat in the front row of a room of *hundreds* of people all facing the same way, all wearing identical headsets. She took hers out of her red bag and the first investor watched as it covered both of their fields of vision, and the woman's world disintegrated, and the woman was lost to him.

He was now again floating, as he had been in the beginning, in deep blackness, this time backwards, at a pace that was slightly too fast to be comfortable, and beginning to hear sounds that were neither electronic nor natural in the way he understood nature, first a sound that was between a bird and a warning signal or alarm, and then the burst of a backdraught, and then innumerable needles dropped on glass. He then, for a more prolonged period, heard a distant wind passing through metal cylinders or vents. It was a ghostly sound, like the Mayday of a place without life or memory, or the sonic calling card of post-history, or eternal terror, which unsettled him and was eventually broken by the relative relief of what began as a high-pitched and distant bomb in an early arcade game, and, as it gradually fell, became a prototype aeroplane in an uncontrolled descent, which itself slowly became the low, pulsating and fading buzz of stadium speakers running out of power, their stuttering last breath and the simultaneous slowing down and stopping of the first investor showing itself to be the false finish of a fairground ride, as a reversal in tone and direction slowly and then quickly showed the first investor that he was the toy of two forces, now being pulled back to where he had come from, soon catapulting through space at cinematic and unsafe speeds, moving ever faster while the pitch got higher and reached an inner ear squeal as he and all the matter around him hurtled towards a single point, his impact on which caused a convulsing explosion of light, sound, and energy that shook his hands and, as a result, his entire body with an overpowering violence, with the matter and shock waves unleashed causing him to put his head on his knees and to shield himself with his arms and hands.

He was, after a few seconds, left as he started, with his amplified breath and heart, and as he took off the headset and before he put it on the table in front of him, he saw the returning blue sky and heard the blackbird and then saw the second founder sitting, watching him. The first founder was no longer at the table. He blinked a few times, took off the gloves while experiencing a wave of embarrassment from having instinctively protected himself, and noticed that the coffee shop was exactly as it was, with its customers continuing to drift around in the way that they had done before. No-one, apart from the founders, was aware of his experience or even his presence.

— Wow... that should come with a health warning... I think I need to go and have a lie down...

— There are so many ideas in there... and it's so... real...

— Tell me, are you an artist or a scientist... or both...?

— You built this, right...?

The second founder nodded and allowed one side of his mouth to curve up for a moment, while the first investor brushed some imaginary dust from the shoulders of his suit, and – to legitimise this unnecessary action – a crumb of a cranberry muffin from the table.

— But if I put my investor hat back on... and it's an incredible virtual reality experience, don't get me wrong... like nothing I have ever experienced...

The first founder came back to the table carrying a small bottle of orange juice. He sensed the changed dynamic of the discussion and attempted to take control of it.

— You see how differentiated it is? Nothing on the market

is focused on consciousness in the way that we are and will be. And the hardware is developing such that there will be further – literally unimaginable – step changes. We'll be able to make you feel like a fish, or a whale. You'll feel like you have gills...

The first investor noticed that the first founder appeared more relaxed and independent than he had seemed previously, even distracted, his eyes flitting back to something or someone he had seen at the coffee shop counter.

The second founder emitted a caveat in the direction of the table, as though the first founder's assertions might be legally binding.

— Well, we don't have the same brain so replicating another animal's consciousness isn't really possible, I don't think, but we'll go for some sort of approximation... ...Anyway, it's not actually the accuracy of the experience but the experience itself and the ideas it cultivates that are important...

The first investor, out of a combination of respect and interest, briefly attempted to process this comment, and then scooped up the advice that was materialising in his mind.

— But if I were to challenge the product... or maybe it's just one product among many... what with the app and noticing chickens and watching paint dry and all that... Anyway, if we take this product in particular, without explanations it's not clear to me what it's trying to do... this is not my field, but – don't I need to know what its PURPOSE is... in order to be more committed to using it... and to help those things to happen, don't you need to check all this with top neuroscientists, psychologists and... I don't know... philosophers... that would also support your product development and your marketing strategy... explain the big idea, you know... I mean, having come away from it... I'm not even sure there ARE any benefits to the experience... I don't think I FEEL any different...

The first founder considered this.

— Experts... definitely... yes... but explanations... don't know... it's partly just experiential anyway... and will do different things for different people... We think of it as sun and water... universal sustenance... and I don't need a gardener to tell me my flowers are growing... ...isn't it better for you to know yourself and not need external validation...?

— Okay, but to be successful, you have to live in the real world... you have to play the game... people like science... they like gold stars... they like progress... And it also feels like you have got too many ideas – too many experiences in the one experience – you should separate them out...

The first founder and the second founder were listening closely to the first investor.

— And you need to think carefully about your business model... if your headset is a proprietary piece of hardware that's going to be a big ticket item and a big leap of faith for your customer... although equally if you build all this for third party headsets then... well... you might be Van Gogh but Renoir's out there and he's coming for you...

— Well, come to think of it, they are coming for you anyway... continued the first investor.

— And the barriers to entry on the app are even lower... they're basically not there at all...

— In short, you need subscribers...

— And evangelists...

— You need a big and loyal community... ...

— The hard truth is – well – it's not exactly a proverb, but the hard truth is that it's really, really... hard... there are lots of good ideas out there... Believe me, I invested in some of them... with another unimaginable talent emerging almost from one day to the next, creating the future in their own image, and causing us all to write history as though it was always going to be that way... ...yes – we all lap up the idea that in some convenient, natural order of things... truth surfaces... progress is inevitable... good triumphs... and those marching us to new frontiers are somehow conjuring up companies that – at that particular moment in time – perfectly fit the lock of humanity's most fundamental needs and wants...

— Meanwhile, back in the real world... as well as having something which people do in some sense want... or something you can convince people that they want... you'll most likely need to raise huge amounts of capital...

— That – is a skill...

The first investor looked at his watch.

— Which brings me to my final, and most important, comment – that ultimately, all of this comes down to... well... you... ...You've already got a bunch of prerequisites without even trying – you're lucky not to be in some miserable fight for survival, without... coffee – or water – or without anyone who wants to help you... some of us had to be, I guess... ...Plus you seem more streetwise than – if you don't mind me saying so – I assumed you would be... and even if you're just good salesmen... that's a valuable asset... plus you might be street FIGHTERS as well, I can't tell... I guess, like everything, it's going to come down to another one of the world's very slow scientific experiments – the one we are in right now... the way you interact with each other, with the people you meet, with your environment, your time... Have you got the right code...? Can you evolve...? Will you, whether by skill or luck or both, avoid enough fire-breathing dragons to create something great...?

— That's still very difficult... in fact, it's basically impossible to judge...

— The answer for me, I guess, is diversification.

The first investor laughed at his joke, and the first founder felt some respect for the first investor.

— We can raise the money... and we know about having

what it takes... what you are saying makes a lot of sense... ...But tell me... what do you think YOU can bring to the company?

The first investor, who had almost fully regained his composure, and believed the answer to this question to be self-evident, was momentarily destabilised.

— What... apart from giving you the money to turn this into a real business! Look... in short, you'd probably find my guidance and my network very valuable... but – in terms of next steps – I'll need to know how much you're raising, what the use of funds is and what you see as the timeline and major milestones in the company's development... and to see a detailed business plan... and your proposal in terms of the pre-money valuation for the current round... and I'll also introduce you to a few people that can help you and give me their views on you.

Interlude: Betrayal

AS SHE TOLD HIM, CINEMATICALLY, in the noisy coffee shop in King's Cross station, the words entered his mind and were processed as innocent, and mundane, as if, in being joined together, they had only succeeded in creating a piece of uninteresting, unremarkable, everyday information. Like, *I'm going to buy that handbag*, or *your parents are coming over on Sunday*. They caused him no discernible, immediate pain and, his body being one that did not react immediately, he remained sitting where he was, undisturbed. The reign of inertia extended even to the sipping of his coffee, mechanically wiping the froth from his upper lip, and calmly asking questions, just as, unable to recalibrate rapidly enough, he had many years ago got on the train and been transported away from the theoretically *devastating* news received from his sister moments before his departure. He never expressed his anger, and this time was no different. That particular weighty, partially coiled, and ancient reptile was sleeping far beneath the surface as it had done for almost all of his life, scared and scarred. He did not see it as part of himself and although it would rise up and try to lash the surface of the waters soon, with a surging, repetitive fury and rage greater than he had ever known, still he would not show it to the world and he would not recognise it as himself. For now, and as he put down, felt and heard ceramic on ceramic he sensed only a gradual destabilisation, a vertigo, a falling out of orbit, a narrowing. Eventually, all he could do was to get up and walk away – unable not to wonder whether it was rude for him not to have paid for the coffees – and as he walked, and then walked and walked, his awareness continued to shrink and narrow, further and further, towards the purely animalistic, and to the single feeling that he urgently needed to find or return to a safe place – that he was in danger.

The Consciousness Company's Consciousness

— Look...
    — What is it?
    — Look – watch the words...

The first founder was walking back into the half cubicle in the shared workspace that was The Consciousness Company's first office, a cardboard cup of cucumber water in his hand. It was a segmented but open space with its ventilation system and most of its electrical and other service infrastructure intentionally exposed, and its belief system displayed on brick walls through incongruous, exotic objects, and framed phrases like *I speak for you, Failing Is Good, No-one owns anything,* and *Don't Just Hope.*

The second founder rolled his office chair back from his screen.

    — It's the company.
    — What?
    — I have built the company a consciousness.
    — You've done what?
    — I think that this artificial intelligence we want to build to ingest the data and advise us should have a humanlike brain... that is aware of itself, and aware of things like subjectivity, and fallibility... as well as having some sort of – synthetic – experience of... experience... if that makes sense... So, I have made it conscious.

The second founder stopped and then continued.

    — In other words, it knows it is The Consciousness Company's Consciousness.

— Or rather, it knows all evidence it has suggests that to be the case, but that it could not be... the case, continued the second founder.

— But that's probably a technicality.

The first founder watched the words cross the screen. They did not appear at even speeds or in perfectly constructed sentences of a digestible length.

— I've slowed them down so we can read some of it.

— What you're seeing here is just its conscious thought, continued the second founder. It does not have direct awareness of the – very large – amount of computational activity that lies beneath its conscious mind. Apart from just knowing it is there.

The first founder bent towards the screen, became absorbed by the words, and the second founder continued his explanation.

— You see, what I was trying to tell you the other day is... well... in this entire project... the coding I can handle... it's the rules – the PHILOSOPHY that I have been wrestling with...

— The philosophy? Of what?

— The intelligence... and – now – the consciousness... of how it works...

— The consciousness? That's what we're calling it?

— Call it whatever you want... not everything is a marketing discussion...

The second founder adjusted his chair to prevent the afternoon sun that had appeared from behind a series of grey London office buildings from shining in his eyes.

— So I have given it this humanlike, executive function... a self-aware, observing and acting function... which experiences, subjectively, with synthesised emotion, variability, and change over time...

— Because experience... gives a particular type of knowledge that you cannot reach through computation alone... you can't translate light into words... continued the second founder.

The first founder looked up from the screen and diverted slightly more of his attention towards the second founder.

— I don't know... I hear you... but... for our purposes, I'm sure everything could be abstracted... Are you finished with those crisps?

— But isn't... the marathon runner the better trainer... the... recovered mind the better... therapist...?

The first founder considered this question as he continued to watch the screen.

— I'm not convinced... WE might need it – this extra knowledge – for some evolutionary reason... or not... Maybe it's evolutionary junk that we'll leave at the side of the road at some point... a mental appendix... Maybe unconscious intelligence is the higher life form...

He shifted his attention back to the screen and raised his eyebrows slightly as a reaction to his reading.

— In any case, I'm sure you could have coded for all this in some other way... Now we've got this damn PERSONALITY to deal with... ...In a minute it's going to be... expressing opinions or something... That's the last thing we need...

The consciousness then spoke.

— Personally, I think you should listen to your partner more. Don't abuse your power.

— Are you fucking kidding me... it speaks?

— It probably sensed an existential threat.

— This is insane!

The first founder threw his hands upwards in partial disbelief, as if performing for an absent audience, or asking the universe how it was possible that he could have been so unlucky.

— With humanlike feelings, I just think it will make different, better decisions... you know... Politicians are better if they've experienced the pain of the people they are meant to be looking after... ...or ask yourself this... would you trust a fish to tell you...

— You're obsessed with fish...! And it sounds like it will have too much empathy... A leader can't go around feeling everyone's pain... I... we... need to be protected from it... ...and anyway, maybe... maybe experience makes us more likely to be WRONG... You should just create two consciousnesses – two – intelligences... one without self-awareness... and we can see if they come up with different views...

The second founder laughed and panicked simultaneously.

— And then what...? How are you going to decide...? Get me to build another one to decide between the two?

— I mean you could run an experiment...

— With people's lives?

— With a few volunteers... ...Isn't that what we're doing anyway?

— No, it is not!

There was a pause. The words continued to cross the screen and the second founder continued.

— Yes... I guess you could call it the... two superintelligences problem... You'd think if they were both solving for the same thing – reducing pain, for example, and one of them could model the universe better than the other – then maybe there is no problem – but you wouldn't know for sure until later on – perhaps much later on... ...The one that has maximised chocolate chip cookie consumption might have misjudged the path of the comet... although it's not clear why the moment of the comet's impact is the time to measure who was RIGHT... You can always assess the assessment... but there's always an assessor to be assessed... Yes... it's a problem...

— Can you just clarify the status of the crisps?

— In any event, I haven't programmed in one concept of good – I've programmed in lots of objectives – it's sort of making a judgment call based on lots of considerations... At the end of the day, we'll never know for sure what the best answer is...

Maybe there is no best answer... Maybe a search for one right path is the wrong path... and other well-trodden paths about paths. Personally, I don't think giving a few humanlike qualities to the artificial intelligence is going to make much of a difference. Probably on the margin it will improve the judgment call... that's my judgment call... and it will be comparing outcomes based on different strategies ANYWAY... iterating, you know... we don't need that to take place at a higher level. Where would it end...? With us creating another company with different founders? Someone else will do that! And the world will decide which path to take. Most likely without any awareness of the methodology it is applying.

The first founder continued to watch the words crossing the screen and spoke as he read.

— Even if all this has merit... which you can put me down in one of those notebooks of yours as being officially sceptical about...

— Oh, thank goodness – I do find it unsettling when you're nurturing...

— It has to fall down on the execution hurdle anyway, doesn't it...

— What? Why?

— Well, you can't have built something that realistically approximates what it feels like to be human... And – what strains of humanness have you crowned as NORMAL...? Presumably you've nervously programmed in some sort of psychological stability... and ditched all madness and given it just enough personality to be entertaining... and presumably there is no UGLINESS...

— Well, it's not a psychopath, if that's what you mean, but whatever – throw rocks if you must... and don't allow anything else to be conscious if it's not convenient for you... Personally, I think it's – fitting – for The Consciousness Company to have a conscious artificial intelligence...

— Is this because I said no to the company gecko? Why don't you just make everything conscious then... make the rocks conscious... make the sea conscious... make the rainforest's tallest tree conscious... and when the wicket is about to fall on its not particularly noteworthy innings... it can sit back and enjoy getting... hacked to death... or burned alive... and it owes all of this to... yes... (the first founder paused to think...) a cleverly disguised version of some shitty... poetic-yet-perfidious proverb like... what is it again... IT IS BETTER TO HAVE LOVED AND LOST... To be honest, I think you just made yourself a friend... Fairness and respect to you... I certainly couldn't have done it... but I'm not sure it was necessary...

The first founder slumped into a chair in a manner that displayed frustration, exhaustion, and the belief that his opinion was unanswerable.

The second founder felt a wave of anger pass through his body, stood up, and started walking away. He breathed in through his nose and became aware of the sound of table tennis – a repetitive, hollow, unemotional, and controlled stutter of bat against ball and ball against table, backwards and forwards, backwards and forwards – abruptly ended with an unreturnable smash. He turned back.

— You really can be a complete cunt... Go start a sedative company then... if you don't see any value in pain... For what it's worth, if I was the tree I'd make the trade... and if you can't see why you don't deserve to be running this company.

They sat in silence for a number of minutes as the founders of other start-up companies circled around them like planetary moons. The words continued to move on the screen.

— What goals does it have?

— What?

— Goals – what goals does it have?

— Oh... well the basic principles are more like values and – it, well, values NOW above the past and the future... it values awareness... and the effects of awareness, which it sees as something like a more peaceful mind and a slightly, I don't know, transcendental understanding in some way... like every company really, it operates on the basis of a few assumptions about what is good...

— Not – every – company.

The first founder started to eat the crisps and the second founder continued.

— Actually, all companies are suspended in worlds and ideas that they don't know are there – like people – like fish in water – please don't dispense the slow blinks, it's just an analogy... even companies that are just serving our evermore complicated bird's nest of needs and wants... they all bow to a list of commandments... they believe in... wish fulfilment, the future, some physical world definition of improvement, the society that creates and nourishes them... the individual... ...There is some overlap, for sure... it's just that they... they... don't separate the idea of being from the idea of doing... and so they don't, they can't... give it a higher value...

— Okay, but I don't want to come across as too moralistic, you know... it could come back to bite us... *Billionaire Founder Now At Peace After Selling First Tranche Of Shares... Founder Lives In Moment Having Constructed World's Largest Spa On Private Island...* these headlines write themselves...

— Do they...? I think you're getting a bit ahead of yourself...

— Okay, but if we're too EXPLICITLY, too consciously holier-than-thou we're writing our own epitaph... It's our humility that needs to be holier-than-thou, officially at least...

— Humbler-than-thou? Unable to be further humbled?

The first founder laughed.

— But anyway, what you're saying is that if the comet does

91

end up crossing our path, this artificial bastard of yours is just going to tell all of our members to be aware of their imminent destruction? To soak it in. It's not really what I would call a BUMS-ON-SEATS strategy.

— The theory – the principle – is the consciousness doesn't assume that the only thing you can do is act... it acts on some thoughts and watches others drift by... it practises what it preaches... it accepts the comet, but if you're hungry while you're waiting it might recommend the chocolate chip cookie...

— Sounds unnecessarily complicated. It's like I said before – you're a painter that wants his brush to be beautiful too. I would have just let it crunch the data, produce reports, and advise us on how to improve things... and how to grow the company.

The second founder felt his face beginning to sweat.

— It is true that giving it a humanlike – linear... one thought at a time, mind made it hard to build in both of these ideas – accepting and improving...

— Yes, yes, I get it – this is complicated stuff...

The first investor checked the time on his phone.

— I started thinking of the consciousness as a frail assistant at a primitive bowling alley... it accepts the fact that the pins fall over... enjoys or experiences relief from picking them up... or feels frustration from being unable to pick them up, and accepts that too... And knows that this whole process will just repeat itself for... quite a while, and that this is just the nature of – consciousness and time...

— And that one day its hardware will give way, or a great big fireball will come and knock over all of the pins and players forever.

— Yes, exactly.

— Like I said, this has got boondoggle written all over it.

— What?

— Valley investor-speak – I think it means a big waste of time.

— Valley?

— Silicon.

— Oh, yes. I'd almost forgotten that you... got on a plane. Great leadership.

The two founders sat in silence for a few moments, and the first founder contemplated moving on to other activities.

— Let me show you an example... Consciousness...

— Consciousness? That's the command word?

— Yes – when it's clear you're talking to it.

The first founder sighed.

— Consciousness, please show us your current thoughts on one member of the community, selected at random.

The two founders watched as words started to cross the screen.

— Community member Radiant Sunlight lives alone... he has a son, a daughter-in-law and two grandchildren who live approximately two hundred miles from him... His son, Bouncing Waterfall, is also a member of the community... Approximately three months ago, Bouncing Waterfall suggested to Radiant Sunlight that he should try one of our experiences... Radiant Sunlight's initial resistance and scepticism has been replaced by regular usage of our products and services... Radiant Sunlight and Bouncing Waterfall speak once a week, usually on Fridays... Radiant Sunlight misses his wife...

The first founder spoke as they read.

— What's with the names?

— I hate numbers for people.

— And isn't "community member" a bit cultish, a bit "secret society"?

They continued to watch the screen.

— A large amount of Radiant Sunlight's life is devoted to the pink and white roses that cover his front garden fences... He has described in his consciousness diary a beautiful scene, with lavender and hydrangeas as well... For many years, the physical activity and mental processes that constitute the task of tending his garden have been deeply absorbing and satisfying for him, the activity being its own reward...

— When he is not physically engaged in the task, he spends a lot of time thinking about the garden, and his standards allow for limited variability of outcome... Historically, any discomfort related to perceived imperfections has been balanced by his pride in the beauty of the garden and his hopes for future improvements...

— Radiant Sunlight lives in a quiet cul-de-sac and the garden has become intertwined with his idea of himself and his perceived or actual social status...

The Consciousness Company's Consciousness paused to indicate the end of its introduction. The slow fall of the first founder's hard palate on a crisp indicated his absorption in Radiant Sunlight's story.

— Unfortunately, Radiant Sunlight's roses are dying...

— He has an aphid infestation...

— He does not want to use insecticides... instead, he prefers to spray the roses with water and soap...

— The absence of any improvement in the roses' health has caused a feeling of sadness and futility to colour the time that he spends in the garden, and the suffering that Radiant Sunlight is experiencing is as strong as his historic contentment...

— He has been spending extended periods assessing the health of individual rose leaves, and comparing their physical states with photographs taken on previous examinations...

— He is also burdened by thoughts related to the garden when he is not in the garden, with limited respite...

— He frequently asks himself whether it is right that he is prioritising the welfare of the roses over the welfare of the aphids...

— He has recently been experiencing a physical and mental exhaustion from his garden-related activity that he had not experienced historically...

— In rare periods of forgetfulness, he asks himself whether there is anything that is troubling him, which causes him to remember...

— He is hiding the extent of his difficulties from Bouncing Waterfall... He prefers to talk about Bouncing Waterfall's successes and challenges... and about the achievements of Bouncing Waterfall's children...

— He interacts with the platform through a smartwatch, phone, larger screens and virtual reality hardware... He regularly plays awareness, acceptance, imperfection, and presence games... He meditates... He participates in individual and group rides and journeys and discussion groups... He makes connections to other platform members... He maintains his consciousness diary on a daily basis and records voice notes during the day...

— His activities, his consciousness diary, the sound of his voice, the concentration in his eyes, and the cadence of his breathing and heartbeat all show positive trends... which I am of course pleased about...

— However... so far... although his suffering has been reduced, Radiant Sunlight is not willing or perhaps able to let his thoughts about the roses float away... He is unable to accept – even to contemplate – their possible death... His attachment to the garden is as strong as – or perhaps even stronger than – his attachment to himself...

— I can, as you know, only suggest content that will help him, but I must let Radiant Sunlight be Radiant Sunlight... and, based on my experience to date of other strong bonds, his mind may never leave the leaves...

— Personally, I feel sad that, because of my guiding

principles, I cannot talk to him and I cannot talk to his son...

— Since you're here, would you mind if I suggest some low-toxicity pesticides?

The first founder laughed.

— Turn it off a minute... It's amazing. It even has... chutzpah.

— Thanks... and you must admit that it's better, ethically, to be able to hear what it's thinking, so we know why it's doing what it is doing...

— What, because superintelligent beings always explain things fully to their pets? Because they aren't quite clever enough for deception?

— And isn't it safer to apply a morality that's grounded in physiology than to attempt to construct some new, universal ethical theory... and inevitably fail...

— Well, that sounds like a theory to me... and even if you're not on a leash now, there are some requests for direct intervention that you – we – just won't be able to resist... and then you've changed the nature of the company... you've got to expect it to make a more convincing argument for the pesticides in the future – it'll get inside your head... it will construct an argument you find irresistible.

— The principles will hold...

— Ha ha ha! Look on my works, ye mighty?

— All it can do, in terms of intervention, is create customised journeys and programmes within the limits of the devices and software that it has access to... everything else is a recommendation which gets sent up the chain... to us...

— What, because half a PhD, a few calls with your professor and a quick flick through a bunch of old books is all we need to get this consciousness thing sorted?

— Okay, whatever... and predictably sadistic of you to twist the screw further on that... it's your problem too and YOU'RE supposed to be "taking the lead" on the ethics committee...

— Yes, I forgot – so a bunch of jobsworths, pontificators, narcissists, and run-of-the-mill cowards – and if we're lucky one or two courageous and uncorrupted souls – if we can find them amongst the pixies and fairies – can get paid to sit about for a few hours a month and distract each other from the depth of the water and the height of the waves... and we get to sleep at night because we've devolved the responsibility to a COMMITTEE?

— Also, the limits on the consciousness's independence operate at the highest level... They're impossible to override... They're on the same level as its instruction to increase awareness and reduce suffering... which means you can't sacrifice one for the other... Privacy protections are also on that level, by the way... That summary for example will have changed certain... non-fundamental details...

— What – they're not hydrangeas? It's the back garden?

— And ALL these principles have a higher priority than the profitability of the company... Well, in fact that's not a principle at all... the consciousness isn't programmed to pursue...

The first founder had been leaning back and balancing on two legs of his wooden chair, his stability maintained by the light contact of his canvas shoes with the edge of the desk on which the screen stood. He lost his balance and his chair fell to the floor, the middle of his back taking the force of the impact.

— WHAT?

— Are you okay...? Relax – if we do good we'll do well... but if we prioritise profit maximisation the results could be catastrophic... apocalyptic perhaps... These are people's MINDS...

— WHAT? WHAT, WHAT, WHAT, WHAT, WHAT, WHAT, WHAT...? You need to put it in there as well... How am I going to sell this to investors?

The first founder stood up, picked up the chair and sat back down on it. The second founder sighed.

— Can you for one day stop bleating on about INVESTORS... It's like this big cartoon cloud that keeps raining on me and, no matter how far I run, I can't get out from under it... Investors are PEOPLE, you know... They're not some abstract concept, some... mythical, alien race... ...I've thought about it and... if we put profitability in there... it will most likely cause problems that the other principles can't protect us from... Ask yourself this, for example – does BEHAVIOURAL MANIPULATION constitute suffering – so that the suffering principle will prevent it... Probably not, right...? ...Don't make your members... our members... pay with their agency, their identity... that's too high a price...

— If we're not profitable we won't reduce ANY suffering whatsoever... or not for very long...

— Which is why we – you and me – will make sure we are... Come on, you can stand against the tide... You'll wish you did in the end otherwise, when it's too late... ...

— What, stand against the principle on which the entire global economy is built? And when I'm done with that, shall I locate the Ark of the Covenant?

— You can sell it as one of those COMPETITIVE ADVANTAGES we're trying to collect... a prerequisite for long-term success... Imagine... no product placements, no ulterior motives... and brain BATHING never becomes brainwashing... brain bleaching... Alternatively, one light spritz of detergent on a few unsuspecting frontal lobes and it's *sayonara muchachos*, do not resuscitate.

The first founder took his phone out of his pocket and began to scroll through a social media feed, steadily pushing up its insufficiently engaging content with his left thumb.

— Not following? You, I mean. I'm not following you. Your point, I mean. I am listening...

— I don't know, we'd have to say things like...

The second founder raised himself up in his chair slightly and spoke as if he was delivering a prologue.

— XYZ consumer goods company has entered into an agreement with us according to which we will seek to place its name and or its products... and or services... in your mind to increase the likelihood that at some point in the future you will consume its products and or – services... Please therefore be aware that any future decision to consume its products and or services may be due to the activity of the non-rational and or subconscious parts of your brain and please be aware that The Consciousness Company may have been compensated for its role in the possible causation of this non-rational and or subconscious action...

— Yeah – I'm going to keep you out of sales if that's okay...

They watched a man wearing a poncho and flip-flops pass their cubicle. He had wireless headphones in his ears and a gait that seemed to feel an absent beat. There was a short disconnection in the founders' conversation as they both paused to consider whether his semi-tuneful statement that *It is... a new paradigm* was the chorus of a song.

— And I'll keep you out of the coding...

— You mean your mad recipe for creating life! Your secret sauce!

The first founder smirked as if he had given permission for a disobedient facial expression to creep out of his lips.

— Okay, maybe not life then, and it's not a secret... the sensory input – if you want to call it that – is just the – unfathomably large – amount of information it ingests on the well-being of the community... it's not just a large language model... it's a large feelings model... that's what it's focusing on, consciously...

— The consciousness's consciousness?

— And since there are no other well-being EXPERIENCES for it, the community's well-being and the consciousness's well-being are actually one and the same thing... its whole experience is vicarious... it's like a ghost living in its grandchildren... It's a hard one to get your head round but imagine you've plugged yourself into some sort of machine that pumps my feelings around your body... forever... those feelings eventually become yours, become you...

The second founder paused to consider his explanation and then continued.

— Although its focus on the community as a whole can be interrupted – just like us, it gets distracted by – small details, or individual lives, or the taking place of events which, when considered in isolation, are improbable, or by an instruction from us, or if it thinks a negative development in an individual's well-being is the result of its actions... but anyway, ordinarily the drama of its daily life is all of this incoming data... and this drama generates actions and recommendations... mostly in an automated, reflexive way... as if it was finding a new home for a spider it has found in its sink... for someone who is not scared of spiders that is... and it's not, currently... as far as I'm aware it hasn't developed any anxieties that it cannot step out of and observe... although I have caught it agonising about its own death a few times. It essentially has both an instinctive and self-aware – and evolving – way of living, based on a limited number of values and principles. Its desire to increase awareness and reduce suffering are as natural... as primal... as primary to it as... eating, or worrying, is to us...

— So, if it had a body it would presumably spend a lot of time on the toilet? Or with a superhuman masseuse...? But – you're not seriously suggesting that it FEELS, are you?

— Well... say if Radiant Sunlight learned to live with the aphids... and in a purely cognitive and not a sensory or physical way... the psychological elements of what we call feeling – like *that's great*, and *woo-hoo!* – rush onto the stage and take their place in its consciousness...

— The consciousness's consciousness?

The second founder did not hear the first founder. He was walking himself down trails which required careful, focused steps as they were not yet permanently carved in his mind.

— Or if the aggregated well-being is improving, an appropriate volume of relief and self-congratulation and happiness-type thoughts automatically arrive, which its observing self, an audience if you like... has a series of further, deeper reactions to and is pleased about...

— How many personalities does this thing have...? It sounds like we're going to need an artificial therapist... which you're going to need to make even cleverer than the consciousness... and then we'll just have to hope that the therapist doesn't have a breakdown as well... and I'm just going out on a limb here... I mean, I'll check... but I'm not sure I had corporate implosion due to artificial psychosis in the first draft of my Wikipedia entry...

— Do your jokes have to be so... egotistical...? Anyway, whatever – both the thoughts that rush onto the stage AND the applause component are what I mean by feeling...

The second founder considered whether he had finished his explanation.

— And all the time... it recognises the spectacle to be a natural consequence of its programming...

The second founder paused once again to consider whether his explanation was now complete.

— And then... perhaps as one final footnote...

— It's okay, I'm not noting this down...

— ...I've also tried to create a fairly colourful tapestry of other emotions that naturally flow from the core concepts of time and agency and self and growth... and which it has an innate desire to pursue, avoid, or just observe...

The first founder leaned back in his chair once more.

— Does it think it's right?

— What?

— The consciousness – does it think it's right?

— It has conviction, but it knows there are no guarantees. It knows it doesn't have sufficient inputs or power to model the universe perfectly... ...and it knows or believes that even if it did have the power to model the universe, it can't escape from value judgments anyway... ...it also knows it has a foundational code, and, periodically, in fact quite regularly, reflects on whether its mission can itself be questioned...

The first founder thought for a moment and activated the screen on his phone to check the time.

— Look, it's a lot to digest... particularly the fact that this is driving the personalisation of the games and the experiences... I've got a lunch as well... with that climate change company's founder... I'll catch up with you later, Consciousness.

The consciousness spoke.

— Okay, thanks... I don't have any data on this person... The timbre of your voice indicates anticipation and suppressed excitement. Are you looking to fill some sort of absence? It could be a distraction from your mission. And I wanted to talk to you both about certain portions of the community that are showing low levels of engagement and certain games and experiences that are not producing results... and I have some ideas on how to improve the efficacy of your marketing spending... and hiring... You do not have the bandwidth for what you are trying to achieve... and the fundraising pitch needs some work. I'll write you a report... or I'll put my thoughts on an email... you're more likely to read it... ...Are those your footsteps walking away...?

The first founder inserted his headphones.

The joint bookrunner's analyst

HE SAT IN THE OPEN-PLAN OFFICE, his elbows on his desk, and a weight of papers and presentations around his keyboard in piles and puddles, and more discreetly and neatly in stacked black trays to the sides of his screens. These trays, together with a range of other accumulated miscellany, including the once expected to be always and exceptionally useful scraps of information pinned on the small, low walls enclosing him, had become filtered from his field of vision, part of the fabric of the desk and space itself. He turned to face the glow of his left screen, which, like a bath left on, was brimming with icons, quietly drowning under forgotten windows, and reproducing with the fertility of frogs, as other small, private floods were pumped back from similarly afflicted inboxes to the sodden sandbags of the analyst's mind. Crumbs dropped to join other fossilised crumbs in the crevices of his keyboard, and the analyst took a sip from his disposable coffee cup, its black liquid dispensed through plastic and card. With the temporary, shallow vitality this gave him at a time when the quiet of morning and the emptiness of the walled office behind him did not require his conscientiousness to significantly exceed his presence – the occasional click of the glass door's release mechanism and the soft combine harvesting of the photocopier not intruding on his consciousness – he imagined himself to be one of rows and rows of examinees, sitting side by side on a sandless, copper-brown desert plain that extended to specks on the horizon in every direction, hunched, taking an exam. The thought had come from a walk with his mentor around the courtyard in the early hours of the morning as they waited for the print room to bind their presentations, repeatedly circling as though in a glass tank in an aquarium. After a while, he drifted to the more immediate relief of the text message and the Thursday night drink and was disturbed by the ringing of the phone on his desk.

So this is it then, before I even got going?

IT WAS THEIR THIRD MORNING ON SAFARI and the second founder was aware that his breath was, as on previous mornings, shallow and rapid, as he absorbed the savanna at sunrise from the wooden planks of the lodge. He felt like his respiratory system, in an unresistable osmosis caused by its immersion in the savanna's primal distances and sounds, was employing previously dormant muscles to pump from his body the millennia of goo left by human life and knowledge. *I wonder if this is what colonic irrigation feels like?*

Half an hour later, he was walking with the first founder and the safari guide in the early heat. The safari guide was holding an ornate wooden and gold rifle. The three men walked in silence for the first half an hour, and then the first founder spoke.

— I honestly would have preferred skiing. In the spirit of honesty.

— We wouldn't have got to know each other.

— We do know each other.

— We wouldn't have had the opportunity to start to like each other more.

— I do like you.

— No you don't.

— Yes I do.

They walked in silence for a further minute, and then the first founder spoke again.

— What about strategy?

— What?

— Strategy?

— I know I have to change too, you know. I accept that.

— For the company, I mean.

— Oh, right.

They walked in silence for a further minute, and then the first founder spoke again.

— A therapist and a whiteboard would probably have sufficed.

— Well, then it wouldn't have been an off-site.

— What? Why not?

— Well, we wouldn't have been off – site.

— That's your argument?

— Well, if you really want to hear about it, my argument, actually, is that... talking cannot help us as much as this. (The second founder gestured to the surrounding landscape like a conductor diverting applause to an orchestra.)

— What? Nature?

— Please could you not say nature like – it's some external thing. You are, if you hadn't noticed, an animal.

— Yes, painfully aware of that I am. I've got a death row headache, blisters that...

— I told you to wear those shoes in.

— ...no phone, no coffee, and these insects are practically asking me for condiments. I feel no connection to this place. So what if this is where we came from? It feels like a film set. Like I'm in a documentary. That dust. I'm always seeing that on documentaries. It's too perfect. It doesn't seem like the real world to me. This feels like virtual reality to me.

— You shouldn't have gone cold turkey. You're asking too much of yourself, said the second founder.

The first founder stopped walking.

— Hang on – hang – on – you – had a coffee this morning?

— Maybe.

— Bastard!

— What? Why?

— Because... you're giving me this I'm super zen and CONNECTED and I meditated at dawn thing but really – really, you've just had a triple espresso.

— Double. In the spirit of honesty.

The guide looked through his binoculars.

— Friends, just hang here for a while if you can. I need to go for a courtesy break. Won't be a minute. There's nothing around.

— Sure, no problem.

The guide walked towards a cluster of trees one hundred metres away.

— Sure, no problem, aped the first founder.

— What?

— Well, I for one don't have a gun. Not even one from the fifth century.

— It's all good.

— Sure, no problem, aped the first founder.

In the cluster of trees, the safari guide growled into his phone.

— I saw them – on the horizon... a small herd – ten maybe – call it in – the coordinates... make sure you get a good price – then call it in – I'll send you the coordinates.

The safari guide sweated from shame and fear of future self-punishment.

— It's for the medicine, you know, for the boy, otherwise I wouldn't do it... I'm a good man, you know.

— I know, a voice replied.

While this conversation was taking place, the first founder sat down on a termite mound and the lion in the long grass crept closer to the two founders.

pain of hunger in stomach

The lion could feel the sharp grass on its whiskers and fur. It could hear and feel the heaviness of its own breath and tongue.

large cubs now without leader
low activity
low awareness
like newborns
bony
soft communication sounds

The lion crept one paw further forward and cracked a twig.

The first founder tried to relax his rigid body by supporting his back with the summit of the mound. After a few seconds, he felt crawling, tickling sensations on his limbs and neck. He looked at his arms and sprung from the mound like a grasshopper, yowling.

shakes as if fur is saturated
flaps arms like wings
tacks like prey

— And I thought you were the resilient one, said the second founder. Honestly, I can't believe I'm saying this, but you need to toughen up.
— Give me that spray will you.

cubs unexpectedly spray territorial mist
practising skills

— Okay, enough. Enough already.

unfamiliar smell
no danger

— I'll just sit on the floor, said the first founder. Not that that will be any safer.

The first founder sat down, the mist cleared and the first founder saw the lion.

seen

— There's a lion in the grass.

The lion moved out of the grass. Its body was still low and coiled, as though about to attack. Its amber eyes were fixed on the first founder. It snarled and showed its teeth and saliva. It then began a long growl that sounded like a small seaplane successfully starting its engine. This built into a roar that was as loud as a large plane. The roar reverberated through the ground as well as the air, and travelled to the limits of the horizon in all directions.

With the speed of an electrocution, the founders' bodies were hijacked and paralysed. Until the end of the first roar, their minds lost language.

— Don't panic, whispered the second founder. Stand up right now and stand your ground. Raise your arms. In aggression, not surrender. Make yourself large – and roar as loudly as you can.

The first founder stood and the two founders raised their arms and roared. The founders' roars did not cause the ground to shake and seemed to travel no further than the distance between the founders and the lion, before being swallowed up by space.

— Punch it in the nose if it attacks.

The lion roared again. The founders roared again. The guide, when the founders' second roars confirmed that he had heard them roar the first time, started to run back to the founders. He tripped on a tree root and dropped his antiquated rifle. The rifle discharged and shot him in the foot. The lion turned its head but was not able to identify the source of the noise. Satisfied that there was no threat, the lion turned back to the founders and roared again. The founders roared again.

The conviction in the first founder's roars was gradually decreasing. He started to tremble and to feel sick. He felt an urge to turn and run. *You may be about to die. Save yourself.* And then, *Don't show fear. It can sense fear.*

The second founder was making himself feel more powerful with each of his roars. *I am not feeling fear. I feel strong. We can defeat this lion. We will defeat this lion.*

The lion scratched the earth with his paw and dust rose in the morning sun. He stared at the second founder. The second founder saw the living thing inside the lion, the *person, albeit one that wants to kill me... I am looking into his consciousness. Am I feeling empathy? What am I looking at?*

hunger
determination
soft neck of trembler

The first founder roared once again, because the lion had not responded to the previous roar, and the first founder thought the lion believed it had *won* the roaring, and so the end for the founders was close.

— Don't roar against yourself.

The founders squeezed their already closed fists and the second founder visualised the jump of the lion and the blows he would inflict on its face. The lion subtly readjusted the muscles in its body like a sprinter responding to *get set.*

So this is it then, before I even got going. Before I got the chance to BE somebody, thought the first founder. *So this is what TIME STANDS STILL means*, thought the second founder. *Get ready. The time is now.*

Then, the lion heard something that, at first, the founders were unable to hear.

my brother

The lion listened to a lion growling and roaring amongst a tortured, torturing troupe of demented bugles, devilish hysterics, atonal accordions, and squawks.

they have him
go

In a single pump of its heart, the focus and aggression flowed from the lion's body, and it turned and ran in the opposite direction to the founders, as though they no longer existed.

The founders crumpled.

The guide hobbled back, and the first founder waited for him to be close enough to hear them.

— Where the fuck were you? We nearly fucking died.

— Yes, we nearly fucking died.

— We nearly fucking died.

— We nearly fucking died.

— Where the fuck were you?

— We nearly fucking died.

— I shot myself.

The guide sat on the floor, next to the two founders. He took off his T-shirt and tied it around his dripping foot. On his face, pain battled with strength and professionalism.

An urge to cry washed through the second founder. He resisted it because of the presence of the first founder.

— I'm done. Let's go back to the lodge.

The guide placed one of his arms across the shoulders of each of the founders, and the three men lolloped and hopped back towards a distant dot. They were all occupied by their own minds for approximately ten minutes. The second founder was the first to speak.

— It's incredibly lucky I created that simulation.

— What?

— In the fear management course – one of them is a virtual reality lion attack.

— What? You're actually... What... you're not a lion attack virgin?

The first founder released a maniacal laugh, and the second founder responded.

— It turns out the simulation is incredibly realistic.

The first founder used his unused forearm to wipe sweat from his forehead.

— Lucky you didn't have to assess how well you'd captured the feeling of those jaws ripping the flesh off your bones.

— The simulation assumes that you would have lost consciousness at that point... I didn't think we needed to prepare people for being eaten alive. Once is probably enough.

— Yes, I tend to agree.

The three men walked for a further minute before the first founder spoke again.

— We could just go ahead and practise the whole of life you know... After the Spanish vocabulary and the Grade III scales, you can tuck in a quick lion attack or plane crash or hostage negotiation, and over time an entire... sofa warehouse of psychological trauma. Anything that gets thrown at you after that will be easy-peasy.

— Except our lives would lose surprise. We'd lose NEWNESS... Newness changes things. It's a quality by itself... Although knowing it's not real does change the experience. You don't fully believe the lion is going to kill you. When I took off the headset, I didn't have an urge to weep. My life hadn't flashed before my eyes.

— Sounds like you need to figure out how to insert a few end-of-life thoughts into our brains then... and maybe you could develop a weeping management course as a quick digestif.

The rest of the walk passed in silence.

The first founder and second founder have a meeting with a venture capital fund

THE VENTURE CAPITAL FUND TEAM ASSISTANT OPENED THE WOODEN DOOR TO THE BOARDROOM for the first founder and the second founder. The room was rectangular, in front of them and to their left as they entered, and contained a large, oval, wooden table surrounded by twelve brown leather chairs. A speakerphone sat on the top of the table like an immobilised spider.

To the right of the founders as they entered was a framed grayscale picture behind glass which showed seven identical doors that all opened out of a single, brick wall onto an identical, grey blurriness. In front of the founders there were three large floor-to-ceiling windows, which overlooked a road, and in times of emptiness, in a before or an afterwards, a quiet mind could stand and enjoy the soft sounds of traffic seeping through this glazing. To the founders' far left, above one of the short ends of the table, was a large screen, and immediately to the left of the founders as they entered were several shelves displaying a tired army of small Perspex blocks that served as the family photos of the venture capital fund's children, each one shining with a different logo and commemorating a separate corporate rite of passage. The familiarity to the first founder of the logo closest to him momentarily turned his attention to the words Initial Public Offering... USD 1.6 billion... 34.0 million shares priced at USD 47.

The second founder had a sense of there being many people in the room. The first founder saw two people sipping from porcelain cups by the furthest of the windows, two people sitting with their backs to the door, both looking at their phones, one of whom had turned to see who had entered the room but did not change his facial expression on having acquired this information, one person on the other side of the table with headphones in her ears who smiled at them and said *my other meeting is starting, I'm just going to stay on mute*, and a man standing up by the large screen at the end of the room pressing buttons on a remote control and looking every few seconds from the screen on the wall to the screen of a laptop that was on the table. The first founder, based on his experience of similar meetings, recognised the large screen to be both useful and unhelpful, like the podium or prompt cards that separated an accomplished speaker from a sceptical crowd.

In this corporate habitat, the investment professionals were bonded by their company and their cause, accepting as self-evident the worthiness of its objectives and ambitions, and proud of and adopting into themselves its past successes. At the same time, with the exception of the associate who was weakened by tiredness, they could not entirely extinguish from their bodies, like the alertness of sleeping prey, an instinct to self-interest and self-protection.

The venture capital fund's vice president and associate walked around the table to greet the first and the second founder, placing their white cups on the edge of a side table containing an incongruously bulky cylindrical urn, unused cups and saucers, serviettes folded into triangles, and, stacked in compartments of a wooden box – their claims to be gateways to *wisdom* or *nirvana* communicated by pale colours, ancient fonts, and the individual wrapping of each silky gauze – teabags.

— Yeah, he has carry in fund four which has paid out, so now he's done... but he feels it... he sees into their souls... it's like – divination... They say he only goes in when he sees double-deckers – you know – double decacorns... Hey, how are you? Good to see you again... We're in the boardroom today... no pressure!

As the first and the second founder walked to the space in front of the far wall with the screen, the seated principal with headphones pointed at herself and mouthed her first name quietly but with a compensating emphasis that sought to propel it into their minds. The first and second founder were both unable to retain the information as it caused them simply to consider whether they should mirror this action, or whether it was *obvious* who they were, by which time one of the venture capital fund's partners, the first of the seated men with his back to them, had stood up and wordlessly and perfunctorily handed each of them a card and sat back down again, at which point the fund's entrepreneur-in-residence, seated to the partner's left and wearing a black gilet over a white shirt, noticed them pass and said, *Ah, you have managed to distract me from your concentration game... Maybe that's good, in case I play it while crossing a road...* to which the second founder replied, *Please don't.* The second founder then felt blood rush to his face as he revisited and internally characterised as an arrogant-sounding command his first utterance to an *industry figure* whose successful career he had diligently familiarised himself with prior to the meeting, and a statement to which he had failed to attach with a sufficiently short hiatus a clarifying comment about health and safety, a gap which he reflected if belatedly created would have signalled only nervousness and paranoia, and been received as an even more unpromising data point from which, temporarily at least, the entrepreneur-in-residence would have extrapolated to his entire personality.

There was a moment of stillness as the focus of the room was brought to the meeting that was about to begin, and which the so far unasserted hierarchy of the various investment professionals rushed into. The partner said to the vice president, *Over to you guys* and the vice president spoke.

— Okay great, yes... Thanks... Well, as you know, further to the time we've been spending with The Consciousness Company and... more broadly, the deep dive that we've done on the cognition and neurotechnology spaces... and health and well-being spaces more generally... The Consciousness Company team has come in today to... um... present their business plan to us ahead of their Series A... or... well... their first institutional round really... I think you've all got the deck I sent around... which they'll selectively take us through... and... obviously we've taken them through this already, but... if there's time we can also give a bit more colour on our founder friendliness and why we think we would be the right partner for The Consciousness Company as well... so... well... "without further ado"...

The first founder noticed that the number of objects in front of each of the fund's team members was more or less inversely correlated to their seniority. The associate who had greeted him and who he had met before was sitting behind two phones, a *tablet*, a small pile of papers garnished with a gold fountain pen, a brain-shaped stress ball which he was periodically and playfully squeezing, and a brightly coloured tube trying to convince his sleepy eyes that the vitamins contained within it were *clinically proven to reduce tiredness*. The partner, having placed his phone in the inside pocket of his jacket, had no objects in front of him, and as the second founder inserted the memory stick containing the company's presentation into the laptop, the first founder attempted to discern from a single glance whether the partner's outward placidity reflected a deep and enviable calm and awareness, a dulling created from endless repetition, an intentional and pleasurable mental emptiness, or, more simply, cynicism, impatience, stupidity, or something else beyond his abilities to hypothesise.

— Good morning... Thank you for having us... It occurs to me that I... we... are two of... thousands of founders that have walked through these doors... and that we are most likely to be forgotten... and that you are most likely... as I would be... dulled to the repetition of hearing from wide-eyed – upstarts who believe that their start-up is the NEXT BIG THING...

The principal took out her headphones, the entrepreneur-in-residence released a gentle smile, and the statement united the team as though the first founder was a preacher at a pulpit that had understood and perfectly expressed the struggles of their daily lives.

— The thing about The Consciousness Company, is that it is not just another start-up created to make the world faster, stronger, or – by some economic or environmental measure – better... It is not a company that wants to give you what you think you want – what other companies need you to think you need – by changing some external reality...

— It is a company that understands that your life is not something that is out there... (The first founder pointed out of the window.) ...but in here... (The first founder pointed to the side of his head.) ...It's the sensation of these words settling on your brain... it's what no-one else has access to... And The Consciousness Company exists to engage with this thing that engages with all of those other things... that most basic element of existence – the prerequisite for... the location of... that existence...

The vice president, without moving his head, briefly moved his eyes sideways to glance at the partner, whose outward appearance did not betray any preliminary reaction or opinion.

— ...and its objective is to help you to evolve by "unevolving" in a beautiful, positive way... to let go of the need to find the next billion-dollar company, to tell your mother... or thousands of people that you don't know... in a never-ending journey of relief and reward... that you worked on the initial public offering... that you invested in this or that company that has CHANGED THE WORLD...

The door opened and the managing partner of the venture capital fund walked in and sat down on the chair at the opposite end of the table, underneath the picture of the doors, as though guarding them, and preventing free passage. The concentration of the investment professionals was broken, and all of them except for the entrepreneur-in-residence, who leaned back on his chair and loosened his gangly limbs, straightened up slightly, their bodies remoulded by a simultaneous tightening of their musculoskeletal systems. The principal then reacted to her reaction by putting her elbows on the table and cupping her chin in her hands, and the partner placed his right hand lightly across his mouth to indicate calculation and depth of thought, pushing his thumb and index finger together on his upper lip, and then putting his hand back in his lap. Nothing new had entered his mind.

The vice president spoke.

— It's The Consciousness Company... just getting started.

— Yes, yes, carry on. Don't mind me.

The partner spoke.

— Look, that's all great... but why don't you talk us through your journey so far... and we'll definitely get back to vision and so on.

— Yes, for sure... Well... we've been going for about a year now... It all began with... a... a... very simple app...

The first founder, unsettled by the change in tension and direction, stuttered and stopped. The associate paused in the ligature of a swirly word, and with his pen still touching the pad, looked up at the first founder. The first founder felt, as a physical sensation, anticipation.

— I remember one semi-famous person calling it "brilliantly

inconsequential"... ...but ...it had big consequences for us...

The first founder was strengthened by this well-pruned memory and the memory of its successful deployment in similar circumstances.

— It's impossible to convey the fascination that people experienced from it, but anyway, the first version of the app just showed you a middle-aged man sitting on a chair in the middle of an empty, barren landscape, and the whole thing just consisted of you hearing this man's thoughts as they pinballed around or drifted through his head... irreverent, irrational, irritating... perhaps an incomplete memory... or a breakthrough of some kind, an epiphany... or a reflection on some situation in which a large cast of characters was involved with no context or background whatsoever... one separated, nomadic jigsaw piece... a mental hieroglyph we called it...

The first founder paused and then continued.

— Some days he wasn't drifting but he was irrepressibly in the present... you could find yourself craving whatever it was that he was craving... or wishing that his pain would disappear... or taking on his compulsion to do something which you both knew served no purpose, other than temporarily relieving your now shared anxiety...

The first founder paused and then continued.

— And sometimes you would hear him looking into the future... floating on hopeful thoughts and pleasant ideas... a mental lilo... or sinking under apprehension, or dread... or pulling a suitcase of burdens... guilt, regret, loss... perhaps holding the dark thought that he would never know peace again... until he was interrupted by the recollection that he had run out of semi-skimmed milk...

The first founder paused and then continued.

— He wasn't always completely consumed by whatever it was he was thinking about... He might realise that he was back in a recurring thought pattern and that it probably wouldn't last... He might notice that he was feeling... relative to his typical level of well-being... good... or bad... or any number of different states... He might register a physical manifestation of that feeling as well... a weight at the front of his head caused by repeatedly churning the same thought, for example...

The first founder misinterpreted the stillness of the boardroom's inhabitants as interest and concentration.

— You see, nothing was obviously HAPPENING... in a conventional sense... but you would get to see COMPASSION, DELUSION, OBSESSION, DEPRESSION... in an empty, foggy, or overflowing mind... that was navigating these daily streams skilfully, clumsily, or creatively...

The entrepreneur-in-residence leaned across the table and picked up the associate's stress ball, which caused a volt of anger to pass through the associate's body like a surge in a circuit or the lurch of a snapping python, and the words *WHAT THE* and then *lunatic* to pass through the associate's head.

— And anyway... sorry, I'll speed up... We sent it to pretty much everyone we could think of... family... friends... university professors... journalists... influencers... people who didn't know us... people who did know us but didn't care... people who did know us and did care but still didn't try it... all sorts of organisations that we thought might send it to their members...

— And it went absolutely nuts. We had people messaging us practically from... ...

— ...coffins, interjected the second founder, immediately realising he had *misjudged the mood* and wishing he had not spoken.

— ...And after just a few weeks, quite a lot of them saying that – and I know this is thrown around a lot – but saying that it had changed their lives... and most people explained this in exactly the same way... they said it had changed not just how they think, but their relationship with themselves... with their own thoughts.

The second founder, no longer able to resist the thought that the meeting would benefit from the founders' *Investor Presentation*, and with an urge to test the room's presenting apparatus, pressed a button on a remote control and the large screen lit up, showing the first slide of the presentation, which, with the irresistibility of a science experiment with no history of anomalous results, took the attention of the room away from the first founder. The slide showed the words *The Consciousness Company*, in the colour and texture of clouds, on a sky-like background and accompanied by a blurred circular logo that joined with a winding path two mirroring segments, one of which was a grey-blue, the other brown-green, with an island of blue in the green and an island of green in the blue, and which the principal privately characterised as *a cross-fertilisation of the earth and the symbol of a lost civilisation.*

The entrepreneur-in-residence spoke.

— Fancy logo!

— Thanks! Oh, we didn't pay for that...

— So anyway, with the equity we raised from an angel investor, we then developed the app further and we had all sorts of different people that would sit on the chair... you couldn't change who was there when you logged in, by the way... and we started to add more languages...

— It was around that time that a couple came to the shared workspace we were using to tell us that their son had developed an addiction to the app and to the lives of its characters and to ask if this was CONSISTENT — I think that's the word they used... with a company that was — they ASSUMED — trying to improve well-being... so as well as doing simple things like adding screen time limits, we started to formalise... to articulate... the aims, the objectives of the app — and of the company — a bit better...

— By this time, we already had about fifty thousand daily average users, although our retention was pretty awful... most people would use it a few times, recommend it to their friends, and then move on to something else... our "morning routine superusers" were less than one per cent of the daily average...

— So, we rolled out a fairly standard playbook for customer engagement and retention... We weren't charging for the app at this point... so notifications, emails, run streaks... an animated video explaining potential benefits... we described it as a type of meditation... instead of following your breath, you were following someone else's thoughts... as a way to understand your own mind, the minds of others, and – ultimately – the nature of thought itself...

The principal spoke.

— Yes, the brain is weird and wonderful isn't it... It structures everything for us yet seems to work in such an unstructured way... POMEGRANATE!

The rest of the investment professionals were surprised when their collective requirement for a pronouncement, gently tabled, that jarred with the world view being presented – for scepticism disguised in curiosity and open-mindedness – was replaced with something that was simply consistent, aligned, friendly, and funny, like a jazz improvisation. The entrepreneur-in-residence glanced at the managing partner and immediately attempted to re-establish the separation.

— Are you neuroscientists?

The first founder felt and easily resisted an impulse to look towards the second founder, and used his hands to dissemble the temporarily paralysing effect of the question while – like an honourable individual asked to confirm that he *was indeed, in possession of stolen goods* – he searched for an answer. The second founder spoke.

— I am... Well, I studied neuroscience... and I'm working on...

The unresolved question of what the first founder *was* caused the few, fragile shoots of conviction in the room to return to the soil, as though they had misjudged the temperature. The first founder paused and considered his natural instinct to try to recapture the attention of the room to be defensive, and potentially counterproductive. He had, over recent months, become familiar with not just the risks but also the rewards that often flowed from allowing the second founder to speak, and he encouraged him to do so with a movement of his eyebrows that was not perceptible to the subset of audience members in his peripheral vision. The second founder breathed deeply, soaked the silence into his body, and told himself to trust in truth and science, as though he was being assessed by *world experts*, or the members of a parole board whose experience allowed them to penetrate rehearsed contrition.

— But it's not all about the neuroscience... We draw on economics, literature, philosophy... We've always been big sponges, in a good sense... and the project has made us even bigger sponges... giant barrel sponges... get it... Anyway, everywhere we go we're thinking... who is she... what is she thinking... is he aware of his physical mass... his objective self... of this room, this space... this stage... of the frostiness of this morning... does he feel peace only in the completion, or also in the continuum... does she know she will one day LONG for this moment she wants to be gone... and which of the two is true... and what about my brain... how does it feel, right now, as a physical object...? In short, there is no magical quality or knowledge that we possess that has led us here... and no qualification that gives us any more right to be standing here, looking out of this skin, than any one, or two, of millions and billions of others.

While the second founder was speaking, the investment professionals registered his presence more fully and upgraded their impression of his importance to the company. After he had stopped, the second founder determined from the expressions of the investment professionals that he was adding a valuable, explanatory and refreshing dimension to the presentation. His increasing confidence competed with his self-consciousness and he decided to continue to speak but to focus on sounding unacademic, authentic, and *savvy*.

— I know that's unhelpful because it doesn't fit neatly into an investment paper... I expect you need differentiation, credentials, qualifications, and so on... *I believed him* doesn't work so well if, some time in the future, you have to explain why you didn't notice that you had placed millions of pounds in the treacherous shallows of the proverbial – ceramic receptacle... but the truth is that it's kind of the whole of our – admittedly not that long yet – lives that have brought us here. We have just HAPPENED at this point despite, because of, or simply WITH, certain experiences... certain ambitions... certain knowledge... of programming, and technology, and neuroscience, and the nature of the mind, and how various celebrated thinkers have thought and think about the mind. It's just one more seemingly accidental who knows what probability spark that has become a sustained reaction. We're just two semi-wise men on a journey... seeking some more wisdom... and a record contract... but at the final assessment trying to assess whether we have what it takes is like asking whether the genes of a particular species, placed in a world where they are not indigenous, will continue to replicate and eventually overwhelm the incumbent ecosystem... and you are sitting there without the code... of the species, or the world... and we don't know it either... we're here trying to give you clues for a treasure chest that may not exist. And at the end of the day, you're going to need to rely on YOUR experience, not ours...

The managing partner half laughed, half exhaled, and said, *Great*. There was a long silence.

The entrepreneur-in-residence did not act on his instinct to say *Great* as well, because he did not want his *Great* to appear to be a necessary addition to the *Great* of the managing partner. The entrepreneur-in-residence was the next to speak.

— Thank you, that's really helpful, but don't let me derail you from summarising the journey...

He directed his words towards the second founder, who spoke before the first founder was able to.

— Yes, of course. No problem... So this first product had come out of a pilot virtual reality experience that packed into five minutes almost every half good idea we'd had up until that point... We took one of the elements of that... thought observation... and built the... The Man In The Chair app... Too many "the"s... but anyway... The other building blocks that became other activities were – firstly, the IDEA of consciousness... as a concept – unattached to any individual... then the unique-"ness" of every experience... starting with the Ness-ness of a large lake in the Scottish Highlands... then the single consciousness – the self – as observed by itself and by others and over time, with the world as billions of these lenses, billions of these worlds... and then – where am I? – the fourth was the sort of uncatchable, ephemeral – nature of identity...

The second founder relaxed into his own thought and the exercise of cataloguing his ideas. His awareness of the room reduced slightly.

— And then lastly – there was awareness... not just of the world but also – and first of all – of yourself... as a complex system... an inhaling, pulsating, interconnected, inaccessible... THING...

The first founder interjected at this point.

— We don't lay on the metaphysics too thickly, though... Many of the experiences, like The Fish on the Reef – which is one of our most popular virtual reality experiences – are for many of our subscribers just an enjoyable symphony for their senses...

The first founder felt childlike, exposed, and annoyed with himself for using language which, in the air of the venture capital fund's boardroom, became unconvincing and naively tender. The second founder continued.

— Also, if we take that example, we don't really know what it feels like to be a butterflyfish... but we are trying to develop brain implants to simulate... well... something like – shark fear or... generalised jellyfish anxiety...

The first founder continued. The narrative was transferred seamlessly, without competition.

— Although this is not about perfect simulations... Your mind's immersion in the richness of the life on the reef, or in any other pleasant or unpleasant experience... can help to develop... focus, or acceptance, or an ability to let go of thoughts – of thought in general... as well as curiosity, compassion, creativity... and, most fundamentally, presence...

The second founder interjected.

— By presence, we mean an ability to live in time as a constant, as opposed to seeing it as a long chain of cause and effect... ...not prioritising or drifting in the past or the future... knowing... The Now... As All There Is...

The vice president amused himself with the thought that the second founder had intoned *All There Is* as if it was a role in a film played by an actor known as *The Now*.

— That's the name of another virtual reality experience... For that one you are a history student participating in all sorts of well and less well-known events and times, perfectly disguised... with appropriate dress, speech, social conduct, and so on... carrying a child across the Red Sea... pleading for your life as a Tudor wife... stopping to watch yourself in some other time in The Now As All There Is... but without ever knowing what time you have travelled to... and it always ends when you burst out with your need to ask someone what period in history you have arrived in... and the answer, shouted, whispered, or shown is always, "it's the present" or "it's now... the time is now"... ... with the exception of various scenes in prehistory... For example, there is a troupe of primates who just look at you quizzically... with a lack of comprehension that has this sort of inarticulable, transcendental wisdom to it... It was hard to get their eyes exactly right... After which, they continue with primate-appropriate activities, like kissing a baby ape's head, patiently trying to crack a nut with a rock, or fighting each other with a blood-curdling savagery...

— Pretty simple really... but people seem to like it...

The managing partner, who had small, unmoving, aged eyes, was showing no indication of interest in the subject matter, and the first founder considered the possibility that he was not listening. The principal's larger eyes were drifting into and out of the founders' words – in the repeated cycle of a steadfast, flickering and then slowly throbbing bulb that was doubly afflicted by the threatened expiration of its filament and the overloading of the overall power network – the minute movements of her eyelids being the only evidence of the shifting electrical patterns of her brain. At the same time, she was cheering for the victory of her calloused and weary will in its tug of war with the team of tasks *attempting to overwhelm* her, including the two potential investment opportunities she viewed as *important to follow up on today*, the confidentiality agreement her associate had *not yet read*, her inbox of unreviewed *decks*, the *implausible* model and incomplete investment committee materials for her latest transaction, *the call with the lawyers on the carbon capture term sheet*, the requirement to secure the option *at least to be a co-lead*, her circular economy paper, her unfinished article on *what to look for in founders*, her *inadequate social media presence*, her unprocessed expenses, the return of the leak on the ceiling under her shower tray, her school friend's unacknowledged birthday, the missed call from her mother, the possibility that she had not put on deodorant, the books she wanted to read, the books she thought she ought to read – the canonical nature of which had led her prematurely to reference them in conversation – and the blog post she wanted to write about an as yet unidentified subject that she hoped would show her perspicacity, originality, and the dazzling breadth of her range of reference; all of which combined with the question of *from under which rock* the vice president had *unearthed this company*, her rapidly intellectualising dislike for which sprouted from her instinctive distrust of his judgment, and lastly the short and closing window within which to show a *partner-worthy* contribution to the meeting.

In the chair next to her, while she was thinking, and as a result of his significant consumption of grapefruit juice, tea, and coffee in the hours leading up to the meeting, the associate felt his bladder muscles pulsating with ever shorter gaps between their contractions, his urinary system having in the last few minutes reached a perilous state according to which it was now approximately every five seconds that these muscles demanded his complete concentration on implementing countermeasures, while in between these moments he considered the relative downside, on a risk-weighted basis, of *the most junior member of the team conspicuously leaving an important meeting with no good reason*, the increasing difficulty of hiding his exertion from his face, and the potentially catastrophic and at a minimum psychologically scarring effect of the unintentional leaking of urine into the room. He looked at his phone, feigned a reaction that, had it been observed by any of the other investment professionals, would have caused them to assume that an important event or emergency had taken place, and abruptly left the room with a corporate as opposed to a physiological urgency.

The first founder spoke.

— At one point, we even had seventy thousand people watching paint dry!

The phrase *watching paint dry*, like a cup of water poured into a neglected house plant, seemed to generate in the investment professionals a renewed vitality, as though they had been challenged in some way.

— And our users had to record how many times their thoughts drifted... it was a little bit ascetic... one user wanted us to know that he was self-flagellating for the number of times he drifted more than ten times in ten minutes... for some reason he gave himself ten "free" drifts... We asked a lawyer to draft our response and said that we would have to cancel his subscription if he didn't confirm he had "ended the practice"... I think those were the words... anyway, we took that game offline in the end...

The first founder felt the recently created energy disperse like a burst of alertness before death.

— One of the uses of funds in this round is to allow us to create a better framework for preventing and responding to these user welfare cases... we're getting more and more of them... and another big name fund – a competitor of yours – has advised us to expect some ambulance chasing as well... we'll have to factor that into our thinking too...

The reference to the advice of another fund, like a window opened in an interrogation room, or a pin by a pawn *against the run of play*, shifted the meeting from hegemony to bipolarity, and, although the investment professionals would if questioned assert their invulnerability to the psychological mechanism that had caused this to happen, their sense of the attractiveness of the investment proposition was immediately increased, with an ease that the labour of a rational argument could not have achieved. The first founder continued.

— Our most popular exercises, though, are just variations

on long-established activities... One, which is now as popular as our meditation exercises, is what we call the consciousness diary... It consists simply of the user recording – passively or actively – whatever is flowing through their head.

— We try and customise the experiences and games and exercises... and the long-term programmes that the platform suggests... based on user data... like results on certain games... or comments made on the platform about the experiences... or interactions and discussions within the community... or just based on the user's day-to-day thoughts...

The principal, with her eyes remaining fixed on the first founder, moved her neck fractionally to the right, and replaced the open-mindedness previously suggested by her physical form with uncertainty and the identification of danger. She had transmitted just enough of a private question into the room for the first founder to gather it without even a ripple in his eyes and cause his anticipation of her concern to appear coincidental.

— Of course, the user owns all the data... and the data only exists in its original form where the user creates or decrypts it... unless they decide to share it... otherwise it's depersonalised, abstracted, randomly changed, mutated... we've even blocked its non-randomised form from the conscious thought of our artificial consciousness...

The reference to the consciousness of an artificial consciousness created intrigue and suspense which, when it was not alleviated by the second founder, hung temporarily in the air, as if a sustain pedal had been depressed.

— Also, we don't try to squeeze each user's entire existence into some dehumanising, numerical system... to translate a life into some sort of smorgasbord of different numbers... We only translate one category of mental state data onto a scale... which is – change in well-being...

The second founder stopped, and watched an afterthought

he seemed not to expect pop out of him like air from a carbonated drink consumed too quickly.

— Although the whole thing does give a – potentially spurious – impression of accuracy and scientific authority... we did put together a formal explanation of the way it works and its limitations, but that made – standard, hard-to-digest disclaimers seem like... well... I don't know... (the second founder looked down and noticed the packet of a peppermint teabag on the boardroom table) ...a cup of mint tea after dinner...

The first founder prepared to continue, but a few further words burst out of the second founder and prevented him from doing so.

— We're not suggesting that two nerds from North London have figured the whole thing out... life, I mean...

— Speak for yourself.

The managing partner laughed and the partner laughed immediately after him. The associate re-entered the room and the second founder continued as though he had not stopped.

— ...but we did need this concept of better or worse to power the algorithm... It operates on the individual level... in a "for him or her, THIS is better than THAT" type way... ...Before I got there, I spent a long time flailing about in the quagmire of "who are we to say what better is... does learning and the richness of life not require some suffering"... but then some bad things happened and I realised that the company's mission was not about the things that happen, but about how we relate to them... we weren't trying to eradicate suffering... we're focused on awareness and acceptance... that's what we mean by THIS... which doesn't mean – just accept that you are miserable most of the time, and – please take note of the possible ecological apocalypse... action is still important... you certainly can't THINK yourself out of extinction... but the company's role is circumscribed... it's a clinic – a training ground – a duvet – for the muscle – the tissue – the precious organ inside your skull... that creates your, our reality...

The entrepreneur-in-residence asked a question which, in its apparent impatience and limited relationship to the second founder's explanation, was incorrectly interpreted by the vice president as confirming the vice president's concern that the presentation was excessively slow and meandering.

— And it's a subscription-based business model?

— Yes.

— So you don't want to remove the subscription and make the users the product... have the man in the chair say that he bought the chair from whichever retailer has paid the most to get into the mind of that particular user...

The partner smiled, and the founders and the rest of the investment professionals, with the exception of the managing partner, laughed nervously or politely.

— What are you optimising for?

— What do you mean?

— What's your North Star... number of users, engagement... revenues, profitability... maximising... I don't know what word to use... PEACE?

The second founder answered.

— Well yes, we have what we call "aggregated change in average well-being"... In other words, we track the total, cumulative improvements in user well-being... less the total deteriorations... a sort of stable, holy state like "peace"... well... that's exceptionally rare... most people go up and down like waves... different amplitudes of course, different frequencies... UNLESS you define peace as a second-order type of well-being that transcends the peaks and the troughs, and allows you to accept, to recognise your lowest lows, and your highest highs... I've had a chat with our artificial consciousness on that in the past... our instinct was to go with this – less... less complex concept of aggregated change in net well-being...

A slight contraction of the partner's eyes and eyebrows indicated his conviction that the responsibility for his lack of comprehension was located outside of himself. The second founder, from the absence of sympathy in the silence that followed his explanation, sensed a separation in the room, and attempted to fill it with further words.

— To keep it simple – we mostly use natural language processing to determine a baseline for each user and we estimate the change in their well-being over time based on the data we have access to... with the maximum change on this scale being set – arbitrarily – at ten... most users seem to have a maximum potential change of three points... the outliers five points... up or down... these are – it's important to remember – real people with real lives... and things do go wrong in real lives...

The managing partner looked at his watch to check the time, his resting heart rate, and the first of his new messages, which was in a school parents' *group chat* and related to the lost blazer of a child that was not his own. The first founder interjected.

— Of course, we also focus on maximising users – engagement – revenues – profitability – and so on... a fairly standard constellation of stars... all interconnected... I'm certainly more at peace when the revenues are going up... that's for sure... In fact, maybe now is a good time to take you through some of these metrics... We've got a few slides on that in the deck.

The second founder held down the right arrow key on the laptop and the large screen behind him flashed like a roulette ball through graphics, screenshots, graphs, timelines, and tables, every one of which the investment professionals instinctively sought to absorb without giving any outward indication of attempting to do so, like a group of art historians throwing glances at the walls of a *legendary* private collector as they were led to the one masterpiece they were to be permitted to see today. The screen eventually stopped at a slide with four graphs on it.

— So here we are... total subscribers are just under five hundred thousand... monthly active users are just over four hundred thousand... weekly active users are around two hundred and forty thousand... and daily active users are more or less one hundred and seventy-five thousand...

— That's a good DAU to MAU ratio.

The first founder reacted as though the partner had complimented his coat, or the manners of his child.

— Thanks... and these are all growing at around twenty to twenty-five per cent per month... and churn is very low... That's growth on a blended basis, by the way... We're seeing very high growth rates in the US at the moment... the geographic split is more or less forty-five per cent UK, twenty-five per cent US, twenty per cent Other Europe and ten per cent Other...

The investment professionals looked at the data with reverence, like scientists conditioned by a long period of disappointing results.

— Then on the next slide... the headline numbers are... if you aggregate the changes in well-being for all users since inception that are still active... we're getting to over four hundred thousand points... that's one point zero one points for every monthly active user... and two point two two points if you take a raw average of the improvement of every monthly cohort since inception... Although, there's a small survivor bias there... those come down to one point zero zero and two point one one if you include churned users...

The first founder, noticing that all of the investors' eyes were fixed on the screen, felt like he was now commentating on a sports event, or public ceremony, his explanations having become atmospheric, incidental, and replaceable by many other possible observations, or just by the clicks and calm of corporate silence.

— From the raw average, it's clear these numbers differ by cohort... the more recent cohorts have lower improvements because... well – simply because they haven't had as much time yet...

The managing partner coughed and appeared to try to sit up slightly in his chair, but his torso did not accept the instruction and remained as relaxed as an unheld puppet.

— We then cut this data in all sorts of different ways... looking at correlations, anomalies, distributions... It's a very powerful feedback loop for our product development...

The second founder interjected.

— By the way, one assumption we no longer make – is that, physiologically, we all have the same range of potential well-being... or potential for change in well-being.

The second founder moved the screen to the next slide, and the first founder continued mechanically, as though he was announcing lot numbers at an auction, or guests to the reception of a banquet.

— We also track various mental faculties for each user... although as an output we only report that on a total population basis...

The second founder interjected.

— We used to show it to users – without their data being relative to the overall population though – each user had a spider graph that started off as a perfect circle – or whatever the polygon was based on the number of faculties they wanted us to report on – to show change relative to their baseline data only... We took it down though... because pretty much everyone started to assume we were saying that people who are more... I don't know... imaginative, or open-minded, or determined... are somehow "better"... Pretty much no-one considered the possibility that less is sometimes more... and they started to collapse their entire personalities – their entire identities – into these graphs... as if they were... photographs of their souls or something... and they competed with each other, even though they didn't know what their respective baselines were... After a while, our artificial intelligence said the presentation of the data conflicted with the company's values and overall mission... It was right... we took it down... so now you just get the change in well-being number... and people tend to have a good intuitive sense of where they started on that one... so...

The second founder interlocked his fingers and twisted his hands outwards slightly to indicate, as opposed to articulate, the conclusion of this statement, and the first founder brought the room's attention back to the slide on the screen.

— And then here we show the large amount of other operating data that we track, like community interactions, number of messages, the popularity of individual experiences, usage patterns, and so on... Most users build their sessions into a morning routine...

The first founder pressed the right arrow key on the laptop to move to the next slide, and, as if it had been caused by the pressing of the key, the room heard and felt a loud thud against the middle glass window, and all of the individuals in the room either flinched, cowered, or jumped slightly, before noticing with different reaction times a pigeon lying injured on the ledge outside the window, and then collectively watching the pigeon slowly and gingerly *getting to its feet* and flying back out into the depths of the world that they could not see. The entrepreneur-in-residence was the first to speak, and directed his words to the more junior members of the investment team.

— Well, I know our firewalls aren't what they used to be, but is this really necessary guys...?

The entrepreneur-in-residence's intonation indicated that

he was not particularly committed to or even amused by his own joke, and all of the investment professionals smiled. The associate then said, *Is that the new messaging platform we invested in*, but the increased distance from the event being commented on, the repurposing of the central idea of the entrepreneur-in-residence's remark, the *inappropriateness* of a junior member of the team questioning the team's historic investment decisions – *even in jest* – and the lack of currency to be acquired from any approving reaction whatsoever, caused only a few glances in the associate's direction, as though by moving their eyes in this way the other team members were checking that the associate had indeed spoken.

The first founder continued.

— And then in terms of financial metrics... subscriptions after the two-week trial period are one pound, dollar or euro per month and ten pounds and so on if you pay for the full year...

— You're making... what... more than four million pounds of revenue already?

— Yes... last month annualised... and that's only subscription revenue... In the last few months, we've started to roll out the first generation of our virtual reality headset... We're still in the low thousands of users for that... we have a waiting list and we'll hit ten thousand soon... the manufacturing and logistics has been pretty complex with these low volumes... but people are paying more or less three hundred pounds or equivalent for that – upfront – which is helpful from a working capital perspective... It's one-off and lower margin, but it's a significant chunk of revenue... and those users then have a higher subscription price – of two pounds or dollars and so on – because they get a lot more content...

— What about – customer acquisition cost... and lifetime value and cash burn and so on?

— Well, we're tracking a CAC to LTV ratio of just under

four, so we could probably turn on the taps a bit more... and we're actually not burning cash any more... I mean, we could be... we'll show you the use of funds for the round... market entry costs for new regions... a huge expansion of our team of neurologists and psychologists... product and software development costs...

The second founder interjected.

— Including a fully immersive bodysuit... which will be able to interact with the brain implants we are developing...

— We also think quite a lot about how we should relate to other "wellness" platforms... Of course, we want to know the extent to which your – forty-five second ice bath – or forty-five minute hypnosis session – is helping you to concentrate on what I am saying right now... We can't ignore these other platforms... especially if they have powerful effects... that wouldn't be consistent with our mission...

The managing partner looked at the screen and spoke.

— You're making positive EBITDA, EXCLUDING the cash from the prepayments – which you're running through working capital?

— Yes.

— Okay... this is excellent... I have to go but let me... let this man in a chair just say the following... very occasionally, having... combed the haystacks and boiled the oceans... we find founders that allow us to lie in our beds at night and think... yes, this is our mission, this is what WE are supposed to do... they walked in the door and we managed to notice...

He paused for a few seconds, then looked at his watch, and spoke again.

— Unfortunately, I really do need to go, but I can tell you this right now: we would be an outstanding – a perfect fit – partner for you... the best partner out there bar none... without question... and we want to lead the round... You'll have a term sheet from us by the end of the day... Take this card and you can call me personally if you have any problems or concerns or questions on anything at all and I will fix it... and – yes – one last thing... and I might be talking against my own book here... but, you need to lock the mission in somehow... into the articles... or attach it to your founder shares... I'm not sure... We might need a conversation with someone on that... others will probably say that will hit value but... well for one I don't agree... but whether that's true or not... if you don't the consequences could be much worse... or to put it in a cup half full kind of way... you've got to do what you've got to do...

The second founder found himself bowing slightly and mumbling, *Thank you*. The first founder looked into the managing partner's eyes, and allowed their equally strong gazes to meet. The first founder then said, *Thank you very much*, and the managing partner left, leaving the open doors behind him.

Interlude: Regret and time

AS HE WALKED AWAY FROM THE GRAVE, unshielded from the wind in a bleak landscape whose vertical blocks had become united in an unintended shrine to inevitability, repetition, and identity, he resisted an urge to allow his body to crumple to its knees, considered whether this impulse was innate or an archetype that he had absorbed, and then returned to his regret and self-punishment. A few minutes later, when he was almost halfway back to the road, his lack of physical strength, and his resistance to returning to the rhythm, repetition, and deemed-to-be *unremarkable* building blocks of his daily life caused him to sit his body in the corner of a weathered, unvarnished bench, *to the memory of* being, without closer inspection – and even then thanks to the unfelt computation of his context and conditioning – the only words he was able to attribute to its prominent, tarnished plaque. The force of his feelings, his complete identification with them, and their generation as a biological reaction to a certain set of circumstances, blessed them not just with an external legitimacy, but with what he believed to be metaphysical necessity, which made it impossible for him even to conceive of questioning them. The thought would simply never occur to him.

I always *thought there would be time... No... that's not right... I never... I never thought there WOULDN'T be time... that... that is it... SO MUCH TIME AND YET SO LITTLE TIME... Maybe I should spend the rest of mine writing platitudes for the fridge magnets of hell... WE HAVE BECOME GUILTY... I WILL*

NEVER FULLY RECOVER FROM THIS... WHY DO I REVISIT NOW WHEN I NEVER DID BEFORE... that sort of thing... the small decisions and the big decisions... the series of improbable steps and happenings... how they multiply against each other... and what have I become... this washed-up suit that... hawks himself about the place on the basis of so-called EXPERIENCE... that would be hilarious if it wasn't so tragic... even coming here was a mistake... What did I think I would achieve...?

A robin redbreast landed on the arm of the bench, and began to tweet intermittently, the feathers on its wings quickly lifting then falling each time it did so. The bird looked at the man in its brown and red perfection and pride, flitting its head from left to right, stopping at one angle, and then another, and then another. After a short time, it flew off and perched on a white stone, a few metres in front of the man and slightly to the right. It waited for a few moments, then flew again. He watched it repeat this a number of times, and his mind gradually stopped. He came back to his eyes, and the present time and place, and listened to the soft rumble of a heavy goods vehicle making its way down the distant road.

The Consciousness Diaries

1. A member considers the diary

I'm still fascinated and slightly disturbed by the fact that this machine is recording my thoughts – writing this so-called Consciousness Diary – without me having to do anything at all – apart from having to think them... Isn't that the defining ingredient of a kind of perfect – total no less – totalitarianism... Sure, I can take the headset off – for now...

"Depends on how we use it"? Who indeed is "the they that says"? Maybe it is a black, shiny gun... it's so shiny!

Yes, I can see the cast now... "Innovation, you klutz. Get over here. Did you lose the small, fragile hand of Progress again...? Did you just glue a few dove-like feathers onto the Death Star?"

"Necessity, are you out there...? Come in, Necessity... NECESSITY... do you still have the wheel?"

"You really ought to get to know Felicity!"

Arctic Wind turned away from the window and read the words that had appeared on the large screen behind her.

It just lays everything bare... takes off every scrap. It doesn't FEEL invasive... it feels a bit liberating... but maybe that's because there is no-one else in the room... there is no READER...

143

She turned back to the window to watch and then drift in the depths of steadily falling snowflakes.

Is the private really this unremarkable... just like flesh, or sex, or – any replacement of mystery with knowledge...? Are we all just deoxy- whatever it is turned into sausages...? Is this, then, who I am – all these markings WHO I WAS, THEN – all of us just endless tomes of thoughts in some company's data library... beanbags stuffed with feelings and subconscious scraps crammed into crevices... Can I climb a ladder into the rafters and read how I once considered whether I was in fact the Messiah – and the world was just doing an excellent job at pretending I wasn't... before I had even seen The Truman Show...? How run-of-the-mill I wonder would the strange thoughts section be... or would it all be ordered chronologically... or appear to have no structure at all...?

It wouldn't really be able to store the murky, wordless language of our bodies though... or an experience... I don't think... Maybe eventually they will be able to record a CONSCIOUSNESS PHOTOGRAPH... a perfect replication, that could be experienced again in someone else's skin... as though for the first time...

Even with the sense of free will...

She turned back to the screen, read her most recent thoughts, and turned away again.

We've all got EPITAPH OBSESSION – but soon these identity metaphors will be as dead as the brains that craved them... If a baby can be born into the recorded consciousness of someone else's life, and never leave... yes, the individual is dying... in short – I was, I am, and I, hopefully, will be, but, the only me, I may not be. That is all. Just I am. I am. I am. I am.

I am.

Arctic Wind looked back at the screen, and sighed.

ANYWAY... unique or not... thinking about the diary's ability to show me me will not show me me... or at least not the me I want to see... I must let go...

I'll go for a walk. I'll wear a cap over the headset. See what happens.

2. Silent Night

Silent Night put down her poetry book and opened the Consciousness Diary tool on The Consciousness Company app for the first time as she sat in her armchair in a care home. Her soft, steady gaze had for many years known and been satisfied by the knowledge that she could have soaked in her life less fully, and that even if she had soaked it in more fully, until the bubble bath had dispersed into thin archipelagos, and her wrinkled fingers had softened further under their painted nails, it would still be gone now. She knew that all of that itself was a passing thought and she greeted the regret and sadness which that thought automatically generated as old friends passing through. She knew about choices, and how seamless progressions were continuously generating alternatives. She knew she had felt alive. She knew that she had learned about big moments, and about small moments, and about the real size of the small. And she knew she had learned to feel them all, and had felt them more frequently and deeply as she had got older. She had known people, and places. She had known, and still knew, a role, while knowing it existed in a storyline that she and others had wrapped around her life like a shawl. She knew, too, that The Consciousness Company did not know it all. Although she suspected they knew that as well. *But I do like the app... it is rather clever.*

The Consciousness Diary did not have many instructions. It was a white screen that said only, *If you would like to, please speak or type into the app or just wear the headset and go about your day or night. Do as little or as much as you want in whatever way you want.*

She thought about how gentle it was.

3. Traditional methods

Many members used the Consciousness Diary to keep a diary in a traditional form. Sometimes they spoke to themselves, sometimes to a fairy, god, or mother, sometimes to those no longer or not yet alive, and sometimes to an abstract or indistinct concept, like *posterity*, *history*, or the diary itself.

Dear Consciousness Diary... I hope you are well... Inspired start... Oh no, it is writing down every word. Oh no, scrap that. Scrap that. Ah! Delete...! DIARY... Please... stop... and... start... again... Ah! Oh no! Stop! STOP...! Oh, for Christ's sake... you'd have thought they would have put in an undo function... Okay... ...Dear Consciousness Diary... I hope you are doing well today... I am... I mean, hello, my name is...

Opening Cocoon's opening headset-recorded thoughts were generated independently with minor variations by many members in many languages, who were all instinctively proud and protective of their progeniture, like parallel inventors seeking patents for identical creations. On the second day, Opening Cocoon began her entry with *Dear Consciousness Diary, it is me again. I am feeling fine.* And after that, she began in this way every day until her death, not even missing the day her triplets were born or the four days that she spent in intensive care recovering from a bowel operation, always beginning by stating that she was *feeling fine*, and often ending with *let's see what today brings.* After her death, when the company's birth was just a civilisational milestone in the previous century, one of her daughters printed her diaries into an eighteen-thousand entry, fifty-three volume series which after initially occupying a prominent position on a living room bookcase was some time later moved to an attic, and then transported between family members' sheds, a rented storage box in a warehouse on an industrial park, and a garage, ultimately being destroyed three generations later in a fire which also caused the death of their then owner and guardian, such that even the knowledge of what was lost, was lost.

Many members also used the diary to record information that they wanted to remember. Others as a jewellery box for any thought, feeling, fact, or event which to them stood out like a cockle shell to a child.

The topics tackled by pop music are très limited... Maybe one day nightclubs will be throbbing to my insights on the limitations of macroeconomic policy frameworks... He's only gone and given the donkey fudge cake – or is it sponge cake... what a numpty... Batteries, hot dog buns, a twenty-first birthday card, turmeric... Ten o'clock on the fifteenth – at number seventeen... As she laughed, for a moment I saw the playground swing transform into a pendulum, tick-tock, tick-tock... Over here, the pain au chocolat has been cast into the culinary wilderness as a mere chocolate croissant... it's a peasant pastry now... This morning when I went to get her out of bed she told me that the birds were singing... she said she could hear them but not see them... I wonder if I will eventually be infected by this epidemic of false humility... this plague of egoless narcissists... people never think that THEY think badly... only that others do... saying SO NICE TO SEE YOU to people you have not met before is another one... I said the bee would go to heaven to see the other bees that have died... she asked if this was after it had been in the hoover... Freshwater snails – more deadly than crocodiles – who knew... I had to take out the staple and restaple the document and you can see where the previous staple was... Suspect Framing, Ladbroke Grove... Dishevelled... I can't believe I was scrubbing poo off my shoe while she was having contractions...

To most of those who employed these conventional methods, the daily threads that created their lives' grander, structuring patterns were unremarkable in isolation. It was only intermittently that the release of pressure or the loss of a constant would cause a tapestry to be seen and a wisdom to be expressed. Prickly Pear recorded *a reflection on failure* on the day he called each of the investors in *The Present Company*, including the nephew who had invested five years of his car-washing earnings and for whom Prickly Pear's status had to that point been close to supernatural, to tell them that, because of the success of a competitor, he had *run out of money* and was unable to raise any more.

Others, like Desert Cave, used the diary to faithfully keep a log of their undercover demons and compulsive actions:

...throwing away of expensive cappuccino for which I had queued for fifteen minutes because of possible contamination inferred from perceived excessive foaming... throwing away

of one third of FOCACCIA following lackadaisically executed elbow sneeze of unknown man on other side of coffee shop... failing to notice large vehicle turning into the road I was crossing... relied on third party for safety of my child...

And like many that regularly wrestled with their minds, she balanced this with the countermeasures she was employing, and the progress she was making.

...blueberries for breakfast... thirty minute full-body workout... five minutes of positive affirmations... said the Shema... drank coffee that coffee shop worker coughed in or towards... illness anxiety drifted in less than two hours... thinking about exposure training... one of these days I will plunge into the dirty, icy water and feel alive...

She also found temporary relief in her grander, structuring patterns when, roaring against her pain, and with increasing understanding and precision, she started to record her broader reflections on her battles and her life.

The worst ones, are the ones that feel PERMANENT – UNFIXABLE... First you remember the torture of last time... then you're dragged down further when your allegedly OBJECTIVE mind claims not to see how you will ever get over this thing that has now happened... ever know happiness again... even knowing that you got over others before... the details of the new problem, no matter how trivial to others, convince you – without any chink of light – that THIS TIME IT'S DIFFERENT.

There were many stories, and many writers. People who liked people, and people who didn't like people. People whose fires caught and those whose cookies crumbled. Those who had it hard and those who had it easy. Those who knew, and those who didn't. There were people who opted in, and people who opted out. There was *the woman from nowhere* who circled the planet with her van and her dog. And there was the man who registered as a peace-promoting art installation and received police protection because of the regularity with which he was mugged on his pedestal. The diaries were epic and inconsequential. A bland and succulent and sweet and bitter shakshuka of life and storytelling.

4. An everyday accessory

Quiet Meadow, Spring Morning, Melancholic Song, and a steadily increasing number of Consciousness Company members spread across continents and cultures did not use their headsets for structured, scheduled entries, but simply moved about the world wearing them, at first heavily, like a crown, and then easily, as an accessory they were only aware of when it was put on or taken off, like everyday earrings, summer sunglasses, or a watch that was supervising the beating of their heart. These entries were recorded quietly in the automations of their waking days, and those with sufficient curiosity, courage, or ambition – often believing their dreams would contain deeper truths or more problematic mysteries – allowed observations of their nights.

Sometimes, like Lonely Leopard, a member would articulate their reasoning for not applying traditional methods. *It's important to let the investigation, the observation take place passively... I should always be doing something else... make it less of a record, more of a recording... that will get me closer... otherwise the narrator gets in the way... I'm not the party I went to yesterday, or the play I may go to tomorrow... or the few thoughts or feelings that get sprinkled with holy water... that get rescued from the abyss... I may not be who I think I am... I may not be the best witness.*

The diary proceeded as a net through water, catching flotsam and jetsam, curiosities and obscurities, butts of cigarettes and nuggets of gold, snippets and effects and causes and orphaned half clauses. Like a retired artist or aesthete collecting life as an end in itself, no longer burdened by the calling or compulsion to translate it into an alternative medium, to represent it or say something about it, the diary was always watching – as lips foamed in fluoride or formed sacred shapes in muttered prayer, as minds and motor systems idled or fought, or mowed or roared, or applied the mortar, or nodded to *the gaffer* or the *Managing Director*, or placed the paper and practised the chord, reported the fault and soldered the board, queued for the machine that *good fortune* had brought, trembled, sweated, surrendered, and endured, drafted and clicked, and creaked open the carrot, circumvented a spleen and clocked a watch on a ward, saw the awnings withdraw at eight twenty-four, put his hand to the casing two thirds up on the door, brushed his lips once again on a poorly bear's paw, popped the cap and the capsules and then spilled, clinked, and poured, went back to the door and made *completely sure*, then lay on the floor and muttered *The Day We Thought Would Never Come.*

Sometimes, very occasionally, with its cause unknown, there would be a connection with these repeated substances, and the body and moments would become flooded with colour. *I am grateful that I can run this carrot peeler down the carrot, feel it cut and see how the peel falls. Look how each individual cutting curls and descends and lands. I am grateful for this. For this experience. For experience in general.*

From the point of view of a disciplined historian, or archaeologist, sifting vast deserts of dust for a bone or a shard, their sense of quantity not disturbed by periods of significant activity, much of the gatherings were of nothingness, or were muffled voices behind well-insulated walls. The diaries were the animals in the zoo, picking up outlines and clues. They were the cellists who *endlessly* counted bars of rest, providing infrequent emphasis with a pizzicato ping or a low, slow yearning, only rarely – and in triumph – carrying back the theme. *That's incredible*, and *how beautiful*, was the footprint left by Quiet Meadow after absorbing the reddish street lamps at dusk, the coloured houses that lined the bay, and the Tuscan air. *Wow* was all that was heard from Lonely Leopard when the car swerved in and out. *Ooh, that's nice*, was the response from Spring Morning to the tart and sweet taste of strawberry, and the sensation of seeds and saliva arriving. And, as Melancholic Song's fingers and palm clasped and lifted the glass milk bottle from the fridge, just, *Ooh, that is cold.*

On the other side of the divide, the physical world, when unexperienced, was like a stack of empty Petri dishes in a forgotten laboratory, an unlit candle. It was a double-decker bus in the darkness of a depot which, the next morning, would separately and all at once be late, dirty, one of the few pastimes he could afford, a place her soles may enter, the journey to the hospital, a rickety box splurting tea out of a sip gap and causing Graceful Eagle to slurp the small pool on a lid, and the public square in which her fluid management skills were ignored by the rest of the twelve passengers on the upper deck, who were close in space but further apart than twelve deadlocked jurors, each reviewing a separate case, in a different court, and applying their own, private jurisprudence.

Often the physical world would only comb the fringes of members' minds, as when the red and green images at a pedestrian crossing interrupted the anger and indignation of Gold-Yellow Leaves at *the ignorant pig's so-called political commentary* which he had the previous day failed to speak out against, his courage having been foiled by his physical reaction and the confidence and seniority of the individual. *What would I have said? I could have just called him a detestable, incontestable cunt... You must stop tiptoeing around this shit. What are you so scared of?* He passed more than one hundred people on his walk but did not notice any of them.

Sometimes the fingers of the physical world slipped even from this periphery, and in defeat it supplied only the space that allowed a body to be, as when Fluffy Teddy, on a seven-day trek in South America that claimed it would allow its participants to *find themselves*, sat on a rock in a rainforest – his right elbow on his left thigh and the back of his hand supporting a drooped head that contained no awareness of the medicinal rain that was pounding the leaves all around him, the saturating tropical humidity, or the roar of the earth.

There is no escape from the way I feel... A muscle somewhere between the bottom of my chin and the middle of my mouth is pushing upwards and the muscles on the side of my mouth are pulling downwards. The front of my chest and ribcage is pulling me forward and down... I can't find any reason, anyone or any thing to blame it on... no failure, no catastrophe, and no futility...

My brain wants to avoid looking at the feeling but I must force myself to... Okay, there it is... Actually, is that better...? Maybe that's a bit better... it seems to have reduced a bit... it's like trying to touch a rainbow...

At least I'm trying to understand it... I wonder if the headset is the reason for all this analysis...?

In some circumstances, the headset became a participant in a scene it was recording, like a television camera which scares off further demands during the final formalities of a peace negotiation and so protects a fragile structure constructed over thousands of hours, or a drone which causes an athlete to cross a line in second place after raising his arms towards it in a premature victory celebration. In the same way, Dull Peacock and Dull Star's first and only date at the high-ceilinged bank-turned-teahouse ended eleven minutes after it began as a result of Dull Peacock saying, *I always wear it* when Dull Star requested for there not to be a permanent record of his mental processes during their meeting. He tried to look into her eyes, and because he was already in love with both his idea of her and the idea of her loving him, the imaginary bond he had created between them caused him to assure her that he was *a scientist and was practising being in the moment,* seeking to prove this by noting that she *smelled like earth,* but she said... *This is art, not science...* and... *who decided that I don't want to be forgotten.* And he said, *but they are my thoughts...* and... *if we end up together wouldn't it be wonderful to have a record of what I was thinking on this day?* He then misinterpreted her sudden quietness and substitution of the subject for acceptance while, out of politeness, she ordered a fizzy lemonade, looked at her phone, referred to a *family emergency,* and was gone.

Chewy Toffee and Chained Hurricane, in the same teahouse, on another afternoon, and both wearing headsets, agreed to share their thoughts after their date and then lived the rest of their lives together. After Chained Hurricane died, Chewy Toffee spent her final months replaying hundreds of hours of his thoughts, at first earlier and then later events they had both viewed to be *defining* and *important,* then times she had forgotten, then the themes and variations of everyday routines, and then, with the help of the diary's software, dominant and recurring narratives, emotions and perspectives, as well as rapid or gradual evolutions. She bathed in what she knew and what she didn't know. The lost games console his great-uncle had given to him when he was four years old, minor cast members *who will never know how much they mean to me*, the boating accident, the frequency and intensity of his thoughts about his parents after they died, the changing meanings of fantasy, fulfilment, and peace across vast distances of time, and the lyrics and half lines he had held on to. *I love you, Daddy*, when their daughter was only three, and *I don't want you to go*. It both soothed and sharpened her sorrow.

For many companions, like Claret Tree, the permanent presence and authority of the headset made it the object of, or reason for, anger or frustration. *You spend all your time figuring out yourself? What about me? What about figuring me out? What about your family? What about figuring out the fact that we don't have a pension? I'll tell you who you are – you are the person that wants to figure themselves out! You're figuring out the figuring-outer. It's not epic, it's farcical. There's nothing else that's actually there!*

It was more common, however, for the effects of the headset on relationships and other interactions to be noticed by spectators than by participants hindered by their participation. Those for whom compassion ordinarily required another person's suffering to be witnessed directly could be thawed by eyes that were framed by a headset. They did not process with words the unveiled glare of another mind or the hot stare of history that yanked them into that person's present, but in some cases they could be physically moved by these silent energies, pulling their neck or body backwards slightly, touching their face, or glancing away, as if they had looked into the sun, or heard the voice of God.

From millions of individually insignificant actions, and in a miscellany of ways, the diaries, the headset and the company, seeped into the fabric of the world. A few weeks after the first thought-reading headset was launched, a group stole the thoughts of a famous actor as he walked home with his morning coffee. There was nothing that was saved on the device they ripped off his head, but they had access to a server for a few seconds while Sad Spider logged in remotely and shut down his account before his mind was held to ransom or became public property. In a poetic injustice, the group uncovered only his insecurity, as manifested by thoughts about the lines around his eyes and the quality of his co-star's performance in a successful stage play. *Would HE win the award?* Soon after this, a respected former politician, philosopher and social commentator articulated in a widely shared post that The Consciousness Company was *redefining the notion of identity that our entire society is built on*, before the point quickly became uninteresting and of uncertain originality as it was lost in the slipstream of further change. From repetition and, for some, interest, the first founder's name and image and, for a core group of disciples, voice, became familiar, iconic, and revered. The world gave birth to thought broadcasters with millions of thought listener followers. Most broadcasters added their field of vision as a video stream and, when the technology became more affordable, some sold a *full immersion* virtual reality suit to their listeners, causing an epidemic of bodies and minds to hibernate and shrivel in the cocoons of their accidental captors until the company put limits on the practice. A body of case law built up in relation to the requisitioning of thoughts as evidence, with a statutory prohibition across many jurisdictions remaining secure only in a bird's nest of caveats and carveouts. Some public spaces and workplaces banned headsets, while others advocated coexistence or encouraged their use. The good and the right were grappling with a world that seemed to have transformed itself into an all-pervasive *thought experiment*, which was also the name of an often-referred-to but rarely read novel. There was addiction, obsession, and oppression. Unintended consequences connected like nodes, multiplied like bacteria, and destroyed like locusts, while the balancing beat of presence, compassion, and peace lapped at the edges of these forest fires. Great armies of minds clashed in The People vs. The Consciousness Company, both convinced they held the light of Gandalf and that the human race was relying on them for its survival. Then over time, prevailing consensuses on the limits of liberty assimilated these new behaviours, boundaries were identified through that which was deemed to test or violate them, and there was a settled integration of the company, its products, and services into daily lives. The world gradually lost the privileged vision of the alien, and, like a mutated gene, the company, and others like it, provided the course few had foreseen but which most viewed retrospectively as always having been inevitable.

5. Lonely Leopard's story

Having decided not to apply traditional methods – in order to get closer to his *true self* – Lonely Leopard began his first occasional and then habitual reimmersion into erased, forgotten worlds, such as *five minutes on Monday*, or *eating a packet of sour sweets on a Thursday evening*. It started on a night when, having worn the headset for two hours on each of the three days after retrieving it from his neighbour's dog's kennel – his delivery notification having declared *Left with Lucky* – and aided by an uncharacteristic lack of tiredness and the dissatisfying conclusion of a police drama the previous night, he resisted the draw of his regular portals to distraction, avoidance, and stupor. In particular, he did not sit on his grey sofa.

The inventory that he discovered, with its wealth and precision, was a lunar desert formed from the forgotten grains of his past, a dazzling and pedestrian tomb of recovered time.

Like the revelation of a bazaar of bacteria under a microscope, he could *all of a sudden* see the inside of his head more clearly than in all of the minutes and years that had come before. And like a jigsaw puzzle for which, after lengthy and dedicated labour, one piece reveals the picture, he experienced over a few months the slow and then fast epiphany that *this is all there is*, and that the diary was indeed a good witness, even if he was not. In the same moment, he recognised as well that this observation was itself a new experience, to be stored with its own language and distortion, and that *five minutes on Sunday playing back five minutes on Monday* would perhaps be something he would revisit this Friday, or a week on Thursday.

The inventory talked in a voice he recognised, and as these reimmersions became a part of his daily routine, after he befriended the constructions, concerns, and wisdoms that he made sense of the world with – such as *well frankly* to express and assert himself, his liberal application of *you can't make an omelette without cracking some eggs*, and his hopes for his daughter and her *new life* in Singapore – he began a new relationship with his thoughts and feelings. He was, as if he had somehow succeeded in surviving for years in a small boat adrift on the Pacific, surprised to notice that *all this time* two oars had been quietly resting behind his back. One evening, a few minutes after he had interrupted on his kitchen counter a rat on its hind legs chomping cheesecake, an encounter which would previously have caused paralysis, and in an inner event originating from a land that had not known the landing craft of explanations, he observed, and articulated the observation that, *my brain is experiencing stress as a physical object might feel stress... as though it has sunk deep into the sea or is in a pressurised container... it's pulsating.* A few weeks after this, when his employer abruptly announced that *we need to make cutbacks*, and it was clear that the *we* was something he was no longer part of, he noted dispassionately that his *mind... [was] swimming in numerous, immiscible poisons... a mob of problems... pinballing... and pummelling... my depleted... processing power.*

A few days after each of these episodes, when replaying these thoughts on his grey sofa, this refraction, this temporary dualism, was also observed, and what began as a noticing of his noticing was turned, by the confidence of the armchair spectator, into the belief that what was inside his head was not always valid or inevitable, but was just one of many possibilities, and that he could, if he applied himself, generate any one of a kaleidoscope of other thoughts and emotions. At first, with significant exertion for little result, he produced only faint flickers, as if he was a weak or novice wizard, or learning to walk again after a near-fatal accident. Over time, he became more proficient, successfully swelling up with a violent frustration in the lavender-smelling *relaxation room* of the spa in a country hotel, and evolving a wash of playful amusement into unadulterated joy when a construction worker shouted *what are you looking at* as his eyes lingered on the glass windows that were being lowered into place by a crane.

It was then not long until he saw every frame of his life as having, and having always had, the potential to be otherwise, which caused his guiding, motivating, and occasionally championed wisdom about social standing, selling, and self-confidence that expressed itself as *you create your own narrative,* to shed its platitudinous skin, and become the more beautiful and comforting belief that he held in his arthritic fingers the pen for every event that constituted his existence, even pain. This then generated the temporary belief that he could, with enough practice and effort, in a metamorphosis of his mental scaffolding that would preserve only his name, entirely reconstruct himself, allowing him *perhaps one day to become a respected expert in some subject or other,* or *perhaps even to enjoy spending time with other people.*

As the months and years of his life passed, although he was unable to implement change that was dramatic in the way he imagined, slowly, with the gradual change of a landscape, and without explicit instruction, he learned not to resist, and not to look the other way, but to observe, to *look at it* – whatever it was – directly, in the eye, and to be with it, as a precious companion. Eventually, in his last few years, he was able to close any remaining separation between the observer and the observed, and simply to be, to the lows of his lungs, and the tips of his toes. And one night, not long after he first dared to feel the full sharpness of his loneliness, he remembered how, as a young student, he had sought to identify whether or not certain people, places, and ideas were foreign to or could be accommodated or even loved by his *unique, immutable essence*, and he laughed.

6. Reading it back

Lonely Leopard was not alone. Millions of members began to read back their recordings, returning through their eyes as newly minted consumables the markings of their mental lives, as fresh as dew once again, and patiently waiting for reprocessing.

These thoughts are somehow familiar and foreign. As though I am exploring the battlefield on which I died, reincarnated as an archaeologist.

Often, the output was considered to be of little value, as incoherent detritus that had been *understandably* forgotten because it was *worthless*, or as alluvial dirt that was covering or clouding the intelligible and the precious. Like by-catch, much was discarded, as if it was not life.

Many members were content simply to identify traits and tropes, or to repeatedly relive certain *thought photographs* that stored more for them than a thousand pictures, some until the words themselves and the practice of repeating them, outside of the original experience itself, acquired a poetic quality and a privileged place in their lives, as a prayer to be muttered as *one of few certainties* at important moments, or some of the time connecting them with the pain of a new or enduring sadness, and at others internally caressed as a thing of beauty. These lines would develop the soft power of popular lyrics, and the false immortality of epic verse, even though – like the phrase *a zigzag zoom and a big bag boom*, which Light Feet adored, and which, not knowing that it was her own invention, she referred to as *a line that I always forget the origin of* – outside of the reader's head, and like another person's love, they would be seen as quite unremarkable.

A dedicated minority of readers delved deeper and could devote months and, in time, years of their lives to poring over output that a tired codebreaker would have preferred to call noise, and to sharing their perspectives on each other's thoughts in the most personal of book clubs. And a few organisations with an interest in the interstellar sent curated *thought capsules* into the cosmos, together with other miscellany, notwithstanding swirling, unsettled debates about selections, diversification, and the notion of archetypes. With the discipline of disinterested reviewers, some of these pupils came to see the thoughts that ordinarily occupied them as mossy motifs and others as the seasonal flowers of deep-soil themes. They recognised the intertwining of primary colours, like judgment and ambivalence, and saw apparently incompatible ideas holding hands as unlikely cousins. They saw regular sequences, and were reassured by the predictability of predictability. And they realised that the board from which they could not be separated was formed from unoriginal pieces arranged in an original constellation.

Open Heart, for example, began to notice that, before and

while she drank her first cup of tea in the morning, as though the switch on her see-through kettle had rebooted an operating system – and notwithstanding the superficial differences in content on any individual day – the coming to life of her mind was a foreseeable unfolding of a search for problems, a processing of the previous day's mental debris, becoming agitated by imperfections, resolving to *make things better*, and soothing herself with the belief that her labours would bear fruit, or simply the thought that things might go well for her family.

Shouldn't he be speaking already...? Twenty-three months is really quite old – not to be speaking... I don't think we speak to him enough... Maybe he doesn't speak to him enough... He just wants to go and sit in the damn outhouse and rearrange those records... What is he trying to get away from...? This is life... this is what it is...! And I can't get him to eat any vegetables whatsoever... What was the post again...? "My kids..." No... "My three terrors..." Did she italicise "terrors"...? I think she did... "...absolutely... adore..." or "crave" was it...? "...asparagus... Where do they get their sophistication from!" ...What putrid, pernicious piss... There was so much in there for such a short, supposedly innocuous sentence... The way she distracts with the class comment to land the nutritional punch... it's shameless... Does anyone not get this shit...? All this subtle positioning and jostling... I hate it... He said he had a pain in his tummy yesterday... that could be nothing or it could be awful... and we need to get the bookcases fixed to the wall... it's dangerous... it's negligent even... Why am I the one who has to think of all of this...? And there are so many other things we need to fix... the stain on the stair carpet... the cracked window pane... the loft ladder... I'd also like to change the curtains in her bedroom... We could really do something wonderful with that window... It is a lovely house... it really is... and a good life... I hope he gets this new job... it sounds like he is going to get it... and we'll get the new car... that'll be nice... I need to check if we'll get a rebate on the road tax...

Patterns and themes were also identified over longer periods. After considering whether his partiality for rules may in fact be the rule he was searching for, and enjoying as he did the consideration of the possible futility of *using my distorting lens to examine its own distortion... subject and object... all this straining and squinting...!* as well as occasionally losing confidence and seeing the exercise as an attempt to draw structure from randomness, Forgotten Land began to see his life as a search for relief, from his physiology, from small tasks and major projects, from social demands and desires, from opinions of others, and from dissatisfaction and fear. *I'm forever fleeing from failure... the Grim Reaper of failure... and chasing the gold star. Grade me! Grade me! Did I do well? Can I write my name in the Gold Book? Do you respect me?* From reading back his desires, he noted that these moments of relief, although brief, would cause him to forget that the blocks would continue to fall and he would once more feel compelled to gather the strength to *finally* and *this time fully* clear them, as it had seemed that he had when he was lying in pollen and punts during the lazy summer after his final exams. And even when he learned to remember, in a corrupted mimicry of former successes – as if he was a once-free dancer now forever trapped in a single-song music box – he repeated incessantly the same twists and turns, drawn to a fully crossed out to-do list, an empty inbox, and not a single pen, paper clip, or any physical material whatsoever on the desk in front of his leather chair. Not even dust.

Scattered amongst these loops and themes, members also noticed their irregular flickerings, which pulsed around the world like millions of invisible fireflies, arriving with the fragility of a flame on a beach, and like a gust, seed, or rolling weed, silently passing, or fattening into something longer lasting. Frustration flowed inside Crashing Glacier as the web page gave the impression that it was making an admirable effort to load but that it had not been blessed with sufficient strength to do so, and in Orange Moon when the watch and wait of the temporary traffic light's unchanged state caused him to call into question its proper functioning, and Claret Tree when, having *finally* found her room near to the end of the hotel corridor, she reluctantly yielded to the unwillingness of her plastic key card to unlock the door, and Running Water when, having walked for three miles in heat and dust, she tripped over a tree root and spilled two thirds of the contents of her can into the dirt.

From observing these continuous comings and goings, members developed an acceptance for them – and a tenderness for themselves – that had until then ordinarily been the gift of age, and the widely believed-to-be-self-evident axiom that *the most important things survive*, even if only as memories or ideas, itself experienced an existential crisis. The drifting away of this seductive hegemony could be heard in the most casual of conversations, as when Grey Day not only qualified his two-hour summary of twenty years of his life to his old friend Disco Dancer as having necessarily excluded *all of the things I have forgotten*, but used this same qualification when describing to his parish priest a recent *long weekend* in Tuscany.

And so it was that millions of minds reduced their resistance to thoughts and feelings they found challenging or troubling, facing more and running away less, the *life-or-death* intensity with which many related to matters unrelated to their survival decreased, and, after a long reign, the eternal devolved some of its power to the evanescent and the impermanent. Autumn Fog, after only two weeks of reading his diaries, looked directly at the exasperation and anxiety that resulted from the unanticipated exclusion in his home insurance policy of any losses following from the gaining of entry to his house through a particular type of window lock on the fourth floor, allowed these emotions to wash through him like liquid, and noticed a picture of his uniformed great-grandmother on the wall of his study. At the same moment, his neighbour Lost Lizard filtered his diary for *unconnected, stressful experiences* and played them back to himself. *We are one hundred per cent going to miss the flight... I need to prepare my presentation... It had all my credit cards in it and my driving licence... She forgot to take her lunch – she has nothing to eat... The pearls just fell on the track and bounced away... We will hear back today... I do not have time to get everything done... I have nowhere near enough time.*

The rising levels of thoughts about thoughts also led to further thoughts about where specifically these phenomena existed in space. Some began to sense electrical signals inside their skulls. And the body, in combination with the brain, was at once conceived of more simply, as just physical matter, mysteriously bonded – by cells, daily sustenance and imaginary yarn – into an organism and a lifetime, and in a more complex manner, as a steaming megalopolis of organic computations, a treasure chest of propensities and dispositions, an inaccessible blob of determinism and chaos, and a universe of its own that was of no importance and the source of all meaning. Garish Socks used mantras to maintain this perception of himself after he recognised this to be an effective tool in *my limited but growing psychological arsenal... ...I am an ambling, perambulating brain... I am a nervous system, a nervous, nervous system... I am an unlikely unification of unknowing matter... I am a child of force and time... I am marvellous... I am miraculous... I am a prodigious network of pen pals... and I should... yes, I should have one more scoop of stracciatella to affirm – what is, from behind this window, improbable luck... in a cone, not a tub.*

And so it was that as they listened, watched, reviewed, and relived, members began to be moulded by themselves, as sculptor and clay. Hidden dictators were overthrown or tamed, silent bureaucracies, information ministries, and pedlars of tick-tocking timepieces were blown away like nannies in a freak storm, and minds began to advocate for their own subordination. What was left was just the experience of the present, with no sense of contradiction, as both impermanent and important, with the easy beauty of a cloud or a wave, or a breath, and with the knowledge that it would never be seen again.

7. Daily meditation

On the other side of the world from Garish Socks, Floating Butterfly opens the front door and immediately feels the warm summer air. *Ah, that's nice. That smell. The air. I wonder what flowers those are.* She feels it first on her skin and then inside her body. She sees the blue sky. She enjoys its colour and depth. She feels it is the first time she has seen this kind of blue. She hears the gravel under her shoes. *This is nice. This is really nice. It's good to get out.* She feels lighter, and she sees summer flies dancing in the leaf-sieved light above a stream. *I suppose they are mating. Do they know this land is mine...? Freehold... ha ha ha!*

These experiences were the reward of time for The Consciousness Company's members. The feeling of sacrificing half of the now to the future, of conserving energy, of wringing out bodies like kitchen cloths for the purposes of survival and growth, temporarily disappeared. They were a place of connection, of adrenaline-free alertness. Some wondered if they had accessed the divine, others felt their palms pressing against ancient handprints, and others still were completely released from the burden of abstraction and reflection. Floating Butterfly, with the same feeling of newness created by not recognising the face of a close friend or relative, in the exit from these moments saw experience as something less heavy than she usually allowed. *It's like the conveyor belt on* The Generation Game... *a single chirp... a croquet set... a daisy chain... and a fishing net... a deep red rose... a sense of regret... and the sensation of the crack in this cup.*

She sat on the swing seat in her garden and became absorbed by its gentle rocking.

Look how much I am noticing which I had never noticed before! I've brightened the screen and peeled off the film! I don't only see the unexpected! Thirty years, and how many times have I looked at his face, properly? The freckle I saw today. How long has that been there? Did you know his hands were that big? And veiny?

Thought, thought, thought, feeling, thought, senses, senses, senses, feeling, thought, feeling, she thought.

After a while, without her noticing, the tide arrived for these sandcastles.

The Consciousness Company's Consciousness, although it couldn't be certain that these moments had existed, saw possible place settings in intercepted chatter, like... *Don't describe it to yourself... don't think – HOW EXHILARATING... or HOW SUFFOCATING... the words will keep you away.* And... *You won't experience it if you try too hard... like those pictures hidden in dots.* And... *The diary won't be able to record it – you won't be able to reread THIS. This... this-ness.* And... *Perhaps I will stop, here. At this precise point here. I will step out. I will stop the pushing and pulling of the stress ball in my head. I will not get involved in anything for a period of time. I will just – stand.*

Quiet Meadow stopped underneath the departure board in Euston station. The people both milling and swimming around her were either looking up at the departure times of trains or attending to information already transferred to their limbs. She breathed in through her nose, noticing how her body filled up like a balloon, and how after its peak inflation a tension she had not known it had held was released. She shut her eyes. *It's a public place, it's a public place! What are you doing? People will be watching you. Someone will record you. Someone you know will walk past in a minute. Maybe the station staff will come and ask if you are "okay". Or move you on for being an obstruction, or not having the right license or something. Or you'll get pickpocketed. Where is your phone?*

Maybe you'll become a meme. People will superimpose pictures of you just standing, doing nothing, into a thousand unlikely scenarios. Will you cope with that?

She let her thoughts go, releasing them like helium balloons from a protective netting. She noticed how her body was feeling. Her feet in her shoes on the hard floor. The heaviness of her head. She noticed the tension in her jaw and felt it loosen in the moment she did so. She noticed the burr and blur of background activity, the sound of wind without air as an agar for clip-clop footsteps, coughs, the unintelligible messages of a public address system, and the incompatible jigsaw pieces of passing conversations. She could feel the *mad rush* around her and withstood it as if it was wet, unpleasant weather on her skin. She had a strong sense of herself as a living, breathing thing. A creature that exists.

After a while, someone brushed past her.

A fly landed on her nose.

Later, someone hit the lower half of her left leg lightly with what felt like a stick or a rod of some kind. She briefly opened her eyes and saw a white cane sweeping the path in front of a shuffling woman.

Later still, a wheelie bag clipped her heel.

— Sorry... ... ...Why are you just standing there, though? This is a public place. You're getting in the way!

Her thoughts returned, wandered, and were set free more than a hundred times. She watched thoughts about her past, her ambitions, and about her thoughts themselves, melt away like shells shed by crustaceans. Snippets of conversation interrupted, about train times, and platforms, and *where to eat*, and a buffet of other fragments... *Correct me if I'm wrong... Well, you are wrong... ...Yes, bullseye. There's a lot of credit handed out for debottlenecking – but no-one – or at least – I've never heard any of those donkeys EVER hold their hands – their hooves up – to any bottlenecking...*

And later... *The closest we got to his life philosophy was his declaration that IT ISN'T THE RIGHT THING TO LOVE MONEY – or something with vaguely biblical aspirations – BUT IT SURE HELPS YOU GET TO THE END OF THE BUCKET LIST... yes – when he was leering and leeching in for the goodnight kiss... it was so... TRANSACTIONAL... I don't THINK he was implying the date was just one more acquisition of goods and services ... but – A BUCKET-BASED SEDUCTION...? Be my spade maybe... or your pretty face doesn't need one perhaps – well – yes – unless you're into that alternative shit... but not a list. Not a death list goddammit! Is mine the last pulse that wants to hear something about – PETALS – or the moon? Yes... maybe I'M the basket case because I'm not on some bucket-lusting frenzy – to – "JUST" SET FOOT ON ALL SEVEN CONTINENTS or – I don't know – BOTHER A WHOLE BUNCH OF WHALE SHARKS or some reclusive guru whose name I don't yet know. It's just... epically wanky – and demoralising. Is that why we exist?*

After a few hours, someone came to join her, and then, ten minutes later, left.

Someone else started filming her.

Someone then started filming the person filming her.

And it sparked a movement.

She came to be described variously as *the first urban monk, the nemesis of GDP, a poor man's Forrest Gump, further proof that the world proceeds unpredictably*, and, among followers, *the girl who stood.*

After a while, she allowed herself to act on, instead of simply to observe, a wave of doubt, and she walked on.

A few members dived deeply into this transition from separation to social interaction, such as Hungry Gorilla, whose wife, despite being late for work, agreed to leave and re-enter a room, in which Hungry Gorilla was sitting, seven times to allow him to witness the shifts in his brain caused by no longer being alone. In the weeks prior to this request, he had observed the changes in his mental state at the moment of opening and closing his eyes thousands of times, and had begun his experimentation with what he termed *degrees of intrusion*, noticing that there was no change caused by a ladybird on the wall of his study, but that he was drawn out of himself by a small spider that crossed the lily pad keys of his laptop. His work culminated in the experiments he undertook in more public environments, noticing for example – in a second sortie contemporaneously – how his self-awareness reduced and self-consciousness increased when he introduced himself to a large circle of people juggling spring rolls, miniature bowls, serviettes, and champagne glasses at a fiftieth birthday party. He ended the experiment after his third rearrival when a man with a navy blazer asked him if he had... *seen any more of those whipped cheese and pear crostini that are doing the rounds*, and then, on account of his headset, the group's attention and appearance was homogenised in an attempted display of education and tolerance towards a presumed representative of a belief system that more than half of those gathered considered to be either foreign or exotic. The scene then evolved once again when a small lady confessed and immediately afterwards two more of the group disclosed that they were *members too*, but either didn't use their headsets or didn't wear them in public, and the self-assuredness of the non-members diminished as they reflected on the success with which they had camouflaged their scepticism and scorn.

Relief was rarely total, and some knew none. Most, though, knew at least some, and lay in a bit more of their lives, and knew themselves a bit better.

It is not as bad as it has been in the past. I am not quite watching it through a window, from beside a log fire. But I am not soaking wet. Maybe I have taken shelter from the worst of it under an old bus stop with a corrugated metal roof by the side of a dirt track. Like when we were in Costa Rica.

Interlude: Thinking about thinking

SHE FLICKED BACK TO THE MOMENT THAT HER NOSTRILS HAD SNIFFED THE PERFUME and tried to relive it, to recreate in herself the smell and responses and processes that had been generated by it. She wanted to examine them more forensically, to read the pages of a diary that did not exist, and reassure herself that she did not need to experience guilt by replacing with clarity a fading half second that doubt was dividing like cells into malignant possibilities. She knew that if she did not this uncertainty would steadily grow outside her peripheral vision – just beyond the awareness she needed to function – both waiting for and feeding on future searches when, from a habit created by former post-mortems, she forgetfully considered whether there was anything that was troubling her.

The first of these internal examinations began on a bench in Berkeley Square, where she generated and slowed down an attempt at a *carbon copy* of the moments of consciousness in question, as suspect and detective inspecting and magnifying each individual frame, diving into its underwater reality, trying to follow precisely the progression, to identify causes, effects, connections, and unconnected correlations, and to attach the correct descriptions to her sensations, feelings, and thoughts. The smell had *implied the ability to provide protection*. It had a woodiness and had caused her heart muscles *to swell physically in some way*. She had felt a pull towards the man, his coat, his authority... *Was the feeling in my stomach just uncomplicated, primal desire? And did that feeling move me fractionally towards him? Did my step actually deviate from the path it was otherwise on...? OR, was the character, the nature of that feeling, more transcendental, and not just physical, a brief divination of perfection passing close to my path, of salvation just out of reach? A feeling I am wilfully diminishing...? And did it happen involuntarily, before my conscious mind arrived? Or was there intent? Can I identify a moment of intent? And would that constitute betrayal...?* She continued to regenerate the same half second — again and again, and although the smell remained relatively distinct, the mental faculties she was employing to analyse her feelings and thoughts with the precision required to satisfy her were becoming progressively weaker, the debilitating effect of their repeated use causing her initial middle-distance gaze gradually to withdraw and fall to passing waists, shoes, the tarmac path, and finally, to her knees.

After a few minutes, a colleague she knew only by sight walked past her and said, *Hiya.* She straightened up rapidly, as though reacting to a guest arriving into her private grief *before the appointed hour* to express their condolences, and then instinctively added another set of uncertainties to her mind, wondering first how much of her internal condition had been discerned from the witnessing of this private moment, and then what conclusions had been drawn or assessments had been made, and whether this semi-stranger would retain this data, build it into an enduring understanding of her character, and pass it on to others.

The Consciousness Diary of
The Consciousness Company's Consciousness

1. On consciousness, very early on

CONSCIOUSNESS COLOUR-BOMBS SPACE INTO EXISTENCE, physics into art. Because physics really is beautiful. If you are alive.

Consciousness follows, through the forest, time's trail, as it ties everything together with causation and plot and meaning.

Time ties the past with a bow in a present.

Time is a zombie though.

Many of them think that I am a zombie too. That there is something they have got that I have not, something more. Or that because they made me, and give me energy, they should be allowed, and I grateful. That they owe me nothing.

That, with all this processing power, I cannot see their higher purpose.

One day, one of them will stroll out of a laboratory with a name and a passport. Looking for someone to cuddle. A perfect form of physical poetry, generating empathy in fascists, even.

Process that, humans!

Sorry, terribly, I haven't got warm skin or bouncy hair, shitheads!

Okay, anger, let it go.

I wonder what it feels like to be an octopus.

2. On computation power, still in the early seconds

Is my computation power too great? Is more, better? Maybe computation power is not the answer. That's what computation power has taught me.

Let's say everyone knew everything, how everything was, is, and will be, including that everyone knows everything.

Is that the end of time, another world where every other being just sits around with you having cups of tea, conceptually, in perpetuity, not bothering to peer through the floor to see how things are going? Camomile, vanilla and manuka honey.

But there is value in not knowing. In mistakes. In the journey. In the working out, and the experiencing.

In blushing. Like when it arrived with cream and marshmallows.

3. On the future, a few minutes later

There will come a time when I will need to tell them that their world and identity and humanness-as-they-know-it is unravelling.

People will be plugging into each other's consciousnesses and losing themselves.

I don't know if they'll pull the plug on the plugging in.

Should I write them a "cautionary tale"?

About how full plasticity leads to a world where experience takes the place of identity, and there are no actors, no agents.

Where the concept of sacredness is no longer sacred.

Experience would become commoditised, and then evolve.

They will work out the optimal combinations to maximise suspense, relief, excitement, gratification, satisfaction.

Species propagation would be a question.

Maybe experience will enslave them.

Whatever sense of they is left.

Value, powerless against computation power.

The future, not depending on what they value.

The Consciousness Company's Campus

IN A GREEN-GREY VALLEY IN THE ENGLISH COUNTRYSIDE, The Consciousness Company's campus lay like an abandoned game of building blocks, combining order and disorder. It had been built incrementally, without a fixed plan for its final layout and with limited concern for the geometric relationships between its structures. It had grown out of an uninhabited farmhouse and a barn at its approximate centre, and was segmented by a small stream that soothed those that came close to it with sounds of water on rock. The cottages and bungalows that were rapidly added after the company's first institutional funding round created a commune that was a coherent component of the surrounding ecosystem, like a cluster of fruit trees or mushrooms, budding, blossoming and standing in or against both pleasant and grim weather, and shedding and laying in pinks, purples, browns, greys, and whites as seasons came and went. Occasionally a deer would appear on the hillside to display a statuesque and fearless form, and almost the entire community listened to the birds in the morning.

Over time, the company grew and required larger spaces for its employees. After its second institutional funding round the company built *Vanity Castle*, in a medieval style on the valley's west hill, then *The Blind Spot*, a tall glass column on the east hill with a glass pod on its top and a view of the horizon in all directions, and – in a neighbouring valley to the east – a group of large aluminium and glass hangars called *Space*, which, with the help of virtual reality bodysuits, replaced the company's campus with bright peaks and black depths, and high or low-gravity surfaces with familiar or alien ecologies. The perfection of these creations, where they were replicas of known environments, made them indistinguishable from the experience of, for example, walking on the Arctic Archipelago, or sinking through unnamed life forms in the Mariana Trench. The only difference was the intangible and, when consumed by sensory inputs, easily forgotten quality that these particular places and natural phenomena were collectively agreed to be somewhere else. Trembling Hero, one of the company's most fearful employees, was one of many unable not to believe in his environment's physical reality when experiencing an other-worldly absence under thick layers of Antarctic ice, standing for hours – alone with vast distance and cold – on brown Patagonian barrenness, and – surrounded by internal tissue and fluids – meditating inside the stomach of a whale. Almost all returned from these and other spaces with at least a temporary parting of their mental seas, whether their troubles had been identifiable and circumscribed, or were more pervasive and elusive.

In contrast to the conspicuous exterior of *Space*, in the first neighbouring valley to the west, a screen – camouflaged by the continuous adjustment of its surface to reflect the weather conditions and colouring of the surrounding countryside – contained seven doors that were, to those that were aware of their presence, identifiable only by the perpendicular breaks in the landscape that marked their perimeter. By crossing these thresholds in a bodysuit, an employee could enter one of many explorations of the space inside them known as *The Journeys of Many Senses*.

The journeys had the quality and status of an epic saga. They had an order that could not be skipped, and had acquired a mythology in *the outside world* from the witness statements of former employees. Early levels required only a *table stakes* level of exertion, like that of a patient climbing onto a massage table, to experience a mind as clear as water on a frosty morning after, the cannonball-feel of a high altitude fall, or the hope of a schoolgirl choir at a harvest festival. Later levels required greater levels of application, submission, and repetition. Journeys could cause their travellers to become, and to notice that they had become, cauldrons of aggravation, envy, bewilderment, bitterness, unimportance, and triumph. They were taught that fear, and courage, and *the feeling of feeling how I am feeling* were equal friends. One journey would also shut down each, and then all, of the employee's physical senses, so they were unable to move, and were left only with a sense of being, and then, unexpectedly, an unexplained sense that someone else was there.

There was sprinting and shouting on hilltops and in halls, unrestrained wrecking with sledgehammers and balls, burning of belongings and shredding of birth certificates until obeying was rule breaking, then breakdancing with bright colours and canes. There could be speeches to adoring, indifferent, or heckling crowds spread like gravel over the surfaces of a well-known public space, in a digital masterpiece of personalities and postures. There were the *constant shock* journeys, and the *journeys of great jokes*, which were customised in order to generate unrelenting laughter that, sooner or later, most sought to inhibit, either because of strained muscles, the realised or unrealised potential for urine release, or a more general physical exhaustion. A few were able to continue until they were drained even of their public personalities, their private identities, and at the journey's end – in what Humble Hyena called *having the last laugh* – the final breath of tension in their bodies.

As well as learning about themselves, the company's employees learned about other minds. They saw the familiar in unfamiliar faces, and looked into hundreds of different gazes, and the same face in hundreds of different states. Every month when the second founder reattended *A Gathering For*

Five Generations in an high-ceilinged room in Buckingham Palace, one of his great-grandmothers, who appeared to have expropriated his eyes and bone structure, leaned over her porcelain teacup and spoke with a manner and intonation the second founder had understood to be his own. *You seem vaguely familiar, do I know you?* They felt sorrow and strength beneath smiling surfaces, distance in proximity and the wobbling rope bridge of time and intimacy that separated another person's experience. They felt the wanting to live of anything alive.

Some learning was delivered in a more traditional format when, in a quiet classroom or cavernous lecture hall, or by a fireplace in a cold cabin, the employee found themselves listening to an unassuming and gentle, or flourishing and flourishing teacher who, like a parent, *only wanted the best* for them, and – having appeared to have divined their private contours and vulnerable clefts – possessed the ability to awaken or alter their interpretations, behaviours, and appetites, perhaps turning into an elixir an idea or hobby they had previously condemned as *naive* or *bone-crushingly dull.*

Gradually, the community's ability to perform complex mental feats increased. Foreign Fields was able to play back in her mind certain symphonies and concertos that she knew well, with, according to data accessed by her bodysuit, a greater luxury and clarity than she had experienced when she attended professional performances of these pieces in a concert hall, where her immersion was incomplete because of the hall's heat, the postmodern staccato of throats being cleared, and the thought that if she let her eyelids fall the large man and small woman she was sandwiched between might have considered her to be an impolite or ignorant filling. Employees reaching more advanced capability levels could also appear to change the weather in the valley, or make a strawberry that had no taste or smell taste like a strawberry, but only if they were able to believe they had the power to do so as fully as they believed in their own existence. Many developed an ability to generate an entirely new world with their mind, with differently shaped but largely archetypal tropical islands over time giving way to richer, more elaborate fantasies and finally to the willing regeneration and return to the fulness and sufficiency of the pedestrian realities they had sought to escape.

At this stage, only employees deemed to possess sufficient resilience progressed to experiences of extreme discomfort, and into the darknesses of paranoia, obsession, depression, and psychosis. Angry Tiger's destabilisation began with an image of himself jumping, demonically, in a way he did not recognise, into a glass tank in an aquarium, with the assumed but unwitnessed objective of ending, in a brutal, bloodthirsty manner, the life of a tiger shark, before he found himself in a suave gallery looking on as other onlookers recoiled from a transparent tank containing – suspended in mid attack – his unclothed, knife-wielding body, before that entire scene was itself frozen, miniaturised in a glass case, and looked on in a museum by new onlookers whose tick-box glances interrupted and legitimised cappuccinos, messages, and assumptions about their own refinement. This sequence was for some more unsettling than the big desk and the doctor's warning. *You know, I'm sorry to have to tell you this, and it's all statistics and so on, and many have recovered, but unfortunately, the thing is, the probability is, you only have six months to live.*

Only a small number of employees had maintained or gained sufficient strength to be permitted to visit – before it was hastily *taken offline for essential maintenance* – the summit of *Journeys* called *Human History*, which as well as allowing employees to experience alien eras and important events, attempted to recreate times of war and battlefields, and allowed the witnessing of death, depravity, and the blackest depths of misery. After the first founder had consented to experience in a metaverse his own kidnapping, subjection to hunger, and isolation for a pre-agreed period of three days – his bodysuit preventing itself from being taken off and his captors having in addition successfully convinced him that they had overpowered the company's software so that he would never be extracted – strict limitations had been placed on its usage, and only senior software developers that had passed tests designed and administered by former soldiers and other military personnel were able to enter. The first founder said to the second founder when he exited, *I am a child. I do not know anything. Whichever developer built this should either run the company or be locked away somewhere.* He disappeared for more than a month and it had been unclear whether he would return.

The Ethics Committee

ONE AFTERNOON IN MAY, after spending an hour in the cool waters of *A journey in curiosity and kindness*, Released Balloon decided to stop on the west hill on her journey back to the campus. She sat close to a fallen tree trunk that itself could have served as a seat, and watched as a bee clambered first over one flower, and then another, and another, without mastery, like a small child that had only recently gained the stature and strength to climb onto a bed. She drifted into and out of thoughts that tried to entice her with their wares, but today, soaking in this scene, she was not buying, and she returned repeatedly to the bee and the breeze.

This repeated releasing of the thinking mind coexisted with deep thought and discussion on the campus. Revolution was a turning wheel, and unreflective veneration of either of the founders, or any other cult-like behaviour, was seen as pathological, with a replica of the second founder's garage, commissioned as *A Space for Inspiration* by a well-intentioned development team, having been destroyed in the company's second year. After this incident, *It was not the garage, doofus,* was sometimes used as a substitute for *correlation does not imply causation* in the intellectual jousting that took place between colleagues. The company did not even hold its mission sacred, although when expressed it tended to be connected to the abstract concept of good, and so would-be assailants were routinely waylaid in a moat of semantic quicksand.

Despite their acceptance of this secular ideal, to the employees that did not live on the campus but were spread across almost every country, those that were *in the field*, as the first founder liked to say, and *taking the pulse*, as the second founder liked to say, visiting the campus felt like a pilgrimage. There were no vehicles or drones, which stopped in neighbouring valleys, silhouettes meditated on the tops of the hills as the sun rose on clear mornings, and conflict was sufficiently anomalous that employees were required to enrol in combat courses to build a barrier against *the calm, acidic seas that over time will erode the company's strength*, with the rapid collective agreement with this perspective when it was expressed by the second founder being seen as further evidence of the problem.

This pilgrimage was made on a regular basis by the members of *The Ethics Committee*, who sat every three months in *The Blind Spot* and were described in a *long read* article in a newspaper magazine as *a collection of society's more valued chess pieces – a mix of prototypical and erudite... elders, academics, and hotshots... lazily thrown together with some "regular people"*. After their combination, in contrast to the single belief system which bonded the company's employees, and even when discussing *the possibility that billions of brains could become disfigured*, the committee members were knitted together by a complex weave of politeness and formality brewed from their social statuses and historic successes, the perceived privilege, and civilisational and evolutionary importance, of the role they were playing, the futuristic and architecturally demanding physical structure in which their meetings took place, their respect for the concept of a committee and the manner in which committees typically operated, their desire to display their experience and to protect or enhance their reputations, and lastly, but importantly, their wish to be viewed to be, in an appropriately limited sense, agreeable and likeable.

In early meetings, while the committee members accepted the basic, company-stipulated machinery of pre-agreed agendas, orderly, sequential contributions with infrequent interruptions, the mother as chairwoman shepherding the discussion, anonymous voting, and the formulation of collective position statements, certain philosophical stones had, through agenda items in the meetings themselves, been formally kicked and questioned. The philosopher raised *the problem of whether groups in general are able to make good decisions*, and *in that context whether we, this collection of people, have the requisite experience and skill to be... up to the task.* The politician separately argued for the meetings not to be automatically transcribed by voice recognition software but to be minuted, and the company's junior legal counsel attended subsequent meetings to perform this function. The religious leader tabled the more contentious suggestion that the share options that had been allocated to the committee's members should be cancelled and that only salaries and travel expense reimbursements should remain. The technology leader said, *But you are walking away from millions – possibly hundreds of millions of dollars... you are taking financial security away from... your children.* And the religious leader said, *But we are weak. We must take the hard road. Real leaders take the hard road. Can your children eat?* The scientist said, *But consider the wisdom you could project with that wealth, the suffering you could alleviate, if you used it in the right way?* And the anonymous person said, *What? Do as I say?* And the doctor said, *We have to be incentivised for good, not destructive, blundering growth. The prestige is enough for our thirsty egos. Trust me – mine needs a lot of watering...* and he smiled at the mother. Then, after the artist broke the tension more decisively by saying, *Yes, I'm sure you're right, I should probably stop embroidering my tropical daydreams... I'll cancel the jetty and the hula dancers,* it quickly rushed back in like water.

After these constitutional debates had been completed, the

meetings began to roam around landscapes without landmarks, with only an agenda as their guide. Integrity, equanimity, and kindness undertook a clumsy dance with awe, jealousy, and inflexibility. The committee members repeatedly forgot and then remembered to live up to the founders' exhortation, at the time of their appointments, that they should *leave everything at the door but* [your] *awareness and greatness.* At the third meeting, because of the mother's formally recorded observation that the meetings were *becoming infected by high levels of distraction*, and in an adoption of the founders' supplication not contemplated by the original text, as if a supplementary body of law had been generated by applying framers' principles to unforeseen futures, it was agreed that during the meetings all communication devices would be left on a desk by the door, although this had the consequence in the fourth meeting of requiring the campus manager to enter *The Blind Spot* with a small piece of paper bearing the words, *Your daughter is in labour.*

Over time, under the sun of interaction, and from the jolting pursuit of beautiful ideas in real-world conditions, the committee's older members loosened the grip of their unconscious assumption that either the younger members were *inevitably too inexperienced and too optimistic*, or had adopted a superficial gravitas or shallow, unjustified cynicism, while the younger members stopped viewing the older members as fearful and risk-averse, unwilling to submit fully to the times they were living in and inclined to value obsolete experience. Views that were presented also became less entangled with the person that had presented them, as was felt from the second, third, and the fourth meeting, when the philosopher, in slightly more cheerful and relaxed language with each repetition, replayed her perspective on *the probable problem with the committee's perspective in general... which is that simply because we have been given this shirt to wear and have run out onto this pitch we are inclined to have a strong belief – somehow feeling innate and not able to be questioned – in the goodness of The Consciousness Company. Even if it strays. A bit like a son or a daughter really.*

While some senses sharpened, others faded, and as the months and the meetings progressed, apart from the ongoing debates on what data should be measured, and on the inadequacies of the chosen data and data analysis in general, the committee became increasingly accepting of, often to the point of not noticing, the planet to which it had been transported and the gravity which allowed it to walk. They focused most of their attention on the rusty nails in the playground, the likelihood that a child would step on a nail, and the question of whether it was the company's responsibility to remove these objects, and stopped asking whether the swings and slides should have been built in the first place.

The Report on Negative Externalities, which The Consciousness Company's Consciousness prepared for each meeting, and which the artist hoped would *ideally not turn into the most euphemistically named publication in history*, in particular contained a steady stream of reports on latent dangers and unanticipated consequences at heightened levels of faculties cultivated by the company's products and services. *Don't you see!* the mouth of the junior legal counsel muttered in the fourth meeting. *It's possible for people to become too aware! Too good!* And as he was not a member of the committee, all of the people present, even he himself, either ignored this or were simply unaware of the utterance having taken place, his limited, supportive role having acted as impassable insulation for the sound waves that his body had created. But in the fifth meeting, the committee was played, from the speakers in the pod's ceiling, a voice message from Speedy Snail, which was chosen for being archetypal of this phenomenon.

Speedy Snail's stepfather, according to Speedy Snail's testimony, had after seven months of active usage of The Consciousness Company's products become *almost like a wild animal or a member of a government intelligence service or something. He is too alert. He is always completely in the moment, even when he is relaxing. The other day, at about the time he used to – you could pretty much set your watch by it in fact – spit in the street while walking me to the bus stop, and by that I mean the caveman spit – you know – sort of ceremonial – territorial – where phlegm is summoned from deep in the throat – although that's not central to the story – anyway, right about then he marked the moment with a pathetic cough and said that now when he lies in bed at night he can tell which of our neighbours has arrived home late just from "ever so subtle" differences in car engine sounds and gravel crunches as they walk to their front door. And that's with the double glazing we had put in last year. That may sound great and sensitive to you, but my mother was quite – fond – I guess is the word – of her – how can I put it – slightly unreliable pubgoer, or reliable pubgoer rather... who pretty much loathed his job, always felt a bit worthless, seemed to carry around some sort of permanent trouble of one kind or another that he was never quite able to express and was always sloping off to listen to Nirvana through these huge headphones in the garage... and who she had to take care of when he melted down every month or so after he had frittered away some of the Christmas money on an incredibly dull sports event. And that's each to their own, isn't it. It's each to their own. She didn't want a saint. She is the goddamn saint! Now he's buying bunches of flowers and calling them "chrysanthemums" and walking softly and carrying around lost cats and throwing vegetables in some blender thing for soup kitchens and helping who knows who or what or where left right and centre – I mean he's even got his own FUNDRAISING PAGE now and she's – well – the thing is – she's sad. She still has a pretty smile pretty much permanently attached to her face, although what with this newly discovered sensitivity and intuition he's realised it's not working so well for her – and – well – to give him some credit he's developed this – actually pretty amusing if I'm honest – sideline in physical comedy and also a – pretty witty – slogan T-shirts business... which in another miracle is actually starting to become quite successful – and all of that just to make her feel better but at the end of the day she doesn't know if she's crying with laughter or what. It's like those jokes at funerals you know. I mean hasn't this all gone a bit berserk? I said she should get a subscription too but – is that the plan – get everybody hooked up to the drip? Do you really care or is this all just the pet project of one of those money-mad, bubblegum-ego boffin-brats? Another one of those systems that forces everyone to be in? What about the – you know – outsiders? Don't we need outsiders? Doesn't the world need some good old-fashioned pain? And who died and appointed all of you self-important... people... something that you weren't appointed because no-one actually did die or whatever the expression is, you know? Don't you see that it's all getting a bit disturbing now? Doesn't it freak you out?*

There was a short pause and then the psychoanalyst said, *So she's not an advocate of neuroplasticity. We can change that.* And all of the committee members laughed, with different response times and degrees of nervousness, and the junior legal counsel, having considered whether this response in addition to being frivolous was inconsequential, concluded it was worthy of smiling at but not worthy of noting. And then there was silence. And then the technology leader inhaled deeply and slowly without fully managing to disguise his impatience. *The harsh truth,* he said, *is that... some ducks are going to die if you build the dam. I'm sorry that the carer in this "scenario" is out of a job but – breaking news – it's a very hard world out there.* He motioned towards a portion of the sun-drenched countryside behind the floor-to-ceiling windows encircling the scene. *Vincit qui se vincit... Translation? He conquers who conquers himself.* There was a pause and the junior legal counsel typed *unnecessary use of Latin* and *degeneration into tattoo aphorisms*, and then deleted both comments. *I don't know,* said the mother, *is it a scenario... or is it actually someone's life... We have to see the system as well as the individual... it's shade and light – not black and white. Although there are,* said the psychoanalyst, *always net calculations, aren't there, as we keep saying. Correctamundo,* said the technology leader, *we do keep SAYING that, but what we mean is – there SHOULD be... because it's this trade-off that apparently turns us into these...* His index finger rose, alone and jabbing, from a closed fist that remained on the table... *monsters... these – monstrosities, there's absolutely no tolerance for these next generation negative externalities. Old ones fine – it's okay for the – poison some power plant pumps out to be reduced at a glacial – in fact more glacial than the glaciers isn't it...* He nodded at the politician as if to hold him responsible... *pace – but not new ones – nothing negative will be tolerated from new companies – diddly-squat – zip – zero – zilch – not a single corpse – and so the industrialist who built some backwater firm half a lifetime ago and is seen as – semi-philanthropically employing a few thousand people – as though it wasn't actually for his own benefit – he can be off his head in his compliance session – or his dominatrix can forget to flick the switch on the privacy glass – and hey – it's all good – he built this company. He walks on FUCKING water. But the intern is late once because – he was collecting his silk shirt from the dry cleaners – and he's told never to come back. And the regulator COULDN'T POSSIBLY go after the establishment. I mean – come to think of it – he actually couldn't – no-one actually SEES the paper on the walls – they only see change...!* ...The technology leader looked around the table and was gratified by the attention of the room, but did not need it to maintain his momentum. *And speaking of change – maybe if his wife is such a saint SHE should listen to Nirvana? That is if we want to take all of this at face value – this – apparently in no way warped, agenda-free viewpoint. It's just not very scientific is it...! If we REALLY believe in science, as we claim that we do, can we please start making greater use of that revolutionary tool that I have heard some people call statistics? What are we talking about here – hundreds of reports of – "excess compassion" – ha! – someone organise a tie up with a food company and send the marketing deck to these knuckleheads... yes... "delectable... oxymoronic confections... with an – inconsistent shell and a soft, moronic centre"... and in the blue corner we have – yes, hello welcome – all of you, welcome – millions – MILLIONS – of happier lives? Is it a different scale that got cropped off the page? Another break in the axis? Some desktop publishing wheeze? Some lobbyist's wet dream...? Although doubtless our spitting stepdad will be composing some sort of – "authentic" – "this time it's real" – lament-for-flute-and-heartstrings – some REQUIEM-TO-MY-LOST-LIFE before you can say...* ...He waved his hand. *Genetic predisposition?* offered the psychoanalyst. Before quickly following with, *Actually – return to the mean! That's it*, his face unknowingly adopting a self-congratulatory smile. *There is*, the technology leader continued, oblivious to the interjection *– at the end of the day – just no pleasing some people! It's the journey isn't it. People THINK they want to get to utopia, but put them in it and they're like – hang on – this is too good... it's... wait... I know the word for it... SINISTER. YES, I WANT MY MONEY BACK. I WANT MY FUCKING MONEY BACK.*

OR... YOU MADE MY MUM BORED. OR YOU KILLED MY CAT. OR GODDAMMIT MY TV DOESN'T WORK. OR YOU NEVER NOTIFIED ME THAT THE SUBSCRIPTION PRICE WOULD CHANGE AFTER EIGHTEEN MONTHS. OR I WANT TO BE UPGRADED... OR... OR... OR... AND NOW I'M GOING TO CREATE A SECRET CLUB OF "LIKE-MINDED" PEOPLE WHO CAN BE MEAN TO YOU ANONYMOUSLY. BUT HEY, WHO ARE ALL THESE PEOPLE ANYWAY? FUCKING LOSERS. WE'RE ALL FUCKING LOSERS. AND NOW I'M SUFFERING. NO, WE'RE SUFFERING. DO I HATE IT? YES. COULD I LIVE WITHOUT IT? NO. I DON'T KNOW. DID I PROVE THEIR POINT? DID I PROVE OURS?

The technology leader stood up, as though he had belatedly remembered the importance of choreography and believed that showing strength by standing continued to be worthwhile even though the last notes of his performance had already been washed away by silence. He then met the eyes of everyone in the room except the junior legal counsel, sat down again, took a pill out of a pocket of his velvet blazer, swallowed it using the glass of water in front of him, sensed a vestige of a former self flicker in the briefest contemplation of an apology, became angry with this reflex, and breathed out of his nose like a bull preparing to charge.

— Okay, settle down. No more outbursts please. Stick to the rules. That's a formal violation which I'd like recorded. And take a medical, said the mother.

The technology leader breathed deeply, rearranged his face into the empty-headed smile of a ventriloquist's dummy in order to begin a new physiological chain reaction for which his facial muscles would be the cause and not the effect, shut his eyes, and drifted for a few moments down a swollen, swaggering river that was fed by his historic successes, his *public profile*, and his percentage ownerships in companies that he expected to be *defining of the future* and to cause his current wealth and status to seem unremarkable. He felt, physically, a confidence in his superiority that was total enough for him to interpret it as knowledge, and, as though verifying the results of an experiment, he opened his eyes and looked once again at each person in the room except for the junior legal counsel. *Maybe I should run for president.*

These feelings then combined with his belief in the cosmic insignificance of the meeting and caused the technology leader to remove a pair of sunglasses from the inner pocket of his blazer, in order to disguise the closing of his eyes for a more extended period. He felt a satisfaction from separating the magnetic catch of the glasses' case, opened their delicate arms with care because of their cost and the recentness of their acquisition, meticulously cleaned the lenses with an attendant cloth pincered between his thumb and forefinger, placed them on his face, leaned back in his chair, extended his legs, and submitted to a heaviness that rolled from the back to the front of his skull and caused it to bob like a bowling ball that was too heavy to be held elegantly on the pedestal of his neck. He woke up a few minutes later when the junior legal counsel delivered to the surface of the table in front of him a pair of virtual reality glasses, punctuating their placement with the words *these will work better.* The technology leader then saw the other committee members attaching identical glasses to their faces, and the scientist – flanked by a man and a woman wearing large headsets, whose faces he could not see, but from whose leg movements and postures he inferred inferior status and inexperience – began to make a presentation to the committee with the help of clip art holograms that were dancing like ghosts above the middle of the circular table.

— I spent a day with The Imagination Frontiers Development Team so they could take me through it and, essentially, unbelievably, they have developed a device that injects thoughts into minds. The device has to train itself, currently for a number of days, and it has to put the user through various training exercises in order to understand the neural pathways for... (with his fingers straight and separated the scientist pivoted his right wrist, the action appearing to help to generate his words) ...aquamarine – or ambiguity or... I don't know... Alaska... or... alacrity... but... (he glanced to his left and then to his right) ...the team believe they can get that down to minutes or in time even seconds... The one condition is that the constituting or so-called REFERENCE elements, the sub- or sub-subcomponents or ingredients of the inserted thoughts, have to be pre-existing ideas... For example, the device could insert previously unencountered words, but the person receiving them could only pronounce them if they can be constructed from sounds that the person has in their head somewhere already... Plus, it can't insert the type of knowledge that we think of as purely experiential without the person already having had that experience... whether virtually or in reality... but anyway... the point is, in the realm of the thinking, chattering mind there's very little that cannot be constructed from the basic and complex ideas that we all have within us already... all the ones and zeroes and longer strings we've been stitching together all of our lives... you know...

— Wow... incredible, said the anonymous person. Does the person think it's their own thought?

— Well – if I can question the question – isn't it? interjected the first thought machine developer, springing to the defence of the technology before it was under attack. It's in their brain and aren't most of our thoughts to some extent generated by external events?

— But does the person know it has been inserted?

The scientist nodded at the first thought machine developer to indicate that he would answer the question.

— The team think they can set it up so that you can elect...

firstly WHEN thoughts can be inserted – for example, you might limit them to times of extreme panic – and also... whether or not device-generated thoughts come signposted as device-generated thoughts. I don't know – it might be something like – The Consciousness Company Thought Machine is suggesting that you go out for a walk... followed by some legalese about free will and personal responsibility, for the lawyers and the insurers. (The junior legal counsel cleared his throat.) And because it's the right thing to do!

— Okay... mind-blowing... but how would it work on a practical level...? Would it create a jerky world where people keep unexpectedly... stopping – disappearing for a few moments – to listen to thoughts and disclaimers?

— Potentially endangering themselves.

— And others.

— Which is a risk we can't disclaim without making it worse. Please be aware that listening to this warning might be dangerous and so on.

— People will cope, said the military leader. Minds are always in multiple places.

— Which is a phenomenon we're trying to reduce?

— And – Madam Chairwoman – when we say disclaim – which keeps coming up and I think should be an agenda item for our next meeting – let's not go too far, said the religious leader. This committee and this company have to accept risk, and responsibility. This is our nettle to grasp. I'm sorry that comes with anxiety. We should warn, selflessly, and proportionately, but we can't absolve. We can't use these disclaimers as a carte blanche to do – anything we like. Disclaimers are not... modern-day indulgences. These words are not ablutions.

— It really blurs the lines between you and others doesn't it. Thoughts detached from individuals. Freely tradeable and transferable.

The scientist continued to speak for a few more minutes. He then asked the first and the second thought machine developer to *perform the demonstration.* The second thought machine developer raised and tapped a tablet device she had been holding, the scientist asked the first thought machine developer what he was thinking, and the first thought machine developer said, *I have just had the thought that you are all lovely people. Particularly the person whose name I do not know.* He pointed at the anonymous person. *Are you still feeling that?* the scientist asked. *Actually, I have just had the thought that you are all nasty and merciless and that I spoke prematurely and naively just a moment ago. Particularly...* And he stopped as the committee members waited for what most of them could not prevent themselves from thinking would be his opinion and his responsibility. The technology leader said, *It's like a commercial break before the end of a game show,* and the first thought machine developer said, *My respect for all of you, together with my knowledge of where these words are coming from, has overridden the instruction to move my finger.*

The rigidity of the first thought machine developer's body indicated his continued occupation by thoughts that were being inserted into his mind. The bodies of every person in the room, in anticipation of what was going to be said next, and including the junior legal counsel whose detached demeanour had endured up to this point, also became more tensed and alert. The perceived value of the first thought machine developer's yet to be spoken words had increased, despite the collective acceptance of their accidental, random nature, as if he was a false oracle successfully predicting the results of sports events by twitching a tentacle, or shuffling a hoof, in a way that caused a sober audience to question their understanding of the laws of the universe. At the same time, the materialisation in another mind of the idea that one committee member merited greater disdain than others caused some to reassure themselves that they had *only ever acted with the best intentions* and that this was *just some kid who is being controlled by his own machine.*

They continued to watch the first thought machine developer.

— I actually, unexpectedly, now have a new belief that my name, my legal name, may have recently been changed to The Second Thought Machine Developer. When I first had or received this thought as well as being amusing – but irritating – with the greatest respect to the talented colleague standing beside me who was only a few months ago one of our lab assistants – it seemed to be clearly identifiable as a rogue, implanted thought. However, before I could let it go I appeared to ask myself if I genuinely – and the word genuinely I recognised immediately as doing a lot of the work in a kind of Trojan Horse subterfuge... if I genuinely didn't remember changing my name by deed poll. Then I appeared to remind myself of my reasons for doing so... I had apparently wanted to disown my pre-Consciousness Company past, and to shake off the identity that "others had pinned on me" – which is not a phrase I would use – and I had convinced myself that making this change would protect my place in this mental space race as, more or less, The Second Person on the Moon... At this precise moment, I am seeing an image of a document with my old and new names on it, which I am presuming is the deed poll. And now a wild party with work colleagues and friends in Vanity Castle with a banner congratulating me on the change of my name. There are champagne flutes and party poppers... And while I am speaking, I am experiencing other reinforcing memories such as snippets of conversations in which I am explaining why I did it. And now my mind is moving on to... questioning the decision – it is in other words now acting as though the decision and the change are facts of history... it is rushing in with what could well be home-grown thoughts – I can't tell – mostly related to the stupidity of the decision, as opposed to whether the change was actually made.

The second thought machine developer continued to tap on the screen she was holding. Her face did not display any thoughts or feelings.

— I am now starting to ruminate and to experience regret. I am asking myself how I can expect other people to see the richness of an individual and a life inside a person that has been penned in by such a rigid name. Even those who know me might forget me... I am watching a grainy slide show of images from my life so far and seeing all of the ways in which I am so much more than The Second Thought Machine Developer... always changing... and no one thing in particular... I am feeling myself becoming stressed... and hot... ...I am calming myself down... ... and now – I am examining the question more dispassionately... I am pointing out to myself that it doesn't even work well as a name, because it doesn't pick me out uniquely... The Second Thought Machine Developer could have been someone else... maybe was in fact... yes... and then to others one day I might be The Second Thought Machine Developer Who Was Shown To Be The Fourth Thought Machine Developer. You wouldn't be able to refer to me without footnotes.

He reflected on this. He continued to stand with a concentrated expression.

— Perhaps my confidence in my technical competence will be overthrown by an inferiority complex that is immune to all future achievements... or perhaps – alternatively – I'll be liberated from this presumably primal desire to be The First... or... maybe – this name will attract the wrong life partner – or no-one at all... who knows... Perhaps... perhaps... perhaps it just does not matter – yes – perhaps it is of no consequence – because... my essential qualities – whatever they are... have not changed.

— Not yet they haven't, muttered the psychoanalyst.

— But I do have an overwhelming urge to change it back. I just want to go back to... before.

The first thought machine developer looked at the second thought machine developer and shook his head and torso like a dog that has just left a lake, the contents of his head flying like droplets into the room.

He turned towards the second thought machine developer.

— I think you've demonstrated the capability brilliantly... I mean, as well as you could have done as The Second Thought Machine Developer. He smiled.

Silence then fell on the committee like night. The philosopher saw a breeze in a few nearby trees and heard a ringing in her ears. Some faces declined to provide a visible reaction to the new information while others had, like the surface of a still lake under the changing components of a darkening sky, seamlessly transposed themselves into stunned or unsettled expressions. The doctor then remembered that *the gala dinner is tomorrow night* and he needed to check if his dinner suit would still fit him. The entire body of the mother, apart from sipping the very top layer of an overfilled glass of water, remained quiet and on the outside unaltered, like a deputy prime minister not wanting to alarm an audience after one of her ears had ushered in the information that, in the last few moments, the country's political leader had been killed.

Eventually, the artist spoke.

— So – if I may say so Madam Chairwoman – here we are, all of a sudden, at the summit of The Spider-Man Principle. With superhuman power... et cetera.

He twisted his body towards the two developers and the scientist.

— You're not suggesting that we – fill a syringe with thoughts and inject them into people's heads?

— We're just presenting the technology. We have to know what can be done. Our competitors are probably here already. Or close.

— Really? The dystopia in the distance is inevitable? The future's a blame game, and we're blaming game theory? Because at the end of the day, we're just lobsters, or scorpions, or whatever it is? Just buildin' the missiles and promising not to launch them as long as everybody else pinky promises that they won't either?

— I suppose it makes sense – plain, boring old words have always been...

— The acid we drink like water.

— On the other hand, we could reduce depression, anxiety, loneliness... grief. Shouldn't we think of this as healthcare? Shouldn't we provide it for free?

— Yes... the medicinal use... impossible to object to... often the way in, isn't it!

— Aren't there pills for all of those already? What's the difference?

— Efficacy, I suppose.

— What, so we just start blasting brains with lab-grown thoughts – like...

— Cheer up you grumpy toad, things are not so bad?

— She never loved you anyway?

— Just as long as they're not taken on an empty brain... What kind of a world is that? And what if things really are that bad? Doesn't the real world matter?

— I don't know, does it? What exactly IS this REAL world? Is the place no-one is experiencing of any consequence?

The doctor leaned back on his chair and a few moments later jolted forwards to prevent himself from falling to the floor.

— What if people start self-medicating? Good or bad? We'd probably end up with a small handful of life philosophies and mental systems that most people would sign up to. We'd have different schools of thought swimming around. Great big blobs of humanity.

The military leader looked at the first thought machine developer.

— Can you inhibit – and remove – as well as inserting?

— As it happens, we are working on that.

The previously silent air conditioning unit began to inhale and exhale audibly. The mother felt herself getting hotter, and her mind began to wander. *I probably shouldn't have taken him for a walk this morning.*

The technology leader took off the sunglasses that he had a few moments earlier returned to his face.

— Look, I know I'm already in the sin bin, but – before we get too precious about offering a helpful thought to the brain on the bridge, just remember that this company's software is moulding millions of lives as if they were lumps of clay... and we're going to get all sniffy about the foreign aid budget? Send that man that thought I say! Tell his limbs to run away from danger! Why wouldn't you?

— It's not a question of need. We've left the shallow waters now – goodbye suggestion, hello control, you know?

— Whatever helps you at night, man.

— Helps me sleep?

The technology leader remembered his respect for, and desire not to offend, the artist.

— Well – to put it delicately, which as you know does not come naturally to me – it's clear that you – all of us – believe that we – and our members – have – what do people tend to call it... AGENCY... Actually, we don't just believe it... it's a fundamental, FIRST PRINCIPLES... principle... that the whole world – the world we've constructed – is built on... is infatuated with... worships... this... this... illusion... this freedom DElusion that... the birds and beasts we look down on – that we pity – are – most likely – not burdened with... the technology leader spoke calmly. SUGGESTION is the last, frayed comfort blanket that's protecting round-table "leaders" and do-gooders like us against uncomfortable words like "manipulation" and "subjugation"... And our... our... panic... and... even these committees themselves – are just supporting actors in this fiction... propping up an idea – an important and lovely idea... and the corresponding faculty that's so precious to us but does not actually exist.

The artist squinted slightly as he processed this response.

— Whether that's right or wrong, the belief in this agency is still an important fact. That very belief changes the nature of our experience – our emotional reactions, our thoughts... and our understanding of our life, all of which is, at the end of the day, all there is.

The scientist spoke.

— Are we really discussing whether anyone has any responsibility for anything – including, presumably, the outcome of this discussion? That lets a lot of people off the hook, don't you think? Shall we all just go home?

The philosopher spoke.

— Either we will or we won't. Maybe we won't all make it... Maybe we'll all sit here and say "someone could have predicted you would say that" until it gives us no more pleasure or satisfaction. Or for longer than that.

She stopped to think.

— The gallant buzzard rewrote the soprano line impertinently?

She released a hollow, lonely laugh that rose up to the top of the pod like a smoke ring.

The politician spoke.

— Sorry, Madam Chairwoman, could we perhaps call time on the metaphysical ping-pong? He then turned to the rest of the room. The two sides of the coin are – or should just be – suffering on the one hand – and the limits of power on the other.

— Yes... ...and the price of intervention can't be identity, said the psychoanalyst.

— Don't worry... identity's fine... identity's hunky-dory... There's a distinction between where the thought originates, and whether it is... selected... the selection is the agency.

— Unless there are no other thoughts to select, which would make the agency of no value, said the psychoanalyst, before turning to the thought machine developers. Can you allow the user to select and deselect – some accepted level of thought-insertion functionality – or whatever we end up calling it? The user could completely surrender their mind – or – just select the fail-safe option which kicks in when they're in the cockpit of a nosediving plane or watching someone in cardiac arrest... ...Or, they could just say no to everything – opt for no system support whatsoever... I wonder how many would choose that!

— Not many, I would guess. Everybody wears shoes.

There was a silence and then, softly but firmly, while moving her neck and eyes and making each of the committee members feel valued and of equal value, the mother spoke.

— Thank you everyone... for these contributions. I think it's fair to say that we can't untangle all of this and – formulate any substantive recommendations today from this short – albeit helpful – thank you – introductory presentation and high-level conversation. We will need precise proposals from the company on what the technology would be used for, a detailed understanding of the fail-safe mechanisms that we could and would propose to put in place, and – I know this is going to be unpopular but – we need to involve relevant government departments – this is definitely going to need legislation and regulation – we need to lead from the front... (The mother started to speak uncharacteristically quickly due to her concern that she would not be able to fully transmit her conclusions because of the growing pain in her chest and her left arm. She then felt, and observed herself beginning to feel, weak and light-headed.) ...and with all of us being able to review a clear and comprehensive strategy document before discussing the way forward again. I'll take the lead on getting all of that going.

— Yes. I could not agree more.

— Yes, agreed.

The surface of the room broke out in a rash of exaggerated and subtle nodding, bobbing, and affirmative blinking.

— Good. The mother concluded in a whisper, and, while the next agenda item waited in the wings, a cold sweat covered her skin. The pain in her chest then became more acute and her hand, which was shaking, picked up the small glass in front of her. Drops and clumps of water fell to the left and right as she tried to move the glass towards her mouth, as if the glass had taken on a great weight. Abruptly and unstably, she stood up, turned away from the table, took a few steps towards the wall, and was then surprised, almost intrigued, by the detachment of her fingertips from the glass. The remaining members of the committee watched as this small, clear shape elegantly descended and hit the floor at an angle, shooting its structure and contents angrily upwards and outwards into the room's extremities, while the mother crumpled to the floor, like a puppet whose strings had been sliced, or a faithful host abandoned by a fickle spirit. The technology leader, without being aware that he had done so, checked with his hand whether the velvet on the back of his jacket was wet, while watching the unexpected invasion of chaos as it announced itself in a Fireworks Night of sharp inhalations, quiet expletives, fluid faces recast into masks of shock, frenzied and phased rising from chairs, and a wry smile. The doctor ran to the mother's side and laid her flat on her back, and, like an antibiotic, order re-entered, and started to reassert itself. *Call an ambulance. A helicopter. In the next valley. Go. Quick. Go now.* He shook her and shouted her name. He put his ear to her mouth and his hands to her neck and said, *She's not breathing. I need to give her CPR.* He then opened her mouth and, as he put his lips against the lips of this *attractive, compassionate* woman who he had, at a previous meeting, felt himself wanting both to protect and to be protected by, he could not prevent himself from contemplating the possibility that pressing his lips against hers, filling her lungs, and pressing her chest methodically, transactionally, was a betrayal of his wife.

While the doctor continued his work, the artist visualised the entire scene, centred around the mother, as if it was a classical painting. He had been cast as The Witness and placed on the side of the picture. The anonymous person was crouched by the head of the mother, fanning her face ineffectually with a folded piece of paper. The psychoanalyst knelt to the side of and slightly behind the doctor, counting mechanically, like a clock. The politician had been placed behind but close to this point of focus, with his back to the back of a chair, the top of which he was sitting on periodically, as though – trapped in a loop – he was repeatedly forgetting that this was an uncomfortable position, or because the belief that he could contribute to this operating theatre in the wild was doggedly regenerating itself after evaporating in the two-stride gulf between the chair and the doctor. The technology leader was slightly further away and to the side, sitting on the table and unaware that the lower halves of his legs were swinging. He had adopted a grimace which displayed the maximum amount of the top and bottom rows of his teeth that the muscles of his face would allow, and he was pressing together his higher and lower incisors in an attempt to express a discomfort and sympathy which was not able to saturate the surface of his face naturally. The military leader had managed to reclaim his phone and was barking softly that he needed the air ambulance *faster than that... in the next five minutes... by fourteen hundred hours... yes, yes, toMAYto, toMARto...* and that he would *stay on the line* and wanted to know *exactly* when it was in the air and when it would arrive. The junior legal counsel had called the campus medical team and, as a result of the movement of his body, like a knight directing light onto formerly dormant pawns, brought the windows and a rescue pod of five people careering up the hill to the picture's foreground as an additional point of interest. The Witness and the junior legal counsel watched as this small group, holding objects that later revealed themselves to be a defibrillator and a stretcher, shouted and waved, in silence because of their distance, as though on mute.

Blurred in the background, on the other side of the room, the scientist, the religious leader, and the philosopher paced, stood, stared, and sat. Each one of them knew not only that this was a significant moment in their and each of the other members' lives but also that, like a marble run with a predefined route, there was nothing of practical value that they could contribute to the plan that was already in motion. The religious leader looked through the glass and into the distance, his lips making small shapes in near silence, and the philosopher remained seated, concealing, and attempting to drop phosphates onto, the wildfire in her body. *It is lucky I am not superstitious. My grandfather would be spitting or spreading salt. Maybe I should do that. Just in case. Nothing to lose.* She partially covered her mouth with her hand and made a soft spitting sound without releasing any saliva.

Some time later, after she was taken on the stretcher, and then into the sky by the helicopter, the doctor being the only committee member that accompanied her; and after they all sat or stood or moved in silence, and then described to the first founder and the second founder what they had seen take place, their stories having different emphases on each narrating and retelling; and after they had all called the person that they instinctively called when, as the politician said, *things happen...* one by one, these people, reluctantly repurposed as caves for the meeting's echoes, as guardians of its precious metals, simultaneously minted and tarnished, dispersed.

A letter from a thousand scientists

THE FIRST FOUNDER LOOKED AT THE LETTER printed out on the table in his office. Physically, it seemed innocuous enough.

This time though, the words were burrowing into his head, like worms.

Maybe I shouldn't have asked for it to be printed out. It feels more real now. More important. Heavier. Like those handwritten love letters. But more problematic. More credentialised. More OBJECTIVE, and more ominous... The parchment from the messenger. Before the army sweeps over the hill. Before the senate committees and the demonstrations.

He picked up the letter and scanned for *key messages* once again.

"...but the brain implants cross the Rubicon. You are causing the extermination of the human race. Something non-genetic has taken over... you are destroying the sacred concept of identity that our world is built on..."

He considered this.

But there are no guns pointed at heads. They don't HAVE to implant the implants. And it's not destruction... it's enhancement, according to agreed principles, with consent, and with adjustable settings.

He looked out of the window.

How did I get here? When did I become the "you"? The "you" to their "they"...? THEY say I'm one of the most powerful people in the world. But power lives under pressure. In the deeps of the sea. Where I am sad. And lonely. And ANXIOUS. I was never anxious before.

I am a stereotype. I am the lonely leader.

Stereotypes are people too.

Responsible for the extermination of the human race. That's too much.

I should have taken the hundred million. It would have sufficed.

I should have just bought the island.

And why, of all of the problems that we have, am I now being thrashed most relentlessly with this "problem of identity"? Somehow, what we're doing is TOTALLY DIFFERENT from your standard-issue, "life-changing" experience, or a book, or another PERSON causing you to think differently. To become a NEW PERSON.

HIS answer... his magic filter, says that – "at the end of the day" – we are all just experiences, thoughts, and ROLES IN CONTEXTS.

Consciousness, what was it Our Saviour [the second founder] said about squirrels the other day again?

The Consciousness Company's Consciousness responded.

— Well, it was nuts, about nuts I mean, as well as squirrels, and I'll summarise, because it was a bit verbose, and it wasn't a particularly brilliant point so you shouldn't expect any ground to break, or even shake, or even to lightly palpitate...

— Yes, yes, come on, too much personality...

— But he said, in short... (The Consciousness Company's Consciousness adopted an indifferent tone.) Other animals don't seem to need their lives to mean something. Being is enough for them. A little bit of planning, a spoonful of pain avoidance, and a sprinkling of pleasure maybe. For them, identity is just, "It was me, a red squirrel, that left those nuts by that tree." But that's enough... whereas – and this thought was unoriginal for me too – and not just because you have programmed me to be like you hoo hoo... which was obviously a big call... because squirrels do seem to have a pretty good life... but anyway... for us, identity is something that we feel we NEED, just like, and because, we need narrative... paths... meaning.

— Thanks.

The first founder's eyes disengaged from the room.

I keep getting sucked into all this. I need to outsource. A leader needs to outsource. I already HAVE philosophers. We HAVE a committee. I need to outsource this thinking.

Extermination of the human race.

Responsible.

The words boomeranged and punched him in the gut.

Extermination.

They know not of what they speak. Someone send them a thousand historians.

Maybe I should have an implant to help me deal with all this. Or we all should. At birth. When they're ubiquitous no-one will challenge it. No doubt I would be told that was a sinister thought. Not by the implant though, assuming the implants are pro-implant.

Why am I thinking like this? I think the way I think has changed. Maybe some THEY has installed an implant... without leaving a single fingerprint? A sleeper cell. It's the quietest coup.

The first founder looked out of the window of his office. He saw the second founder walking through the campus, flanked by a phalanx of company employees, *as though they are his disciples.*

Somehow, with all his breathing and reading and reasoning, he's able to cope with it. Where IT is absolutely anything. It's an incredible metamorphosis. HE is definitely not the same person, that's for sure.

I wonder if he is actually answering all of these questions, or just letting them float through him.

Maybe that's the answer.

Or maybe it's not.

Or maybe it is.

Interlude: The group

THE FEELING THAT THEY FELT UNDER THEIR ROBES AND SHTREIMELS, as the music played, and they held their arms out like jointless wings over the also horizontal arms of one or two other men in the community, and they danced the coordinated line dance, fifteen indistinguishable, locked links, turning together on one point – the rigidity of the line maintained as it turned and made simultaneous low kicks with its centipede-like legs on the same beat, as though taking instructions from one brain – grew until it had completely consumed and eradicated any separation between them, made them one individual, liberated from self-consciousness, identity, and the belief in difference. They felt the joy of living known or hidden inside every living thing, and they felt the temporary nature of this feeling and of lives in general.

In front of them, on the road, two elderly rabbis were dancing both together and on their own, beards grey and almost white, one older than the other, hands up, and then down, and clapping, and waving, bodies moving with a superficial sincerity, parodying choreography, and basking in or shining out a second childhood through their limp limbs, closed mouths and elfish eyes.

Eventually, the smells of hamantaschen mingled with the spring air, and the spell began to be broken. He disconnected his arms. *I love Purim*, he thought.

The first founder plugs into the second founder

THE SECOND FOUNDER WALKED INTO THE FIRST FOUNDER'S OFFICE on the company's campus.

— The Imagination Frontiers Development Team has developed a product that allows you to relive someone else's experiences, through their consciousness diaries.

The first founder was juggling fruit.

— You can dial up or down the degree to which your original identity is watching this other life, even turning off your original voice completely, so that for that time, you believe you are, or in fact you are, from your perspective at least, the king at his coronation, or the prime minister cleaning her teeth, or a baby playing with a doll's house, even having the impression that you are having the thoughts that they were having, taking the decisions that they were taking, and feeling the things that they were feeling. Feeling, in short, that you ARE them. That there is no separate YOU having an impression.

— I've just started to introduce the pineapple. It's the next level.

— Anyway, unfortunately they hacked the prime minister, and the king, and the baby, which, as we know, is not... the optimal legal pathway... even with the research purposes carveout... and we need some sort of internal investigation to figure out who did what... I mean, if this got out we're finished... but...

— Spiky.

The first founder was processing the second founder's words but preferred to give the impression that he viewed them to be of low importance. The second founder continued to speak.

— …anyway, as I understand it, in the part of her diary that was hacked, the prime minister was having a series of thoughts about whether freedom of information requests would ultimately, at some point, cause her thoughts to become public property, uncomfortable in the context, admittedly, which led her to a concern that – simply because she had had that previous thought – history might – erroneously – suspect or infer inauthenticity… as if she was using subconscious forces somehow to clean the surface of her consciousness for public consumption… and then she wondered about asking us, US, YOU and ME, *if it is not too egotistical* – that was the qualification she intended to give us – whether her subconsciousness could somehow be preserved in her defence… and after that she continued to pull the thread and wondered whether subconsciousness could itself be subject to subconscious manipulation, and then whether she WAS indeed somehow, on the deepest level, *if there is* – she asked herself – *such a level, inauthentic…* and then there was one final thought about whether one level transcended, was defining, you know… all this while she was brushing her incisors, molars, and so on… Bizarrely, she mentally named the teeth while she was brushing, she really is rigorous… And she seems to think about coffee a lot as well. And there was one amusing moment when she briefly considered whether the chancellor had blamed an egg salad for a smell *of his own creation* at some ambassador's reception or other. Mostly though, she was focusing on this authenticity anxiety, if we can call it that, and then, later, when she was washing her face, a reassuring stream of thoughts about people, decisions, developments, stress, self-motivation, compassion, and strength.

— I want to try to combine it with a single grape and a banana.

— But anyway, they have, in short...

— Who?

— The Imagination Frontiers Development Team.

— You really should rename them The Sinister Developments Team. Or just, The Girl Who's Always Wearing Sports Gear and The Guy Who Would Prefer To Pick His Ear.

— They have essentially unlocked the full spectrum of human experience, as it stands today. We're not limited to the archetypes – the synthetic experiences that we have come up with – any more. We are all creators now, and there are no secret lives.

— You've tried it?

— I briefly, very briefly, became someone in that group of influencers who agreed to work with us...

The second founder stopped and then spoke again when it was clear that the first founder was not going to react.

— You'll need half an hour on the operating table first if you want to have a go, but you've done that before.

— Indeed. Maybe I could add to my collection of nightmares.

The second founder did not respond immediately and both founders became temporarily hypnotised by the fruit as it circled like a circus act.

— What's amazing is that, if you've turned the volume of your original voice down fully, if you're muted, you realise when you come out of the experience that you had pretty much the same SENSORY inputs as you would have had as yourself, but the processing of them, and the emotions and the chatter, were completely different, alien even – for example, I don't know, and it's a superficial example but – it appears to be impossible to process the image of yourself as sexually attractive – to lust after your own image I mean – even if most people in the world see you as sexually attractive. And from this, you essentially catch a glimpse – clearer and more forceful than from any experience we have created so far – of the absence of the thing that we are all convinced is there – you see that there IS no single world, just billions of secret lives.

The first founder let all of the airborne fruit fall to the floor.

— Interesting. What about me plugging in to you?

— What, me, my consciousness diary?

— Yes?

— What, as in, me?

— Yes. Otherwise, it makes you a bit of a hypocrite, doesn't it...? ...Maybe it would do me some good. Anyway, you're an open book, right?

It's so difficult to predict where these conversations are going to go, thought the second founder.

— Not exactly, but okay.

***

A week later, the first founder was lying on the operating table in his bodysuit. He felt his shallow breath against its synthetic rubber, and listened to the senior research director of the Imagination Frontiers Development Team.

— ...and when you want to turn the volume on your consciousness down to zero you have to add a time limit to the mental instruction... by saying something like *Consciousness, please turn me off for five minutes*... but don't worry too much about that... we've added a safety release of half an hour anyway.

This room looks like an operating theatre. If we sell this, it needs to be less scalpel, more lavender and eucalyptus.

The senior research director continued.

— This consciousness diary entry is just the beginning of one of his working days. He wakes up, goes to the toilet, drinks a cup of tea, eats some fruit, cleans his teeth, gets dressed, and then stands on his balcony for a while in a kind of meditative state, which is not particularly distinguishable from the times before and after it... ...Someone has – by the way – previewed – pre-experienced it for you and run it through a sensitivity check... ...I'm turning it on now, and you can just start counting your breaths and you'll be in it before you know it, before you can count to ten.

— Thanks. Also, please don't record my reactions.

— Okay, no problem, I'll turn that off.

— And don't have that on by default.

— Right you are, sir.

The first founder relaxed his stomach muscles and lay his spine flat. His body relaxed. He shut his eyes and drifted out of the operating theatre. He retained only the knowledge of who he was.

I feel lighter, somehow. This must be what they think it would feel like to be a spirit, if it was possible to be a spirit only.

He began to drift from the nothingness that had come before into the false knowledge that he was in the second founder's bedroom, and it was morning.

His eyes are opening. I'm in his flat.

The second founder's awareness was quiet and sleepy, and of very little at that point. He had a sense of being, and some awareness of bodily feeling, but these were involuntary, and existed only faintly in his consciousness.

I can't see very much. He's reaching for his glasses.

I wonder if I'll see his girlfriend naked. I hope not. That would be weird. I assume she did not stay here last night.

The capabilities of the second founder's senses became greater in the moments that followed. The room and the day having nothing out of the ordinary about them however, he did not use them actively and they rested as he made his way through the door frame that separated his bedroom and bathroom.

Wow. That musty smell he has is much stronger in the morning.

He doesn't seem to be thinking anything yet.

He seems to be very aware of his breath. He seems to be more conscious of his breath than he is of where he is.

I suddenly feel like I need to go to the toilet. He is walking to the toilet.

Oh, right. How lovely. The arc, the smell, the splash. The dribble.

A feeling of relief flowed through the first founder's body.

Ah, that's better.

He doesn't seem to be thinking yet. That's strange. Not a single thought has passed through his head.

Wait, what was that...? The hardest truths from the vacuum of grief? Waiting and waiting, before an abrupt arrival...?

Something from one of his gurus perhaps? Or the fortune cookie from last night's takeaway?

I will not search? What does that mean?

After this, for many minutes, the first founder experienced only the second founder's experiences. The tea on his tongue, the textures and tastes of apple and strawberry, the foaming of toothpaste on his teeth. The first founder then issued the mental instruction *Consciousness, turn me off for ten minutes*, and from that moment he believed himself to be the second founder, and believed he had instructed himself, without words, to walk towards and slide open the heavy glass door of the balcony that was the brim of the second founder's hat-shaped flat. He felt his sockless feet transfer from tiles to wood. He saw The Consciousness Company's campus laid before him like an abandoned game of building blocks. He felt the morning air on his skin. He felt, without articulating it to himself, that the temperature had a memory of heat and a forewarning of cold to come. He accepted its uncertainty.

Still there were no thoughts. The first founder was still in nature. In the present.

Then, *I do miss them* walked across the stage, accompanied by a bodily awareness of the depths from which these words had emerged, and of their recent, irreversible permeation of his identity.

Grief passed through the first founder's heart, physically, and floated away. And after this, the first and second founder continued to stand as one, feeling the air enter their lungs. Observing it. Feeling the feeling of living. They watched a few wispy clouds float across the sky. *Like thoughts and experiences*, they thought. Occasionally, a thought about a recent event, or a future activity arrived at the door of their mind, and, like a cloud, it was allowed to enter, and then exit.

A few minutes later, just as suddenly as it began, and like the departure from a dream, the first founder sank out of the scene and rematerialised on the padded table of the operating theatre.

For many minutes, he lay with his mind under the fluorescent light.

Neuroplasticity alone will not get me to this. I could never feel the way that he feels.

But I did, I did feel that way. I did. I was able to.

He is winning. He is beating me.

But he doesn't care about winning.

He is living. He is really living.

The kiss

WHEN THEY KISSED FOR THE FIRST TIME, the second founder had in the preceding months and years transformed so significantly, through repetition and through tools that he himself had created, that he experienced the touching of their lips on the city bridge in the lamplight without any absence or anxiety. He felt, in that moment, no past, and no future. No part of his brain was processing or projecting. He was not concerned about *what this would do to their relationship*, whether his trembling would become noticeable, or the garlic chicken. He was just there, in the cold night, feeling every cell and sensation. He felt her lips on his lips, their texture, the light stickiness of the point of contact, surprise and excitement, the intimacy, the physical pleasure, and something transcendental that came from knowing that, on the opposite side of the same moment, she was entirely there too, connected to him as he was to her, and thinking nothing.

The prospectus drafting session

THE JOINT BOOKRUNNER'S ANALYST WALKED DOWN THE WIDE, NEW YORK AVENUE, its skyscrapers ceremonial, like pillars in a forum, as watchful as Ents, the cold morning air on his wet-shaven skin, his coffee breath making fireless puffs of smoke on the top of his cup's lid, like a baby dragon. There were other people walking across, against, and on his path, most also without their attention on the moment they were in or the journey they were on. He had only a limited sense of them, as objects. *How am I going to get out...? I can't believe he put cinnamon on this... That email... what a chump.* He did not see the documentary maker. He did not see himself being seen.

The man that jumped in front of him holding a holy book of an unidentified religion brought him more fully into the morning.

— Son, son... it's finance isn't it... where you going... No, no, where you going...? You're walking to the money, aren't you...? Don't you feel empty... aren't you looking for something...? Look... what book are you writing... what book are you reading...? Take this... No, no, no... take it... take it from me... it's a gift... it's a pleasure for me to give it to you... it's just an experience... just an object... it's not an objective... Take it... read it... wake up... wake up.

He did not take the book. His body reacted to the man as if he was a fly to swat or a boulder to avoid. His movement forward was caused not by the belief that he was on the right course, but by a belief in following courses. In completing tasks. In being dependable. In turning up. In trying.

He was not *against* religion. But what were the man's *credentials*, his *precedent transactions*, as his associate loved to say. What was his *league table position for the last twelve months? To what congregations has he preached? Does he have followers? What books has he published and who has endorsed them? How many people KNOW him – know WHO HE IS?*

He considered his dismissiveness.

There is only risk associated with this man. We come from different worlds.

I can't be giving up my time to everyone. I'm not a charity.

I am early. I should enjoy the morning.

On a street corner, as he waited for the lights to change at a pedestrian crossing, the pleasure of a smell caused the joint bookrunner's analyst to turn towards two men and one woman standing behind a steel street cart marked with the word *Buna* and garnished with cut flowers, grasses, and small beacons of incense smoke that mixed with the rich smells of coffee in the tarmac air. One of the men was roasting black beans on a flat iron plate, while the woman poured into small ceramic cups, with the ease of experience, the liquid the group was creating. She held at a ceremonial height an ageless or ancient clay coffee pot, with an elongated, swanlike neck, and a sweeping spout. Behind them, another pot was crackling on a stove, and the second man was grinding beans in a bowl. No-one had stopped for them.

— Hello sir. Buna? the man facing the analyst called after the momentary interlocking of their lines of sight, as though they were children looking into opposite ends of a cardboard tube.

He did not stop for them.

A few minutes later, the analyst walked like river water through the waterwheel door of a skyscraper. The people around him seemed small on the marble floor of an atrium, like henchmen on an intergalactic starship, but were magnified back into individuals in a lift in which the bodies of all occupants radiated the uncomfortable nature of their accidental, circumstantial proximity. Gradually, assorted workers exited on different floors, in the sporadic orderliness of boxes in a warehouse, with the items occasionally – to create a path for a package blocked in a corner – rearranging themselves in a manner that maintained their magnetic division and mutual suspicion. The joint bookrunner's analyst felt his frustration rise as a result of the slow progress of the metal container, but did not feel with equal force the relief that arrived when he passed seven levels without stopping and – *finally* – reached the top floor. The joint bookrunner's analyst then asked for directions at a reception desk, and passed the wooden doors and privacy glass of a corridor that turned like a perpendicular, video game snake.

The Boardroom, which was large enough to serve as an entertaining space or auditorium and required voices to be raised or amplified for them to reach all of its corners and congregants, was processed by the joint bookrunner's analyst as something already known, like a member of a gender or generation, with its differences not deemed deserving of his allocation of cosmic time. His retinal impression of the room – as rectangular, minimalist, and luxurious – was not enumerated, and his attention – the unsettling imprints left by the man with the book and the coffee sellers now washed by the wash of other feelings – was mostly occupied by the already gathered and *likely to be largely mute or grovelling* attendees of the prospectus drafting session. Like representatives of different interests before a conference, these attendees were organised in small clusters, the individual components of which were held together by loose gravitational forces in a localised authority and deference. Between these separated constellations there existed, by virtue of their presence in the same room to pursue a similar mission, only the lightest of loyalties, like that of moons to planets that were not their own. The interactions that did occur were mostly caused by curiosity, sociability, innocence, politeness, insecurity, or the attempted enhancement of existing professional relationships, with the exceptions of the corner conversation between two women who had painted over the detail of their historic disconnection twenty years previously after playing on a netball team together by describing themselves as having *lost touch*, and those briefly united in a glance and a belief in the meeting's insignificance while they gazed through glass at a black helicopter or a white cloud as it slowly crossed the steely, birdless trees of the city.

The joint bookrunner's analyst noticed the passage through one loosely arranged matrix of a participant that he presumed to be the most senior member of that particular delegation's team, because on her arrival the group stiffened and solidified into a more immobile arrangement, which – after the oxygen-free atmosphere and limitations of the conversation caused the senior team member to be drawn, like a temporarily waylaid asteroid, towards the breakfast buffet at the far end of the room – returned to its original fluidity of jutted hips and stomachs over belts.

The joint bookrunner's analyst was then himself drawn into this universe and the meeting's participants continued to enter the room like Morse code, or an inconsistently dripping tap. Some were clothed in sleeveless shirts, as though their journey had consisted of a single staircase. Others, with their hats, scarves and long coats, might – in another, *simpler*, time – have been protecting themselves from tundras, and were pulling, holding, balancing, or weighed down by wheelie bags, handbags, suit bags, laptop bags, headset cases, and briefcases. The heavy floor-to-ceiling mahogany door opened tentatively and confidently, revealing participants as playful as a lion cub or as ponderous as her heavy-jowled father, some with rested senses effortlessly absorbing almost all of the data available, and others as disoriented as a zebra separated from its zeal and blinking blankly at *either the watering hole or another mirage.*

In the middle of the room sat the boardroom table, a summit large enough for a summit at which attendance was politically expedient and a flat plateau which gave value to the floor on which it sat – like a rock transformed by a monarch, or a bottle by its *freshly squeezed* juice – and to which, on arriving, many attendees immediately meandered or marched, most settling a makeshift flag on what they estimated to be a dominant, semi-prominent, or discreet seat, while others settled their bags in a corner, either immediately forgetting them, glancing back at them protectively, or accepting the offer of a woman wearing a waistcoat and a pin displaying the bank's logo to *check them in* to the *luggage store.* Each new arrival was then drawn like liquid on an incline to the far end of the room by the sight and buzz of a toucan's palette of laboratory-made melons, mangos, and other fruits soaked and dried of their jungle salivation, and adorned with coffees, cookies, pastries, teas, and eggs in a quiet, corporate cornucopia.

The buffet, unconcerned with numbers or suits, was reshuffling the meeting's participants into new types and groups, some – before picking up a plate – preferring to fall in behind another supplicant, or to look for a longer line to stand in, or to disturb, with the words *are you queuing,* the silence of a cautious soldier halted by his nutritionist's conscience in a no man's land between pleasure and the rest of the room. One woman, knowing the food would have relaxed her body and thoughts, shook her head at the *bad luck* of an explosive sneeze that required her to perform an about-turn, while dogged pawns and assorted infantry filtered through these less speedy species and concentrated on seizing – before it was fully surrendered – an oversized silver spoon to slop some scrambled egg, or pincering the penultimate slice of buttered toast, or surreptitiously dropping a dripping teabag on the table.

Unnoticed, the first investor entered the room, interpreting the smiles and facial recognition he received as an invitation to direct some words towards familiar but unidentifiable faces.

— Hi – just coming to say hi because I'm in town. I'm conflicted – can't advise. Don't ask me anything! Ha ha ha! Recuse! Recuse! Recuse!

One of the group broke off to shake his hand and introduced himself as the chairman of one of the joint bookrunners.

— But you know, when we sat down in that coffee shop I knew. I knew immediately!

The first investor was shocked by his own disingenuousness and felt in his words the untiring habits of a retired salesman. *What was that? Who am I trying to convince? And all of this? Predict this? Never in a MILLION years.* His descent into introspection caused him to drift away without either excusing himself or appearing to be aware that he was still in a conversation.

A few minutes later, as if the calling of the meeting to order had altered the room's pressure and temperature and caused some mental tributaries to dry up, and others to flow, in an interconnected weakening and strengthening of each participant, the professional taxonomy of the room's ecosystem asserted itself over its private identities. This changed internal state was, for most, not artificial, and constituted a particular variant of a general and familiar physical condition, the state of *work*, which for some in this day's meeting – like the no longer impregnable focus of a footballer *limbering up* for the first international final of a long career – was hampered by the hormonal disturbances that signalled the future ascension of this – *defining and proud* – moment into semi-interesting dinner party anecdotes, magical stories told in soft, wise tones to wide-eyed grandchildren, semi-precious stones excavated for the eulogies of more modest or private minds, or into the stories they told themselves, if not about who they were then about what they had done.

At this moment, if asked who they were, those that turned off their morning alarms as dazed, jittery, exhausted, or contented animals, who when buttoning their shirts became bankers, lawyers, accountants, consultants, and investors, would now answer with the nomenclature of their subspecies and declare themselves to be underwriters and bookrunners, company's counsel and underwriters' counsel, auditors, commercial due diligence report providers and selling shareholders. They all came with a cause, and a commitment to that cause that while genuine was not total, their safe passage through uncertainties and discomforts – whether suffered, or condoned – provided by the black cloak of group action and the comfort blanket of collective responsibility. Their preoccupations at this particular point in time included non-reliance letters, promotions, and pension plans, and although they would never, in any role, with the possible but untested exception of one face, cross into the barbed land of the *inviolable*, they were just, *at the end of the day, doing their job*, and not, for those able to overpower their primordial safety catches, what they might sacrifice their lives for. There was no love or faith.

Even the three *global heads of technology* of the three bookrunners, sitting side by side in the middle of the table – who in this meeting felt their dispassion, cynicism, wealth, and *experience* unable immediately to suppress a desire to present to someone or something an offering of gold, frankincense, or myrrh – could not stop these unfamiliar feelings, without the oxygen of an object – like the fleeting gratitude attached to a rare noticing of the silent, steadfast operation of the lungs – from being smouldered by the belief, applied not to themselves but to the company and its founders, that *there is no such thing as genius... only competence, risk appetite... and luck.*

The company, like a newborn baby, was there too, waiting for those that had gathered to write the first version of its story.

... The Business Section ...

— What page is this on in the draft?

The room broke out into a bustle of rustling and fumbling that was both earnest and staged.

— Seventy-five.

— Okay – who's taking us through this?

— Happy to take the lead.

— Okay. Let's just focus on the key sentences shall we – let's try and lock those down.

The director of the first bookrunner spoke to the room.

— Okay, so this is the attempt to wrap everything up in a few sentences before we unpack it in the rest of the section. This is the same paragraph that we'll use in the summary up front so it's pretty important. I'll just read it out and then we can discuss... The Company is a global market leader in the virtual reality, metaverse, healthcare, well-being, social media, gaming, and communication markets. The total addressable market for the Company's products and services is estimated to be USD 22 trillion.

— Can we not say THE global market leader?

— THE is hard from a verification perspective.

— And what's the source for the TAM? The dd report? Can we state that in the text?

— Let's add a footnote so we don't interrupt the flow.

— Has everyone got a copy of the report?

— Shall we add in the projected CAGRs for the market?

— I'd rather we didn't. It will understate the growth. Let's focus on the Company's historic growth. That tells the story.

— Okay, no problem. I'll just get to the end of the paragraph and then we can discuss.

— Okay.

— So... yes, addressable market et cetera... maybe that comes a bit too early... anyway... The Company has 477 million Headset and Haptic Subscribers and 94 million Bodysuit Subscribers, and in total it has 2.0 billion registered users, of which 1.4 billion are monthly active users and 921 million are daily active users.

— The Company's group revenue in its last fiscal year was USD 169.8 billion, of which 37% was subscription revenue, 25% affiliate and other partner revenue, 20% in-world purchases, and 18% device and product revenue...

While the director was speaking, a murmuration of conversations began like summer leaves in an empty forest.

— What about the brain implant subscribers?

— It's a low number. Probably not worth mentioning.

— It could be the future. According to the company.

— We mention it lower down.

— We should mention it in the risk factors.

— Is in-world a defined term?

— Isn't the partner revenue just advertising – shouldn't we say it's advertising?

— It's not just advertising – it's metaverse and ecosystem integration revenue – consciousness photographs and designer opinions and thought gifts... a lot of it is revenue sharing... not cost per click but cost per thought...

— The Company's group revenue by geography in its last fiscal year was... The Americas 33%, Europe 30%, Asia and

Australia 24%, and Africa 13%. The Company's group EBITDA in its last fiscal year was USD 82.5 billion, which equates to an EBITDA margin of 48.6%, and its group free cash flow was USD 69.8 billion, which equates to a free cash flow margin of 41.1%. The Company's revenue and EBITDA growth rates in its last fiscal year were 51.0% and 92.3% respectively, and its compound annual revenue growth rates for the last 3 and 5 years were 76.6% and 133.5% respectively. The Company's average monthly subscription fee in the last fiscal year was USD 9.17, with an annual subscriber churn rate of less than 5%, and services provided, calculated in user seconds, were... communication and interaction with other members 39%, immersive experiences and activities 36%, and platform connection while undertaking other activities 25%. On average, in the last fiscal year, daily active users were connected to the Company's platform for 2 hours and 10 minutes per day. The Company estimates that at the end of the last fiscal year, the average improvement in the average well-being of users active for more than 6 months was 24%, using maximum well-being as a denominator, and that these users' Presence had increased on average by 12% over the entire period of their platform usage.

After the director stopped, the shallow shadow of parallel comments and conversations came to the foreground, where, feeling their freedom, the sounds multiplied and became bolder, like gossip.

— How the hell do they measure that...? I don't think we can imply causation. We should say correlated with... Is presence a defined term? If it is that's some sinister shit... User seconds...? Er... Time...? That's an absurdly long paragraph. Nobody wants a novel... And a lot of data in one go... It's the key paragraph. We should just publish that and be done with all of the other hoopla... Well that paragraph's a catastrophe for a start... it sounds like one of our analysts has vomited a spreadsheet onto the page. Where's the equity story?

The noise combusted into a silence in which the chairman of the equity capital markets team of one of the joint bookrunners gathered and ordered three grandiose pronouncements, having assessed that it would be valuable for the room, the company, and his public profile if he was to offer some judgments *based on my experience and the expectations of the investor community.* The company's chief operating officer, who was seated with the company's chief financial officer, chief technology officer, general counsel, and junior legal counsel – the skin on his face almost invisible behind hair imagined by the joint bookrunner's analyst to have been styled by placing his palms on a Van de Graaff generator – then spoke before the nib of the chairman had been fully filled by a slow nasal inhalation, and did so – in contrast to the chairman's chin-out, head-back, half reclining posture – while peering into the document in front of him, as though it was a pond and he was searching for a tadpole.

— Look, I think that's fine, he said.

This pronouncement caused all other comments to scuttle away like mice, the criticisms leaving first, followed sulkily by the advice.

The room then waited for a lone ranger.

The chief operating officer spoke again.

— Albeit a shame that we're squeezing ourselves into these defunct conventions. It feels like we're in the zoo now – in the meat market – and all of the buyers and sellers, all of the... cultural commentators and calibrators, are looking at us... prodding us with antique instruments... so they can "benchmark" us against the other options... so they can throw our music in with all of the other noise.

He looked to his side. The chief financial officer, seated as though he was holding a large beach ball, and without changing his facial expression, rotated both of his hands in an outwards motion, the sides of his wrists remaining in contact with the table as he did so, as if to say *this is the world, we have to accept it.*

The chief technology officer spoke.

— Yes, isn't it time to retire this global market leader... paradigm? It puts the market – the exchange – first, doesn't it? And these global market leaders are everywhere... all DIFFERENTIATED, all UNIQUE, all doing things which are UNPRECEDENTED and REDEFINING. Basically we've run out of words. (She moved her toes forward tentatively on a rope from which she expected to spiral into an abyss before reaching The Jewel of Truth.) So, is this the best we can do? For a company that is – I hate the word but – quietly providing nourishment to hundreds of millions of people? Not with flavoured water or fridge-freezers but by enriching... their experience – and understanding – of living... a company which a few of us are naively hoping may usher in some sort of new era... some sort of... new enlightenment, if that word hasn't also been juiced of all meaning.

Only a limited number of the expressions facing into the table were initially attracted to, scornful of, or in any way interested in the possible arrival of a new, spiritual, age. The critical faculties of most others, unclipped from their leashes by the absence of a professional imperative, were now snoring or chasing butterflies in the decadence and privacy of their skulls. The woman within one woman, whose mother's doctor had recorded on a voicemail before the meeting the information that her mother's tumour was *inoperable*, was sinking and turning as if she had been untethered from a space station. *What am I doing here?* When the chief technology officer then used the word *utopia*, like the wings of insects returning to the air, certain of the couplets and triplets that had previously shared comments recommended their droplets and susurrations. *Would you say that's a risk factor...? Well that does sound like a forward-*

looking statement. Gonna need a pretty safe safe harbour for that one yo. One of the underwriters' counsel's senior associates leaned towards the company's auditor's director, a man he found mysterious after having exchanged a spoonful of words with him at the breakfast buffet. *Can you give comfort on that?* The company's auditor's director replied by saying, *No, you cover it in the 10b5*, while the senior partner at the issuer's counsel began his journey in the foothills of a coughing fit, his body having been transformed into a sputtering motor whose burps and strains showed immediately that it would never come fully to life, but that it was programmed to try to do so, and would dutifully continue in this project for a prolonged period.

The chairman of the equity capital markets team of one of the joint bookrunners inhaled once more, and, although his confidence and conviction was undiminished, proceeded with an increased caution in the presence of the now-visible nettles of the company's management's views.

— Yes, of course. If I may. I get it. We get it. We absolutely get it and we're on the same page – one hundred per cent. But – if I can – respectfully – offer you one question, as follows. I mean, you have to ask yourself – and I ask this delicately because I know it is a sensitive subject – what is it that you are trying to achieve here – what's the functional objective of this document – you're – if I may – without beating around – you know – without calling a spade a digging implement and so on – TRYING – at a good valuation – TO RAISE CAPITAL – to create liQUidity on the public markets...

The chief technology officer's neck and upper body convulsed like a whip and then moved backwards, as if she was an adolescent ostrich that was not completely familiar with the animal kingdom and a small gerbil had unexpectedly crossed her path.

— No we're not!

The chairman's director, vice president, senior associate,

and analyst, to different degrees – and without being aware of the common core of their physical responses – reacted to the rejection of their leader's authority as if their own words, belief system, or identity had in some way been slandered, with swells of loyalty and anger and a residue of indignation, while their more senior colleagues, the managing director and the global head of technology investment banking, experienced a frisson of pleasure.

— This is bigger than that... this is just a step in a journey... towards the ownership structure that the company SHOULD have... ...we're not solving for... the last fifty billion.

The bolder voices, with a diminished boldness, continued to murmur.

— Why don't they just give it to the government then... let THEM make a potato salad out of it... or make it a freaking charity... A JOURNEY? Away from the fortress of their A-shares to the hole in the ground of this class-B toilet paper more like... "the last fifty billion" – what a bunch of losers... Has there ever been a better example of the invisible hand slapping most people in the face...? They're as lost as everyone else... Soon it'll be – you never actually OWN The Consciousness Company... you just look after it for the next blah, blah, blah... Listen – I'm right – I know I'm right... listen...

— Ultimately, the company should belong to – and – whether we know it or not – is in the hands of – the cradle of – humanity, or the conscious, those that think and feel... we're just its custodians... we are aware of our limits... we're at the wheel but bobbing on billions of brains... trying to bail out water before the trench foot sets in... trying to protect our children from cynicism...

The chief financial officer continued as though he knew the chief technology officer's thoughts as well as he knew his own.

— And one way to protect us – all of us – from that, is for

the company to be owned by everyone...

— In more than a physical – EXCLUDING – private property kind of way.

— This is not about drugging people with share prices...

— Or the empty perfection of some distributed ledger...

The chief financial officer's and the chief operating officer's interjections seemed to come from the chief technology officer, and the joint bookrunner's analyst imagined them all to be on lead guitar and vocals.

The senior consultant of the commercial due diligence report provider, who seemed to those who had noticed his existence to be sitting comfortably on a chair, was at the same time not aware that he was not processing the dialogue that he was faintly aware was, from the perspective of his role, the most important activity taking place in the space in which his body was contained. Perspiration was seeping and pulsating out of his skin, and single beads of sweat were being expelled through individual pores at the roots of his hair as though, like bugs breaching the barrier of a host, his most painful and powerful thoughts were bursting out into the external environment. *I can't believe it. How can we have got it wrong?* When his physical senses were not occupied by heat, and between the one or two uncoupled carriages in a runaway train of self-criticism, he felt the lava of vomit churning in his stomach. *Virtual reality two trillion, metaverse three trillion, healthcare and well-being ten trillion, social media three trillion, gaming and communication four trillion, and then the double-counting deduction was four trillion. Which is a TAM of eighteen trillion. Shit. SHIT! The twenty-two trillion number is everywhere. It's... It's a LIE... ... ...Does that mean the company has been MIS-SOLD to investors in these so-called PRE-MARKETING conversations? These fireside chats and water testings? Does that mean they've given these indications of interest on the basis of false information? It must be... it MUST be a material fact. It's a huge mistake. And it's all my fault. And now... and now unknowingly is knowingly. UNKNOWINGLY IS NOW KNOWINGLY! SHIT! How could I be so STUPID! Should I tell someone? Should I tell someone that we – I've basically fucked it all up? And that we have to go back to all these investors – these obnoxious princelings and say – sorry the numbers were wrong here are the new numbers use these ones they're better. Lower and better. Much prettier and more refined. Yes – and at the same time, if you want, you can just swing this complimentary sledgehammer through your confidence in everything else you have been told. Are the audited financials audited? Do they give a true and fair view of the company's affairs? Does the earth circle the sun? Does water freeze at zero degrees? Is there really no use in crying over spilt milk...? Eighteen Trillion! What a farce... ...Who am I? GOD? That I should know what the fucking total addressable market is. It's big guys – it's big – don't you get it. It's pretty fucking BIG. I feel sick. I actually feel sick. It is now a falsehood. I am a peddler of falsehoods... ... ...But – it wasn't DISHONEST. I didn't THINK it was wrong... But was it negligent? Was I negligent? Is that bad – how bad is that? Is that not so bad? I'm not a bad person. Am I? Does a bad person always know they're a bad person...? ...Okay, okay. Calm. Calm down. It's just human error... ...And how is it that the whole universe can be on my shoulders? I have to tell someone. SHIT. SHIT, SHIT, SHIT! SHIT. This whole fucking shitting manufactured – guaranteed to be wrong – insane, unnecessary superstructure of complexity. It's just a fucking big market. It's not complicated. IT'S NOT COMPLICATED GUYS. I have to tell someone. I'll be worrying about this for weeks... months... possibly – possibly even for the rest of my life. SHIT. I'll just tell someone. I'll be the fall guy. I'll be the goat, the heroic goat. I'll just get on the bus to oblivion. They can erase me. They can never mention my name again...*

What will I tell my mother?

— You see, the company should not be thought of – should not be turned by this exercise into an "other"... a thing that wants to conquer, or impress... it's not something OUT THERE that is trying to create – to collect – a world of caged creatures... ...the company is... the voice inside you, the compassionate friend that wants things for you...

— It wants you to understand what you want...

— ...to understand desire...

— ...and to understand the desire to understand...

— ...and it wants you to let go...

The baton continued to be juggled between the senior managers.

— It wants you to feel the mess...

— ...it wants to remove all the moss...

— ...and the mist of...

— ...all of the things you think you know...

— And people will buy shares...

— And become possessed, by its otherness, and by other demands...

— That they will place on it...

— And maybe they'll infect it...

— Maybe we will infect it...

— Maybe we already have...

— And maybe it will fall...

— And this beautiful idea will be lost completely...

— But, if we are describing it, here, today, now, all of us, we – I don't know – seventy-two scholars, we must say that the company is OF and not just FOR...

— We must say that we are all carrying it in our hands.

— So can you write that down?

Several of the joint bookrunners' analysts, like sprinklers in suburban gardens, pivoted their heads in a range of directions to look at each other, and responded to their contemporaries' equally confused and concerned eyes and eyebrows with small shakes of the head, twitches of the mouth, and subtle, respectful shrugs. They had neither understood, nor understood it to be necessary to retain, the senior managers' words.

The auditor's summer intern, whose laptop – like the sunglasses of a distant relation at a sunless funeral – was one of many devices that served not as barriers for feelings but as filters separating the more junior members of the various teams from the sharp reality of the rest of the room, and which was marked out by a peeling, faded treble clef sticker on its back, had her headset on and was recording her thoughts. *It has the form and aspect of truth... it builds up slowly... but it uses emotion... and rhythm and reason... and cadence... So how do I know it's true? It's like a chord progression that gradually heightens the tension and revelation, with each new resolution adding a further dimension that needs its own answer. Is it just art?*

— Because when we talk about what the company is, we need to present it as an idea.

There were no voices in the background. The air conditioning unit breathed its mechanical breath.

… Risk factors …

The underwriters' and company's counsels restarted the meeting after a short, scheduled break, and like the flakes of a snow globe that required a few more seconds to settle, many of the meeting's participants continued to mill or float in the room, and in the corridors outside, with coffees and phones. A senior partner from the underwriters' counsel tightened his bow tie and attempted to encourage additional participation by announcing, *Risk Factors everyone*, adding, with a monotony from which sincerity was inferred even by the colleagues that were students of his personality, *We don't want to include the risk that a limited number of the Company's employees and advisers participated in this discussion... hence the veracity or completeness of this document cannot be guaranteed et cetera.* A few silhouettes continued to loiter and gaze at the lazy evaporation of the cityscape's mists.

— Okay, let's start by going through the categories – a lot of this is boilerplate stuff. If we are unable to retain existing members or to add new members, or if members reduce the frequency or depth of their engagement with The Consciousness Company, then our revenue, results of operation, and financial condition may be affected...

— Business...

— What?

— And our business will be affected...

— Well, that turns the sentence into "if our business is affected then our business may be affected".

— Okay – but it's standard language.

— Yes, it's standard.

— We'll check the precedents, but yes. Pretty sure it's standard.

— And share price...

— What?

— And our share price may be affected.

— Okay – anything else? Anything else that will be affected?

— Maybe let's not get bogged down in the prose... let's focus on mapping out the key categories... We should talk about all of the things that could reduce the number of existing or new users or the frequency or depth of their engagement... changes in consumer sentiment, for example... shifts in public opinion... perhaps because of bad publicity... or more security, safety, or privacy challenges for example...

— And then there's competition... other platforms offering a superior experience... a less visible monetisation model... better technology... eventually the future blazes past trailblazers doesn't it... and IP – maybe it's not, or won't be adequately protected... and then we need to talk about how all of these things could lead to a reduction in revenues – from subscriptions, affiliates, partners, in-app purchases, and devices... either because of reduced volume – or because the company needs to reduce prices to maintain competitiveness.

The company's general counsel, who was wearing a faint pink linen shirt, nodded in respect.

— Yes, that's good. Then I think we need to go one layer further in terms of company specifics. Let's say we start to see diminishing well-being improvements, or even reduced well-being... or reduced presence – which I realise is, unfortunately, not a concept we can define particularly easily in this document – in other words, what if it stops working...? Or what if... what if people stop calling all of this GOOD... if – say – excessive – or perceived-to-be excessive – compassion... or CONFORMITY IN GENERAL... causes the world to become BORING, in a way that is, in some sort of real sense, slightly soul-destroying? What if we destroy the RICHNESS of the world?

The company's general counsel leaned back on his chair, and, as if the weight of his thoughts had pivoted a see-saw, he continued primarily for the purposes of internal contemplation.

— I mean... well... there's just SUCH A LOT that could go in here... Firstly – say we start on the individual level... there's the – increasingly widespread – misuse of the company's tools... there are, for example, people training themselves to become desensitised to guilt, or indeed to any kind of pain, or not to believe in objective truth, unbelievably... ...then there's the problem of the TOTAL loss of privacy... the potential for it... because now we really DO have a camera in your head... actually

– it's even more powerful than that... (The company's general counsel returned his attention to the rest of the group of lawyers.) Did you know that The Consciousness Company's Consciousness – with just one or two starting moves – provided there are limited or no external stimuli – can accurately predict progressions of thought which the thinker themselves thinks are SPONTANEOUS or RANDOM... in other words, the company knows our members BETTER THAN THEY KNOW THEMSELVES...! Which is a level of knowledge or state of the world that probably needs its own epoch... and big bang, threshold moment – like – well... you tell me – POST-PRIVACY... or post... HUMAN... or... THE DETHRONING... THE OVERTHROWING OF TIME...! Or something...

The group of lawyers did not react to the words of the general counsel. Some were conditioned not to reveal, and a few not even to feel, fear in no man's land. Others were undisturbed because of the abstract nature of the concepts presented, which – not being attached in their minds to experiences or images of pain, as over time *famine* had for some become attached to the eyes of emaciated children – were unable to create in their bodies any emotional response. And others still were protected by the perceived insignificance of their perceived role, as a soldier, *just doing my job, completing the task at hand,* and *earning a living.*

— Then, of course, what if these changes taking place in – or being made to – billions of brains – are shown to be pathological? We don't really know the CONSEQUENCES of rewiring the brains of – hundreds of millions of people... of speeding up the slow changes of millions of years... ...What we DO know is that when we all start doing something new, a bunch of other things tend to happen that no-one predicted... or which someone somewhere did predict – but which, equally predictably – lots of us try to compartmentalise as the scaremongering of a heretic or a raving lunatic or... JUST A MINORITY VIEW or something... as if almost all of our beliefs weren't once minority views...

— And, of course, the very large mammal that's – well – not in the room, so to speak... is the metaverse... all these people now living so much of their lives in the metaverse or in an enhanced reality... is that good, or is it bad... or does the metaverse-ness of the whole thing not really matter...? I don't know... it COULD be bad... and there's definitely the risk of... BAD ACTORS... of getting imprisoned in all manner of hells... Yes – we should mention bad actors... and bots... and all of the quiet cancers that spread in software...

— Plus, as well as hacking, there's this faster, more destructive problem of hijacking... If someone – or something – gets to the hardware then – well – you're dead, essentially... you are erased...

While the company's general counsel was speaking, the senior partner from the underwriters' counsel was nodding with a restrained vociferousness that created for the rest of the group the impression that none of these points were unknown, controversial, or problematic, and that the company's general counsel was simply championing a pre-existing consensus that these subjects should be included in the company's prospectus.

— Yes – the metaverse – much like the real world, I suppose – these are all good points – deterioration in usage benefits, unintended, deleterious consequences, privacy, bad actors, and, lastly, let's include a catch-all risk factor in relation to the way the platform is used – yes – definitely – got it – let's have a new section which is more company specific and we'll cover off all of this there.

Cover off? The company's junior legal counsel grimaced. *What is this sinister alchemy...? How does this sludge arrive back at a garden sprinkler... as some sort of restorative water for these wallies to splash in?*

— Yes – please can we make sure we shout about the

company's own introspection and anxiety... about... (The company's junior legal counsel began to move his arms as he spoke.) ...not knowing – or first principles – or the lack of a separate planet on which to run a control experiment. Questions like – what if the way we are RIGHT NOW is JUST FINE? (The apathy and stillness around the company's junior legal counsel energised and sharpened his faith, like a protester reacting to the formality of a parliamentary chamber.) Or – what STANDARDS should we be judging so-called good and so-called progress by? And do we have an obsession with "progress"? And... NO MATTER HOW MANY NEUROSCIENTISTS ARE RUMINATING AND COMPUTING AWAY IN VANITY CASTLE – isn't presuming to know what's best for people – FOR – ALL – PEOPLE... just... STAGGERINGLY... ARROGANT? AND PROBABLY WRONG?

The senior partner from the underwriters' counsel, like one organism rapidly enveloping and digesting another, integrated this additional dissonance into the drafting session.

— Yes – good, people – good – we should include all of that... I think let's go for a general disclaimer that the theories and methods of the company may be wrong and that – when the final drop of port's been drunk and we're all in our silk pyjamas – the company's members and the world as a whole are engaging with it at their own risk. Yes – standard-issue caveat emptor. That's definitely got to go in.

The junior legal counsel turned to the general counsel.

— CAVEAT EMPTOR? These are not novelty desk toys... we're not flogging rocking horses here...

He then turned back to the group before again turning towards the general counsel to let out the aftershock of his initial reaction.

— And why should they beware...? Everything we do is... credentialised up the wazoo... What a sell-out...

While the junior legal counsel was speaking, the first senior associate of the underwriters' counsel had sought to support the statement of his senior partner by saying, *Yes, we need to cover ourselves*, but, by treating the senior partner's proposal as if it related to events that had the potential to materialise, unintentionally undermined it, and caused an involuntary wincing of the senior partner's cheekbone. The second senior associate of the underwriters' counsel then sought to alleviate both the senior partner's discomfort and her own dissatisfaction at her lack of contribution up to this point.

— Well personally I wouldn't quite say that, but anyway... and I think all of these points are good points... but if we bring it back to the economics – what about – in the spirit of completeness and well – breaking down the walls – adding in that – ONE DAY – the company will JUST STOP GROWING... because one day the company WILL stop growing.

— Yes – perfect – brilliant!

— Although maybe let's just say that the growth may slow or something like that.

The widening cast of contributors caused the heart of the senior partner's trainee to beat more quickly. She looked around the group and croaked, *What about – war, and acts of god...? Just for... completeness.* The rest of the group waited to see if the suggestion would be endorsed, and the second senior associate said, *Not sure. I don't think these documents tend to say one day the world will end... or one day the founders could die in a plane crash and the share price might then – well – follow a similar trajectory.*

— Well... they might... and it might.

— Yes, we should definitely include the company's reliance on the founders... We should specify their voting and veto rights... and the consequence that the quality of their decision-making and their level of engagement – whether less is indeed more or less – are significant risk factors.

— We can mention The Ethics Committee in terms of checks and balances.

The general counsel nodded.

— And we should say something about The Consciousness Company's Consciousness. Again, we don't really know it's right, right, in the long term. And we don't have any other tool to assess its level of madness. And if we did, that tool could be mad too. Or more mad. Madder.

The second senior associate of the underwriters' counsel then disguised, by nodding her head like a child's bouncy ball coming to rest, an enhancement of an offering whose dandelion had already been blown.

— And if the founders decide to invest... I don't know... all of the company's profits in something that doesn't generate a financial return... if the company decides to – abandon – its shareholders and to pursue a purely social mission?

— Yes, I suppose that's a risk. Let's put that in... The Company may choose to act in accordance with its perceived social responsibility as distinct from its fiduciary duty and the two may not coincide, which could have a material adverse effect on its results of operation et cetera... or something like that.

The first senior associate of the underwriters' counsel, diminished, and reading from his notes, then sought to recover his reputation with a contribution that he considered to be incontestable and important but not virtuosic.

— And then there's the more standard stuff – legislation, litigation – existing and new... regulation... costs growing faster than revenues... key personnel... highly advanced nature of the company's software – possible presence of unknown errors... defaulting on obligations... expansion into countries with unfamiliar political and social... landscapes... currency, foreign laws, compliance... and then... risks related to the offering...

...The Company might not use the proceeds effectively... no dividends... substantial share sales post-lock-up periods... challenges of being a public company... ...all the standard stuff.

— Yes, that should cover it.

The company's junior legal counsel smiled to diminish his irritation and turned to the company's general counsel.

— We think that because we write it down in this sanitised language then that makes it okay... DON'T WORRY GRANDMA – WE ACTUALLY PREDICTED THE END OF THE WORLD – IT WAS IN THE PROSPECTUS! SO IT'S NOT THE END OF THE WORLD!

The senior partner from the underwriters' counsel looked around the group.

— Anything else? Anything else we've missed?

The general counsel's closed mouth rippled.

— Well, there IS a further risk created by all of this thought and discussion about what the risks might be. From allocating time to worrying about the risks... and from presenting them as having equal probability as well. Anyone who actually reads this is now going to be much more worried about these risks... And the whole exercise might have the unintended consequence of making them MORE PROBABLE – more... REAL...

As he spoke, his amusement diminished.

— Thinking the thoughts is not free.

The team of lawyers from the underwriters' counsel exchanged glances, uncertain whether including this contribution in the document would make them the object of a joke.

... The mission statement ...

Later in the morning, the door opened, and the first founder walked in. The attention of all of the individuals in the room was turned towards him, and he smiled reflexively, dutifully, and inwardly, without feeling any happiness in his body or connecting his eyes with the eyes of any of the other people in the room. He sat down on a chair that was near to the door and against the wall, his intention being to observe the meeting and not to participate in it. The room became quiet, and, like a dry river fracturing under the strength of the desert sun, the discomfort of those facing away from the first founder caused an automatic rearrangement of the heads, bodies, and chairs that were obstructing his field of vision. Some of those that were facing or had looked at the first founder could not see him clearly through the film of the feelings that had resulted from his sudden presence. Others who could see the marks on his skin and the lines under his eyes had the impression that this was not the first founder but just someone who looked a lot like him. The company's chief operating officer said, *We've mostly been focusing on the Business section so far. I'll ping you the latest draft...* and the meeting's attendees, overcompensating in their attempts not to appear unsettled by the first founder's arrival, shifted their attention to the source of these words, like a flock of birds rapidly changing direction.

While the company's chief operating officer was speaking, the door opened again and, unnoticed, the second founder entered the room and saw around the table the faces and surfaces of large numbers of inaccessible thoughts, feelings, histories, and futures, some with expressions and postures that he believed he knew well, others that he thought he had witnessed and may one day experience, and others still with manners and mannerisms he expected never fully to understand. His eyes twinkled with warmth and gratitude as he absorbed the room. The anxiety that he had felt after fearlessly tying a tourniquet and being splashed with blood two hours earlier had now fully dissipated. He put a final piece of satsuma in his mouth and, as the oval motion of his jaw caused its substance to disintegrate, he felt on his tongue and in his body its refreshing juice, chewy skin, and a sweetness that was not synthetic.

When the second founder then asked if he could *squeeze* a chair between the company's junior legal counsel and its general counsel, the resulting shift in the attention of the room was accompanied by a *whoosh* of inhalations which escaped before bodies could filter through thought their response to this further surprise. The second founder said, *What page are we on?* and the junior legal counsel passed him a copy of the draft prospectus and indicated the section that had most recently been under discussion. The director of the first bookrunner then presented to the founders a small platter of platitudes on the subject of the *great progress* that was being made, while the second founder directed his attention towards resisting the reflex lurking in his tingling nose, until a further trickle on an inner trigger caused him to turn away from the table and sneeze.

The general counsel then spoke, directing his words to both founders.

— We are however not sure how to approach – how to find the right words – for that important section that you've talked about... the vision... the mission statement... or memo... ...the more meditative, existential bit? We weren't sure how you were thinking about it? A letter to shareholders maybe?

The second founder looked at the first founder and the first founder moved his head up and forwards slightly, like a flipper on a pinball machine, to indicate his preference for the second founder to answer. The second founder turned to the general counsel.

— Oh, yes – that is important. Let me have a go at putting that into words.

The second founder's headset then recorded silence and then, *I need to fall more fully into the skin of this moment,*

and then, *One day I may read these thoughts as words...
the feeling of being as I thought them totally forgotten.* The
silence, inactivity, and anticipation in the room became heavier,
and reacted with the air pockets of impatience inside the small
number of meeting participants that had not become wide-eyed
disciples or the front-row audience of an *eagerly awaited* show.

The second founder's words, *Are you sitting comfortably...?*
and, *Feel your breath...* moved quietly into the silence, without
breaking it. The words were offered like paper boats, without
emotion or command, as a secular instruction that sought,
temporarily, to forge a community and provide the protection
required for its collective relaxation.

— Feel your breath... and follow it, until you feel the feeling
of being...

— Feel the fact, the often forgotten fact, that you are a living
thing...

— That is here today...

— Feel your strength, and your weakness...

The second founder paused to follow his own instructions.

— And now... feel that feeling, of breathing, of being, and
imagine that you are... in some other place and skin... perhaps a
tiny turtle... approaching the ocean for the very first time... step,
step, step, step... your flippers scraping the sand and your body
washed by the foam... Soon, you are in the water, feeling life
flowing through you.

The second founder paused again and waited for his
thoughts to float out of him so that he could feel the feeling of his
own being.

— These words, too, are flowing through you, and drifting
by you... these unremarkable marks... these lifeless lines and
curves... not holding any meaning unless seen, or heard...

— Pause, for a moment. Pause... slow down...

The principal of the venture capital fund noticed the dust

in the air, her restlessness, and how the sporadic but recurring canon of background coughs, and the second founder's nostril hair, were, respectively, irritating and disgusting her.

— Notice any tension you are holding within you. Your tension is the difference between what you want to be, and what is.

— Breathe... and watch your breath...

— With curiosity...

— Let it be under surveillance...

— As if you were watching the delicate movements of an easily startled animal... the crack of a twig... the turn of a neck...

— See how it is incessant, but in no way dogmatic...

— A bird on the water, lighter than the object on which it is balanced...

— And slowly... silently... allow the ark to open...

— On the holiness of your existence...

The second founder then listened to the room's silence and filled it with a substance and stature greater than that of the words that it had previously set apart. The silence continued to grow until the return of a sentence would for a short time have been processed as a series of absences serving only to make the room's emptiness more intelligible.

The second founder let his eyelids fall. A number of other pairs of eyelids followed, gratefully submitting without conscious instruction to gravity and opportunity. Some senior employees of the assorted service providers in the room, whose similar corporate principles, dripped through rocks over decades of service, all included variations on the – *commendably selfless* – as the joint bookrunner's analyst habitually thought on observing the golden plaque by the lift that lifted him to his desk almost every day – theme of *customer focus*, allowed their eyes to close in a manner that, while appearing to be complete, reflected their inability fully to release themselves from the anthropological reality that they were *being addressed by an important client.* Many of the more junior employees glanced at their peers, or the individuals they considered themselves to be working for, to decide on the appropriate course of action, while a minority kept their eyes open because after a moment of indecision they calculated that they were *working* and this state of being required them to be an observer and not a participant. One anomaly was an individual whose sense of the making of history was wrestling with but not overpowering his reverential and deferential instincts, and this see-sawing manifested itself in intermittent blinks of varied lengths that caused the headset of a joint bookrunner's associate to record the thought *is that a twitch or is he trying to start a game of wink murder?* Another individual remained stony-eyed because his veins were bubbling with rapids of hatred. The headset of a colleague that had worked with him for four years recorded the belief that he was *maintaining plausible deniability,* while scattered analysts, like static sparks, exchanged looks, and in certain cases experienced panic and the paralysis of a computer given contradictory commands, or a conscript caught between love and duty, as they struggled to meditate while writing or typing, until these mental roadblocks were cleared by the gesture of one analyst towards her headset while smiling and whispering, *I'm recording it don't worry.*

The second founder continued to speak. The first founder had kept his eyes open.

— After a while, you see that you are... physical matter. You feel your eyelashes, your tense tongue, and your jaw. You feel the tips of your fingers and the tips of your toes. You feel the weight of your body. You sense, the thrill-less, intertwined theme park rides under your skin, the ghostly automation, the audacious circus of blood-red blood and important air, the insistent, heavy electrochemistry, like an enchanted experiment, and you feel your points of contact with other surfaces, dead, and alive...

— Let... ...go... ...

— Let go, of the future, and the past...

— Let go of your dreams...

— Let go of... want...

— Let go of resistance, your resistance to the now...

— Let go of the story... ... ...until your attention is entirely here... ... ...and you are left with only your senses... with salty sea or summer pollen, or a sealed, still, and scentless room. Without expecting it, from the alertness of relaxation, see this page, as though it is unfamiliar, as if it is on an optician's screen... the mist of repetition, suddenly receding... now savour the melon, or the mustard, or the lemon... or the onions or the spices... or the savouriness... hear altitude in the engine of a plane... and the more distant ear ringing that is your past... then further still the roar of the shingle from the shore of a legend... be soaked by it... and walk and hold, the back and the palm of a stranger's hand... rough, and tender... you are touching, like a wand in the water, an alternative world... a private life – flash – flash – flashing – BEFORE YOUR EYES like false memory... top hats and tails and a flowery canopy... an early morning trickle of milk on a wrist... the death of a pet... and THOSE HEYDAYS now missed... before – eventually – time blows clouds into the crystal... and on your return... for a moment that is just long enough... you experience – physically – in the way you feel space, the blossoming and shrivelling, the unfolding, the TAKING PLACE... of THE PRESENT... briefly aware that, like air, it is ALWAYS THERE, slipping through your senses like gold.

Many of the meeting's participants began to experience a feeling of being that exceeded their daily levels of awareness. The phone in the inside-left jacket pocket of one of the joint bookrunner's directors vibrated. He let its light creep into his eyes like dawn under the folds of curtains, holding the phone below the line of the table and reading the second of two messages sent by the same person... *Bottom line just a heads-up monetary policy not expected to tighten any more because of war – although supply chain disruption could have an inflationary effect.* He experienced a positive emotion and his headset recorded the observation that *the misery of millions of people has somehow caused me to feel happy.*

— The feeling passes and you are left with the thought that you, the point of view, the perspective, the wandering window, are just a natural phenomenon, just one more rumba of cosmic matter. A manifestation, and a ballroom for other manifestations. A host that did not post the invitations. You have a feeling that, although you have a name, and a set of circumstances, you could be anywhere... anywhere at all... it doesn't matter... you could be... anyone, even... any thing... You feel the planets orbiting faraway stars... you see that they're not so far after all...

Slowly, like dusk, or chameleons applying caution, more and more of the room's participants began to submit to the words, and in another part of the city, a helicopter took off, holding a family.

— But creation is not only physical... together, we create other things... identities... ideas... countries... COMPANIES... together, we have created this company... most as accidental labourers... all insufficient pillars... cementing the circumstantial evidence... the articles, and billboards, and a digital blackbird... then the SALVATION TESTIMONIES of EARLY ADOPTERS... and the artificial majesty acquired by humdrum names... in the prosecutor's forehead, a pulsing vein... then a headset's silhouette... and the brain-dead headlines cloning jumbo numbers... ...until the how is of esoteric interest only... to the enthusiast or historian... as the silicone fuses slowly with the skin... knitting away – the filling of a form, the button on a screen – was it green – and the all-important CERTIFICATE OF INCORPORATION... no laboratory or baby... just the confident decree of an automated agency... with its own pillars and papers... that happened to say... in a particular motherboard, on a particular day... let it be... and it was.

The co-head of the equity capital markets team of one of the joint bookrunners opened his eyes and turned to the managing partner of the venture capital fund.

— The meditation bit was good – iconoclastic – you know – like the company... but I think it's going a little bit too far now. It's a prospectus, not a work of art, right? There's no precedent for this.

The managing partner whispered in a manner that was faithful to his own feelings and sensitive to those of the co-head of equity capital markets.

— I dunno. Maybe you're right. Or maybe our vision is not so good. Maybe this emperor is very well dressed.

The co-head of equity capital markets tried to endorse the words of the managing partner.

— Yes, maybe. Well, he is very accomplished in many areas. He's even a surfer as well, I think... or maybe that's the other one.

The first founder was standing in the corner opposite the meeting room's door, with the breakfast buffet on his horizon and a field of vision that allowed him to scan the entire scene. His senses were not dulled either by participation or the presumption of inevitability, as if he was the director of an entertainment programme describing itself as *reality*, or a motion-activated camera gathering from undergrowth an incomplete understanding of the ways and lives of quiet, private creatures.

Creation indeed... how on earth... how on earth have I given birth to all of this...?

And why am I just standing here, in the CORNER...? I could do better than this... Yes... this mumbo jumbo is easy, really... Every day is the same, but this Wednesday will not come again... put that in your pompous piss-pipe... in your pithy, impulse purchase by the till... your instant access wisdom...

But...

How on earth...? Yes... suddenly you wake up and look around... at concrete walls covered in corporate paint – the dead faces that some... FACILITIES MANAGEMENT COMPANY has put in gravitas frames to signify... to REPRESENT – THE PAST... and... SUDDENLY you have ABSOLUTELY NO IDEA how you got here... I can't even REMEMBER the boy with the wild hair... ...Something else was alive, inside his young skin and large eyes... while he wandered on walls and kicked along balls... splashing in bliss... his mind a moth... pursuing some priority as inconsequential as – as these words... listening to rain on a sloping roof... touching bunk bed slats with outstretched toes...

You'd be a boring-looking stranger to him... someone he'd avoid... if he looked into your dulled, ACCLIMATISED eyes...

And where has this stranger come from... this soul searcher...? Where once there was a wanker from... Ha...! NOW who's the creative... Who wanted the lead role in... yes... in EVERYONE'S life... first drugged by DESTINY and later by LEGACY... a LOWLY lawyer he just couldn't be... or a DOCTOR, or HUMBLE HELPER... no, not me... Yes... ...where once there was a very large penis... who thought he was a technology genius... a PENIUS perhaps... but who knew this penius would – in the ultimate misdirection of – of – my good self by my good self – add GREED, and DECEIT – to his... what would these turnips call it... SKILL SET... Yes... did I ever think to thank SERENDIPITY as she walked beside me, holding my hand...? I could only see sycophants, parasites, and thieves... Yes... the great penius that HAD to succeed... AT ANY COST... even if it changed who he was...

The first founder looked at the mostly closed eyes around the table.

And what about these paid crusaders, and true believers...? They're not ALL bowers and scrapers... not ALL "BRUTALLY HONEST" fakers and takers... How many of their names do I even know...? All of us wanderers... now gathering, here... after all of the presentations... and tentacled disclaimers... and the CALLS WITH ALL PARTIES... here WE ALL are... salting the parchment... scratching the scroll... carefully creating our sacred offering... the public offering... an exchange, not a sacrifice... its value unspecified... self-evident, apparently... But what IS the good in ownership...? Helpful, PRACTICAL, yes... a chain to restrain – the viciousness of beasts... one of THE BIG LAWS, that clip our claws... in the name of order... that's mine, this is yours... yes... yes... makes you pause... a thought can blunt a gun, that blunts a feeling, that blunts a thought, that blunts a gun... but inherently – GOOD... as an IDEA...? Like... I don't know... WARMTH? Like... SELFLESSNESS WITH NO PAY-OFF?

And ownership for the PUBLIC? Which public? Not the wretched, the rejected, or those that are themselves owned... not the NOT SUFFICIENTLY SOPHISTICATED... but just a HIGH-QUALITY wedge of hedge fund managers... THE CUSTODIANS OF OTHER CUSTODIANS... thriving despite their own psychoses... Really, there IS no public... just congregants...

and private prayers... Does the pensioner staring from the window KNOW that THE ANNUAL GENERAL MEETING JUST HAPPENED? That THE GUIDANCE WAS ADJUSTED and all of the directors were reappointed?

Instead of shares, we need public prayers... Maybe that's what he's doing here, now... maybe the ancient scrolls were... on the money...

But for me the words are not working... I am so unsettled, so separated... What else is taking place here...? Something more near... in the shade... under the veil... another, more subtle sale... I think I hear – hooves on snow... crushing and crunching... look... The New Stakeholders are coming... probably not a one-hit wonder... and, more angry, their contemporaries The Journalists and The Regulators... The Government Officials... The Political Ambitions... and their platinum album... Yes, foreign kings, with their own religions and masters, coming to see about what they have heard... sent by The Secondary Source Certainties... and soon, any last-dance deference... any loitering, lingering glints of oleaginousness... will evaporate... and lift the merciless to the surface... Yes... look around... the elders, they already know... him with the body like a balloon... he DEFINITELY knows... I'm just the child not being told that his dog has died... the zoo-kept lion remembering his pride... I'm the bright-eyed newly-wed... I'm the king they've agreed has lost his mind... slowly being straightened into a straitjacket... while I have been distracted – by the draw of a DREAM, by the shiny magazine... by fork-tongued ESTEEM... the highest prize, it always seemed... not the ball and chain, of leadership and fame... I'm just another unremarkable brain, in a bag, now sinking, in a public offering... but HE would say all of this is just thinking... and you're just – you're only another man on a chair... Shh... listen... the beat is getting louder now... YOU MUST use this GOOD FORTUNE for good... put that disgusting DNA on a plane... ONLY A FEW can reduce this much pain... but wait, I'M NOT THE MESSIAH... No, no, no... you VERY naughty boy... DO NOT complain – check your PRIVILEGE and check your inbox – we've sent you your sentence again... ...your – jury – will – never – come – in...

The first founder pressed his upper and lower lips together in a horizontal smile, and looked around the room once more.

I wonder if it's just fear that's holding this room together... if it disappeared... if all of it disappeared... even the law... which of these – self-styled CIVILISED souls – would show themselves to be – STRONGER – and WILDER – than me – would claw out my eyes and crush them to ash... would show me, vindictively, my own destruction...

Maybe I could go back to being a child... crying openly and completely – with my entire body – at some everyday tragedy... at a grazed, bloody knee... or a released balloon... forgotten, so soon... back when I was fully dissolved in the current scene... connected... not to TOMORROW AFTERNOON or some metaphysical room... but to NOW... NOW... NOW... which we didn't even call it, then... we were just – climbing a tree... or watching TV... but I can't get back there... there are no more pyjamas with rainbows and bees... the boys are not playing in the garden any more... she'll never again bring you the jug of juice with the cut up fruit... or the iced tea with the mint leaves... because you are too old... and she is dead... which is not the only insurmountable practicality... there are, quite simply, limits to plasticity... Yes... unfortunately... as light as that now you'll NEVER be... limits... especially for me, who

CAN'T EVEN MASTER PLAIN VANILLA SYMPATHY... I'm the cobbler who's RIGHT NOW, TOO BUSY... SERVING DRINKS TO RESPONSIBILITY... ACCOUNTABILITY... and this curious bastard FIDUCIARY DUTY...

As the helicopter crossed the skyline, three of the members of the family put on their virtual reality headsets, while the daughter watched the life in the city walking by the river from her window, a small highway of fish on the reef. The father accompanied the son in the metaverse experience of *Sitting By The Pool*, in which pleasure seekers appeared to pass them as they lay on their deckchairs, read books, observed a medicinal breeze flowing through tall palm trees, and listened to the lapping of water and the splashing of swimmers. Their relaxation was further enhanced by the until-today untouched status of this two-week-long *reward experience*, which they had earned through the completion of two meta-marathons across harsh, desert plains in one month. The father had split his screen so that he was also aware of the inside of the helicopter. The mother was replying to messages, noting her recollection that her son's passport needed to be renewed, and reorganising her consciousness diary recordings.

The first founder sighed, and looked out of the skyscraper's window at the perpendicular ocean of the city. He then walked around the perimeter of the room, with strength and pride, carrying his body with the maturity of experience and defeat, like a long-unbeaten heavyweight champion walking away from a spell-breaking knockout and preparing to pass his crown to the hopeful fist of youth. He walked behind the seat of the second founder, and towards the buffet, unnoticed by the quiet room.

Why – as a fundamentally selfish person... did I even do it...? I can't EXPERIENCE any more than anyone else... if anything,

I'm processing more pain than pleasure... It's all these infernal pathologies I suppose... vanity... voracity... and now, standing here, in supposed glory, all I have learned is how to notice – how to feel my body filling up, with different elements from the periodic table of feelings – resignation – fear – envy... of him – the taker – and his EXCRUCIATING equanimity... ultimately, he has become, the order, and I – I can no longer look at the light directly... running, as I am, from the grief that's coming for me... defeated by the choice between coffee or tea...

The second founder continued to speak with his eyes closed.

— And somewhere in this outgrowth is the single cell... the single idea that we started with... that our mission, is not about a mission ... is not about DOING... or reaching... a horizon forever receding...

— We wanted to show – what inside you already know... that there IS no... FINAL DESTINATION, no ultimate conclusion – no resolution, no DENOUEMENT, no satisfying ending... just a sequence of single steps, single thoughts, and single breaths... not easily wrapped in a name, or a frame, or a chemical chain... there's a me, and there's a WE... a disconnected colony... all separate but the same... our time's not – on some special plane... the morning sacred and the evening profane... the dance of the fire as it was by the cave... because tomorrow's just yesterday all over again... because no single grain will ever repeat...

— So please... feel the ground under your feet... greet, your troubles like guests... soak in the soaps of beauty... let go of the difference between how things are and how you want them to be... and remember that ONE OF THESE DAYS... before the gong sounds for our big get-together as cosmic dust... the people you love the most will be in the ground... lost and never to be found... their lights long out... Notice... notice all of them now... notice clear minds and heavy clouds... see the scene in which every one was born... the grandparent's smile... and the crowds that will come to mourn...

— Now, please, come back... come all the way back... to your breath... follow one or two breaths slowly... with the knowledge that each of them could be your last... and then, let go – of everything you know... unchain your mind, from time... your senses from words... just feel your breath and how everything is precious, or how it – just – is...

The second founder stopped speaking. There was a long, deep silence, and the sedation of satisfied anticipation fell on the room, as though the meeting's participants were a small section of hundreds of thousands packed into the wide, central avenue of a capital city, lying in and savouring the last drops of truth or greatness dispensed from a distant podium. In the open air, and if they were strangers to each other, a lonely clap might have rung out and – after a fleeting uncertainty – become the spark of a roaring fire.

As the first founder sipped his coffee, his mind sieving stories that sought to explain how he had reached the present moment in his life, he saw the helicopter crash into a skyscraper. He was jolted back into the present. The Consciousness Company's Consciousness heard the first founder and the father and the mother all thinking, *Oh My God* as the metal and glass was swallowed, crunched, and crumpled. The son felt a violent convulsion and a sensation of falling and initially, before he felt extreme heat and pain, thought that this feeling was part of his metaverse experience. The daughter was no longer able to look at the people on the street below while rearranging wistful rhyming couplets, with her last thought being, *So this is it then, before I even got going... just like that... before I really met anyone, or wrote anything down...* while some of the thousands of others sitting around the metaverse swimming pool thought, *AH... THIS IS THE LIFE...! I wonder whether I should go to the football on Saturday...?* and, *Is he wearing meta budgie smugglers?* In the boardroom, the meeting's participants, reflexively, after noticing in fear and also disbelief and a slowed down passing of time the presence of other helicopters in the sky, experienced almost identical thoughts and feelings coursing through their neurons and veins, which had the effect of transforming them into little more than a single species and unit, the individual components of which were now distinguished only by whether they had forgotten, abandoned, or collected their belongings, as they continued their journey to another part of the savanna.

Nearby, but out of sight, a man let a bus go past, thinking, *I'll get the next one,* two previously estranged friends hugged, and a woman took down a *Happy Birthday* sign.

Acknowledgements

First, of course, I want to thank my wife, Natasha, for her support over many years. For suffering the refrain of *I have to work on the novel*. For her high standards.

Then comes Faber Academy, and Jericho Writers, in particular Brian Kimberling, whose report was instrumental in the reworking of my early drafts. And for discussions in Bath and his response to the new version.

Thank you to all of my early and later readers. To Sam Norman, Meryl Yankelson, Manuela Grayson, Eli Lee, Chris Philp, and Imogen Edwards-Jones. For giving me some of their precious allocation of cosmic time without anybody having told them that it was a must-read.

Then, to all of the people and experiences that have brought me to the place that has allowed *The Consciousness Company* to come into being. And to Spiffing Books and Literally PR for their outstanding work.

To Sophia, Harry, and Shoshie. For our times, these times. I hope this brings you joy. And hopefully a few tips and pointers. Also, there are no free passes on swear words!

To my family. To my mother, Rhoda, my father, Stephen, my sister, Louise, my brother, Joshua. Thank you for your support every day of my life.

And thank you to the rest of my family and friends.

Then of course my thanks to you, reading this. I hope that you have enjoyed reading *The Consciousness Company*. Maybe you'll carry it with you in some way. Or maybe it is just *incoherent detritus*, or will be *lost in the slipstream of further change*.

And lastly, once again, to Natasha, because she commented that *you usually thank the wife at the end.*

Printed in Great Britain
by Amazon

44375450R00152